Broken, But Healing

Casey Power

Broken, but healing

Copyright © 2025 by Casey Power

All rights reserved.

No part of this book may be reproduced in any form or by any electronic or mechanical means, including information storage and retrieval systems, without written permission from the author, except for the use of brief quotations in a book review.

Edited by Valerie Jones

Cover Design: Tori Epps

As always, I owe my writing career to my mom. Thanks for putting up with all my nonsense over the years.

And one more thing, Dad: thank you for not being ashamed of this new adventure of mine. Your praise and support go further than you know.

Love you always, Mom and Dad

~ Casey

Table of Contents

Introduction   7

Chapter One - I Can't Go on Like This   10

Chapter Two - Wake-Up Call   16

Chapter Three - Once Upon A Hill   23

Chapter Four - Long Time, Much Needed   31

Chapter Five - Sun Always Rises and Sets   38

Chapter Six - Steps Forward, Jumps Back   53

Chapter Seven - Coping 101   62

Chapter Eight - Face Your Fears, Child   74

Chapter Nine - The Devil Has Many Forms   84

Chapter Ten - Sweet Like Honey   99

Chapter Eleven - The Plane All Over Again   111

Chapter Twelve - Insecurities Surface   124

Chapter Thirteen - How Could You Not?   144

Chapter Fourteen - The Touch That Burns   157

Chapter Fifteen - Roles Reversed   167

Chapter Sixteen - Safe Space   172

Chapter Seventee - Thin Line of Lies and Truths   177

Chapter Eighteen - Surprises Can Be Good or Bad   199

Chapter Nineteen - Unexpected Turn for the Better   211

Chapter Twenty - Reveals Aren't Always Happy   216

Chapter Twenty-One - Risks Pay Off   230

Chapter Twenty-Two - Thanksgiving Thrills   233

Chapter Twenty-Three - Unsettled Changes   242

Chapter Twenty-Four - New Point of View   246

Chapter Twenty-Five - Run Like a Girl   249

Chapter Twenty-Six - The Failure of a Brother   256

Chapter Twenty-Seven - Paralyzed Dreams Return   259

Chapter Twenty-Eight - Different Connections   264

Chapter Twenty-Nine - One Hell of a Fighter   270

Chapter Thirty - Happiness You Can't Take Away   276

Chapter Thirty-One - 1 out of 20   278

Chapter Thirty-Two - Hole In Your Heart   284

Chapter Thirty-Three - Good Vs. Bad   290

Chapter Thirty-Four - Vanishing Like Smoke   296

Chapter Thirty-Five - Hiding In the Tundra   298

Chapter Thirty-Six - Trauma Changes You   305

Chapter Thirty-Seven - Once Upon A Time   313

Chapter Thirty-Eight - Palm of Her Hand   318

Chapter Thirty-Nine - Choose The Right Answer   325

Chapter Forty - Courage and Bavery Are Parallels   333

Chapter Forty-One - Reminder of Mine Own   341

Chapter Forty-Two - Anger Is an Unpredictable Emotion   344

Chapter Forty-Three - Surprised Reaction   353

Chapter Forty-Four - Swallow Me Whole   362

Chapter Forty-Five - You Can't Save Her   369

Chapter Forty-Six - No Heaven or Hell   374

Chapter Forty-Seven - Defy the Odds   377

Chapter Forty-Eight - The End?   381

Introduction

Maggie

Every day was the same. Wake up, throw clothes on, take medicine, run until you can't breathe anymore, sit in the shower for an hour, nibble on a piece of bread, mindlessly watch the TV, take medicine, crawl into bed, and close your eyes.

Every week was the same. Monday: Jackson would be at home all day. Tuesday: Mom would take me somewhere to get out of the house and take me to therapy. Wednesday: Calvin would run all day long with me. Thursday: I would go to Jackson's house and see the work that had been done. Friday and Saturday: Skyla will be with me. Sunday: I was left to my own on how much I wanted to eat or run.

Every month was the same. Third, I would go in to see Dr. Loggin. On the sixth, I would go and visit my dad's grave. On the eleventh, I would go and sit at Maxwell Fath's grave and leave flowers. On the twenty-fourth, the news would replay and discuss the shooting. Then, before I knew it, the month was starting over.

There were always whispers that followed when I would be seen in public. There were always awkward moments with Jackson. There were always fights and screams with Jackson. There were always tears with

Skyla. There was always nonsense being spoken with my mom. There was always silence with Calvin. There was always something or someone did that kept the cycle of every day, week, and month being the same.

My life had become nothing more than an endless cycle of feeling nothing while everyone else around me felt something. I had become nothing more than a hollow shell with no life. I was a robot. My brain and heart were dead. I was equal to someone who was living in a coma. And the fucked-up part is: I wished and prayed to be in a coma. I wished that one morning I just didn't wake up or that someone would come and shoot me while I was asleep. I wished and prayed for death because what I was doing was not living.

Kelly had said my depression was back, and it was hitting me harder than ever. She understood this was part of my healing process. I had been broken before everything, but now I was shattered into little pieces. If I thought I had been unfixable before, shit, there was no way to repair me. However, Kelly's point of view: I was healing myself. To others, it looked like I was relapsing or committing suicide, but Kelly saw it as a hurdle and something that could pass. She believed that there was still a part of me in there, but she knew it wasn't just going to magically reappear.

In everyone else's eyes, I was dying. They all thought that one gesture or life-saving act would be able to bring me back. Seeing Jackson scream and beg for me to say something or do anything was one of the few times

I felt sadness. Watching Skyla hold herself together so I could be broken apart was sadness. Looking at myself in the mirror, I felt nothing. I saw nothing but a person who was not living.

I had become nothing. I was nothing. I was just another number to the world.

Chapter One

I Can't Go on Like This

Jackson

The weather had certainly changed these last few weeks; the sun was out longer, and there was warmth. May had come within the blink of an eye, and it was hard to imagine it had almost been one full year with Maggie in my life. Maggie.

Maggie may have smiled once in the last four months. She refused to let me touch her. She could barely maintain eye contact with me. I had lost her because the person in front of me was not Maggie Kensinger. She didn't even look like Maggie. It broke me all over again, when those lifeless eyes would look at me, small tears falling out of them.

There had been many times I considered taking pills. Many times, I had to go running AA meetings because I was afraid of relapsing. Most nights, I found myself looking in the mirror, hating everything there was to me, and silently crying myself to sleep. As I would cry, I began to feel selfish that I thought I had it bad. I felt guilty, and it only made me cry more.

Everything that had gone on with Maggie was taking a toll on everyone, not just myself. Skyla had dropped weight and was looking more and more like hell. She seemed to be drinking more and working less. I can't remember the last time she tried to pick a fight or even put makeup on. Calvin barely spoke and always had dark circles under his eyes. He didn't have enough in him to flirt and be an asshole.

Maggie was doing everything she needed to do: taking her medicine, going to Dr. Loggin, seeing her therapist, and getting out of the house. Somehow, in my eyes, there had been no improvement. If anything, Maggie had grown quieter and more lifeless. She barely could hold onto a conversation with me, let alone the fights that would happen.

The fights were not physical, and truly, it was just me screaming and yelling at Maggie. I felt utter shit every time a fight would begin, but there was only so much I could hold in. Only so much I could take before relapsing on my own. The way our fights would end was when Maggie would stand up, maintain solid eye contact, and say: "Go, I am sorry. Leave."

When I heard those words, my stomach would drop, and I could feel my body breaking down, inch by inch. No energy, muscle, or oxygen would be left. It was as if those words were bullets that had entered my body in various areas. The worst part of it was Maggie's face. Her lip would curl, her right hand trembled, her left hand formed a fist, and her eyes emotionless.

It would be a dead lie if I didn't admit that I believed Maxwell Fath deserved to rot in hell. He had broken Maggie, taken what pure innocence she had. It would be another lie if I didn't say that I was pissed that Mitch Kensinger chose to die that day. Being a doctor, I know it's nearly impossible to pick when to die, but the fact that it had to be that period pissed me off. The last thing I would never admit out loud: Daniel scared the shit out of me.

Over the last few months, I have been trying to figure out what was having the biggest impact on Maggie. She had been hit with three blows: the shooting, her father's death, and Daniel. On the twenty-fourth of every month, she would sit and watch all the replays and broadcasting from the shooting. There would be no emotions from her, and my stomach would twist and turn. At her father's grave, she would just sit and stare. Whenever the name Daniel was spoken, she would break into a crouching position and sob into her hands.

From what I had been able to gather from various people in the hospital, Daniel Dobson was rumored to be the head of the psychiatry department. No one knew for sure, and no one knew when it would even happen. He had not been back in the United States since the funeral and hadn't attempted to contact Maggie. I knew it was a matter of time before he would return, whether it be for good or a vacation.

Maggie made it very clear that she still didn't want to speak out against Daniel, and neither could we. Skyla was furious, trying to explain to Maggie there was no way she could work in the same building as him without trying to kill him. I even tried telling Maggie there was no way I was going to sit by and let him roam around free. She didn't budge, telling us she would handle it. By the way, she reacted to just hearing his name, I knew her handling of it wouldn't be what she needed. However, to keep what little trust she had in the world, I would let her handle it.

The truth was, I didn't know how much more I could handle. Maggie was vanishing through my fingertips; she barely was a person at this point. It killed me from the inside out to see the woman I had fallen in love with disappear. Somewhere, deep inside, was Maggie. Just how long would it take for her to resurface to the world?

It was a sluggish Tuesday; the sun was shining brightly, the school was getting out, and the tourists started coming. The weather had slowly reached the high sixties, still relatively cool for me, as back home, my mother talked about how hot and gross it was.

There were only a few surgeries for me, and then I would have the night off. I begged and pleaded to pick up extra hours but was sent home. No one would even give up being on call. I showered and changed in the locker room; I was going to head to the house before I went to see Maggie.

The house had been completely gutted, and the only thing that had been done was the floors on the inside. The kitchen and bathrooms had hardwood floors, and the rest of the house had soft carpet. I didn't want to move forward on anything because I wanted Maggie to be there through the whole process. I wanted her to have the same excitement as she did before about the whole house. I didn't want to move forward until she was ready, and a small part of me feared that she never would be.

For the last few months, I have been staying at Maggie and Skyla's. Calvin was there almost as often as I was, seemingly sleeping over every night. There was still confusion about what Calvin and Skyla were, but in my eyes, it was more than friends with benefits. They hung around each other at the hospital and even sat together in the cafeteria when they both had time.

Maggie had very little to say about it, other than Skyla was happy, so she was happy for her. I know it had been a big step for Skyla; she lost the love of her life at twenty-three. She had been convinced that Bently was her one and only. Now, here she was, all these years later, in some sort of relationship. I also know this was just as big of a step for Calvin. In all the years I had known him, he never had a serious girlfriend. He only had Kara, years before I knew him. She had died, along with their daughter they shared.

Everyone has a past, whether we want to or not. Even the people you least expect to have a past are sometimes the ones who have the worst past. Some of the kindest people are some of the most hurt people. Broken people will always love more. I still remember Maggie telling me that; I was amazed at how wise and pure that statement was. I was now just beginning to wonder if even broken people had their limit.

Chapter Two

Wake-Up Call

Maggie

Mom had taken me to get breakfast, and then I sat with Kelly in therapy for an hour. Typical Tuesday. However, the only thing that changed was when Mom picked me up; she was not alone. In the front seat of the BMW was Skyla.

Getting myself settled into the backseat, Mom did her typical run-through of how Kelly was, how it went, and did I need to talk about anything. My typical answers remained the same: good, fine, and no. Skyla shot me a look through the mirror, knowing that at least two of the answers were complete bullshit. I gave her a look back, trying to figure out why the fuck she was here in the first place.

"Before you complain," Mom started, "know this is for your own good."

Skyla whipped around, "You look like shit. I look like shit. Your Mom looks like shit. So, buck up, we're going to not look like utter shit."

I raised an eyebrow, "So you're telling me we're going shopping?"

Sensing the distaste in my voice, Mom turned around and smiled, "And spa day," she said with way too much enthusiasm.

"Since when have you been into girls' day?" I asked Skyla, ignoring my mother, who was clearly excited.

"Since when do you not give a shit about yourself?" She fired back at me, and I frowned. "You've been rotting away and pushing anyone you have away. So, you're going to get your hair treated, a facial, nails, and go shopping. You are going to get up and start working on yourself. You know damn well when I was in your shoes with Bently, you were not going to let me depression or grief win. Here I am now telling you I am not going to let that beat you." Skyla shook her head. "I am sorry I didn't do it sooner."

Slouching back into the seat, I let Skyla's words pierce through my body. They hit deep, and suddenly, I had the rush of all these emotions again. My mind, fixed on how useless I felt trying to help Skyla cope with something. How it broke me to see the person I loved the most crumbled, and there was nothing I could do but hold her.

The memories of picking her up off the floor, the phone calls with just breathing, and holding her hand as she stood in the water came back vividly. She was not only losing herself, but she was losing the war within. She was letting the illness will, the broken and fucked up part of the brain, win.

It took her months to get back on her feet after I held her, crying and trashing about. It was a slow progression, but every day, she inched closer to the person she is now. It didn't come without consequences; she had fallen behind in school and didn't get into her top choice for medical school. She had lost a lot of weight, her hair was falling out, and her skin was blotchy. Every day, she had to commit to herself, taking care of not only her brain but her body as well.

Skyla struggled over the next few years with confidence, something that she had never experienced with Bentley. He loved her, and she loved him. It was like a fairytale of their relationship, but no one but the insiders knew the dark side, Grimm's version.

Skyla and Bentley met in homeroom "freshman" year; they sat next to each other. It took him a while to break through the ice with her; she was distant and rude. He would come by her locker every morning with an iced vanilla white mocha and walk with her to homeroom. They would talk about likes and dislikes, but they would also discuss the meanings of life and deep shit. I think because they could have those kinds of conversations, Skyla finally let him break through.

Bentley was a hockey and baseball player, so he fell in the category of the jock. That was one part Skyla did not like, but he didn't act like any of the jackoffs. He was genuine and would devote his time to her and not the guys. Because of this, he got teased and left out of things, but it didn't matter because he had Skyla.

He was the kind of guy who made heads turn, not because of his looks, but the goofy smile that would always be on his face. He could walk down the hallway and high-five every person and say hey. Everyone would look, smile, wave, and talk to him. It was the kind of person he was, and I think Skyla was terrified of it, but eventually, it became one of her favorite parts of him.

Now, just like with any couple, they fought. They fought in private and kept all of it out of the gossip. A lot of the fights started when Bentley was caught with alcohol in our sophomore year, and he got suspended for the hockey season. Skyla couldn't understand his need to drink every weekend and the need to always have beer in the back seat of his truck. Skyla and he would get into screaming matches over it. Another issue was Skyla's mom couldn't stand Bentley and would do everything in her power to cause tension between the two of them.

Despite the fights, every morning he brought her that damn coffee; every Friday he would surprise her with flowers or jewelry or some sappy shit; every Sunday morning he would take her to brunch, and every day he woke up and struggled with depression. It wasn't until junior year that he finally got diagnosed and put on medication.

Skyla was there when he got the news; she held his hand when he went and got his medication for the first time, and she always held him when his thoughts would go dark. Most nights, Skyla found herself opening her window for Bentley to come and lay with her. The first few months were hard on him; the medication changed his personality and energy. He stopped playing sports and barely could make it to the fourth period. People noticed the change; they whispered and made rumors. But even with all the shit going on, Bentley still brought her the coffee, the gifts, and took her out.

I know his family was extremely grateful for Skyla because she stood by him. That was when I knew she loved him. Sure, she had the young love or puppy love, but when Bentley went through this change, and she stood by him without wavering, she loved him with all she had.

The summer before senior year, Bentley worked hard to get himself back into shape and gained his personality back. This was also the time when he started to get possessive of Skyla. If one guy looked at her the wrong way, it was game over. Bentley would get into fights over it. He was never mad at Skyla, but as nice as it was to be protected, it made her feel like her loyalty wasn't there.

"It's like he assumes that I am going to leave him," she said as we lay outside in the backyard of her mom's house. "I don't understand how he can think that."

The sun was shining, and we were trying to get the vitamin D we needed. "What if it is more about him than you?" I suggested as I turned to look at her. "Maybe he is so insecure with himself that he can't understand why you're still here."

Skyla groaned, "Now I feel like shit for making it about myself."

"I wouldn't," I said as I flipped to my stomach, "it is a valid feeling to have."

In the end, all the possessive shit ended when Skyla finally sat down and talked to him. He was hurt to think that she thought he was doubting her loyalty. Bentley made it clear that he never had and never would doubt her loyalty. That was the thing with Bentley: he saw Skyla as more than just his girlfriend; he saw her as a person, someone who deserved respect. Sure, he would call her beautiful and crap like that, but it was the way he viewed her.

Bentley wanted to give her the fucking sun, and he wanted her to have everything she deserved. They talked about marriage; it would have to be a small wedding and no church. They talked about kids, two boys, and how they would raise them. Skyla and Bentley had gone ring shopping a few weeks before it all happened.

In the years after Bentley's death, she struggled with herself. She wore baggy clothes, refused to wear shorts, and always self-criticized herself. She would stand in front of the mirror, pointing out the small imperfections, and let herself be ashamed of who she saw in the mirror. Because this was not how it was supposed to go, she was supposed to be engaged, have a wedding, and have kids. All of that was gone because of the biggest nightmare she had had.

Now, all these years later, I sat in the backseat of the car, ashamed of who I was. Skyla was watching me carefully as she reached out and squeezed my hand. Her touch brought warmth and a healthy shock of energy. She cracked a smile as I squeezed her hand back and let myself smile.

Chapter Three

Once Upon A Hill

Jackson

My car was parked on the middle level of the parking garage. It was a solid ten-minute walk from the locker room to my spot. One day, I swore I was going to count how many steps it took me, but my mind was always preoccupied. Because my mind was spinning with all these thoughts, it took me a second to realize someone was standing by my car.

By the time I realized there was someone there, the person turned around. My heart skipped a beat, and I stopped walking, afraid to move any closer. It was at that moment when everything froze, and my eyes locked with her. The sudden warmth was spreading through my body, the same feeling I had when I saw her for the first time.

Her hair was down with waves and looked bright; it did help that the sun was shining directly on it. Her skin looked smooth and soft; the sunlight made it glow. Those beautiful eyes were where I got lost in the shades of blue and hints of green. The way they could get me to stop dead in my tracks and forget what I had to say was the power they held.

Taking in the rest of her, she was in a white and blue flowy dress that fell barely to her mid-thigh. The shoes were tan sandals, and you could see the white nail polish on her toes and the fingernails matched. The lips were covered in a light pink gloss, and she wore the smallest earrings.

It all seemed like a mirage, a vision; she had goddess energy, and there was no way she was there in front of me. That body was not hidden; the sun and color from her were there, and most of all, there was the smallest hint of a smile. Her body had changed; there was more muscle in her legs.

My eyes lingered on the scar on her inner right thigh; it was bright against her skin. I remember the bandage and how much blood was soaking through it. I had not seen it healed; she was very careful to make sure no one would. Quickly, as I felt guilty for staring, I took the remaining steps to her. The scars on her arms had faded in thin lines, with a light red hue, those I had seen as they were more of a challenge to hide.

Maggie Kensinger stood in front of me, perfect, even with scars. I couldn't help the smile that spread across my face as she adjusted her dress. There were tears dying to escape my eyes, but I was not going to let them show. All I wanted at that moment was to bathe in her warmth, as it had been gone all these months.

"Mom and Skyla suggested a girl's day," she shrugged, "Mom picked out the outfit, and Skyla picked out the rest. She even convinced me to cut a few inches off."

That is when Maggie did a little twirl to show off. When she met my eyes again, I laughed, and I watched as a smile naturally formed on her face. My heart felt like it was going to explode; here she was in front of me.

"Well," I said awkwardly, "I think they did a great job."

She smiled and shook her head, "Feels weird, but nice," she squeezed her left hand into a fist, "can I show you somewhere?" Her body tense at her words.

I smiled at her, "Yeah, that would be pretty perfect."

As I was putting my backpack in the back seat, I watched as she carefully moved her way into the front seat. Watching, there was a sudden rush of nerves; how long would this last? Was this a dream? Was she breaking up with me? How long will this Maggie be here?

Squeezing my eyes tightly, I numbed those thoughts out and made my way to the front. Sitting this close to her, I could smell the strong scent of vanilla, with just the tiniest hint of lavender. I let myself smile; the happy memories with her flashed through my mind.

Listening carefully as she guided me to a side of town I had not really been to. She kept her focus on everything going on outside, watching people and cars. The angle from where I was sitting, I could clearly see the bullet scar, sending Maggie's screams echoing in my head. The painful image of her coming out of the ambulance that day distracted me as I almost ran a red light.

Maggie seemed unbothered by this distracted driving; her body turned more to look out the window. She simply would give directions, sometimes a little too late, but she finally told me to turn into the Buena Vista Ski Area.

"It's like seventy degrees out," I said confusedly, "why are we at a ski resort, and the bigger thing is, why are there even cars here?"

She smirked and hopped out of the car, leaving me confused. I had never been skiing, and I didn't even know there was a ski place here in town. I wondered if the Kensinger's spent a lot of time here in the winter. Maybe it was a special place for her. Whatever it was, she was walking at such a fast pace that I had to jog to catch up with her.

The sun was out longer, and it was getting warm, which meant tourists would be flooding in soon enough. I was excited about my first summer in Bemidji, but I was nervous about the people Calvin kept talking about. In my years growing up, I had such a distrust of others. There were times I found myself not believing in my mother, making me fearful that I could never trust anyone. In my mind, people were looking out for only themselves, so they would do whatever they needed to achieve.

Maggie, as usual, always defied my views of others. Despite the literal hell we had been through, I still trusted her. When she told me she took her medicine, I believed her. Even though there were times when it got so dark, my belief that Maggie was in there somewhere, helped me get through it. My trust in her had been challenged, but she always proved her honesty.

Here I stood, slightly out of breath, on top of a hill clearly used as the starting point for skiing. Maggie was frozen up top, taking in the view that was in front of her, whereas I took in her. There was a spark in her eyes and a relaxed smile on her face. I couldn't tear my eyes away from her; it had been too long since I had seen the color.

"My mom used to take us up here, winter, spring, etc." She said, closing her eyes and letting the breeze hit her skin. "The best time would be in the fall, the leaves changing color, and it was cool enough to wear a jacket." She let a big smile spread across her mouth. "We always would go on this hayride with my mom's friends and their kids. It was a rare time when Dad would join."

I finally looked around to see this view. The sky was painted in vivid and bold colors, with pinks and oranges. The lake sparkled and had that deep blue color, and it was at this height you could see how big Lake Bemidji really was. It was nothing like the ocean by any means, but it blew away my expectations of what a lake would be.

"Calvin hated it because he was usually the only boy." Her voice cut through my thoughts. "Anyways, in high school, Skyla and I would come up here. It was like our secret hideaway at night; we would drink whatever liquor Bentley could score for us. There were lots of tears, but lots of laughs."

The sun hit her hair perfectly, showing all the golden and copper tones there were to her. She looked over at me as she reached for my hand, and shock waves went through my body. I can't remember the last time I held her hand, but right now, my heart was beating so loudly it distracted my thoughts. I could feel the relief throughout my body from just her hand.

"I know these last months have been fucking hell." I brushed my thumb along with her hand as she spoke. "I just want to say I am sorry for all of it. The yelling, the times you cried, but most of all, triggering you. It wasn't fair to you, and it was selfish of me to only think of my pains," she took a deep breath, "what I am saying is thank you, but most of all, I am sorry."

Maggie maintained eye contact as she spoke. She didn't need to thank me; that was part of the deal we made: be with each other even when we're not okay. I was never expecting her to apologize for how she dealt with the shit that was handed to her. I was thankful she did, but that also meant I owed her an apology for pushing her and causing more pain.

Squeezing her hand, I pulled her in for a hug. She did not resist and pressed against me. Brushing my fingers through her hair, it felt like silk and smelled like lavender.

"I am sorry too, Maggie. I know I wasn't the most helpful." I kissed the top of her head. "Remember the deal we made?" She looked up at me, clearly trying to hold the tears back. "Even when we are both not okay, we are still there for each other. I meant what I said that night, and I still do."

I wiped away a few tears that fell down her face. "Jackson, you didn't deserve to go through your pain alone. I am sorry, and I don't know what to say because I feel disgusted that I couldn't help you."

"Maggie, you are getting better; getting yourself back on your feet and smiling is what will help me." She ducked her head away, and I tilted her face back up. "I don't want to lose you."

She smiled as some tears fell down her face, "Now you're getting too cheesy."

I rolled my eyes and, leaned down, and kissed those soft lips. She brushed her fingers through my hair as I guided my hands down to her waist. I didn't want this moment to end. Warmth and chills ran through my body as her hands brushed my neck. The last time we kissed was the day of the shooting; if only I knew what would have happened.

Pulling away, my lips traced down her neck, and I heard her gasp. Fuck. I came back up and smiled as I kissed her forehead. I turned to look back at the view, and she rested her head on me, a smirk on her face. She closed her eyes, and I looked down at her: she was the view and had always been the most powerful and beautiful view.

Chapter Four

Long Time, Much Needed

Maggie

It crossed my mind, while out doing girly things, that Jackson deserved not only an apology but thanks. These last months have shown him how bad my mental health can get. I knew he had been struggling with his pains; while I was out running one day, I saw him leaving a building downtown with a piece of paper. My heart sank as I knew he was either getting help or he was cheating on me. I couldn't blame him if he had been, but that wasn't the case.

When he was asleep that night, I peeked at that paper he left on the floor: the name and number of a sponsor. Instead of being happy he wasn't cheating, I felt a huge weight crush my heart: he was hurting, and I wasn't helping. Fuck, for all I knew, I was the one who was causing the issues. I didn't sleep that night and stayed up watching reruns of *The George Lopez Show*.

Jackson didn't need to stay with me. He didn't need to suffer because my pathetic ass was. For that, I could never express in words or gestures what that meant. Most of it solidified my trust in him. Trust was not an easy thing to gain with people who had been through trauma. As much as we want to believe we are trustworthy, in the end, most people are only looking out for themselves and will use your secrets against you.

I know that is a very bleak way to look at the world, but that was a reality for me. You could go and watch some of those reality or competition shows; they will betray anyone to get to the top and win. In my opinion, secrets are worth more than money. I think this because secrets hold more value and impact. Secrets can be the very thing that makes you or the very thing that destroys you.

The reason behind bringing Jackson to the ski resort was that it brought back such happiness. It reminded me of the times Mom would be smiling and taking so many pictures. I could hear Dad telling me to look at the video camera. The burn in my legs from running up the hill, racing Calvin to the top, tingled my body. Then, there was the view that left everyone speechless, no matter what season it was.

Jackson was lost for words at the view. It still got me lost for words. Overall, the best view was on a clear night, with the moon reflecting the water and the hundreds of stars twinkling above. Skyla and I found such peace up here. It was in those moments we could really let out what needed to be said. We could say the most unhinged crap or confess about the saddest shit. It was a safe place for both of us.

You could tell when we were out shopping and shit, how much this meant to my mother to be doing this.

In the last months, my mom had lost the love of her life. She would never let you see the pain or let you watch her shed a tear; my mother was too strong for that.

Growing up, my mother and her two sisters were left to fend on their own. My grandma had died in childbirth, and my grandpa was a raging alcoholic who could never hold a job or control his temper. My mom took the most beating, defending her sisters. She became my grandpa's favorite punching bag.

Because there was never stable money flowing in, my mom's family was always moved from house to house and eventually had to live in shelters and cars. When my mom was ready to graduate high school, she was top of her class and had a full ride to Dartmouth. Her sisters were old enough and knew how to take care of themselves, yet Mom always said that was the most selfish thing she ever did: leaving them to pursue a career.

With the past my mom had, she really had no time for anything but school and family. My dad had a few classes with her, and he always said the thing that caught his attention was my mom's eyes. In a class of hundreds of students, he zeroed in on my mom and fell in love. Mom, on the other hand, was not so in love; she didn't trust people, especially when it came to men. My dad had his work cut out for him.

It was months before Mom even agreed to go on a date with him. So, all the flowers, walking her to her dorm, and endless notes worked in his favor. My dad, who came from such wealth and perfect family background, did not care that my mom had a fucked past; he admired that she had pushed past that.

By the time my parents graduated, my mom's sisters were in college. They both had gotten into Penn State, one for academics and the other for volleyball. My grandpa had passed away from liver cancer not long before. Everything seemed to be getting on track; everyone was getting where they needed to be.

That fall, my mom's youngest sister, Annie, was walking home late from the campus library. She was walking along a main road when a car jumped the curb, hitting and killing her instantly. The driver was a fifty-one-year-old man, an alcoholic who was driving with a blood content of .13.

It took my mom almost everything she had to not lose herself and wreck everything she had going for her. She took some time from school, buried her younger sister, and let herself grieve. My dad paid for the funeral; the only time she didn't fight him over who was paying.

She was never the same after losing her sister. My dad always said she never had the same smile, like a part of her died with her sister. Looking at my mother now, another huge part of her died. I felt a strike of guilt hit me; I had not even stopped to realize how much my mother lost in these months. That is even not to mention her daughter nearly dying twice.

I curled my lip and squeezed my eyes shut. In the last months, I have been beyond selfish, caring only for myself. I had been too self-absorbed to realize how much those I loved around me were crumbling.

"Jackson," my voice cut through the cool air, "I love you."

We turned to look at each other, our eyes locked. His eyes glistened in the sunlight, and his smile caused my heart to stop beating for a second, a feeling that hadn't happened before. The way he looked at me sent my body into relaxation, taking away the pain and shit this world gave. When he looked at me, he healed small parts of me. If only I could do the same for him.

The house was empty; both Skyla and Calvin worked the night shift. Opening the door, immediately Jackson's hands grasped my hips, fingertips skimming my bare thighs. My body sank into his as he slid his one hand under my dress, his fingers brushing my clit. I turned around, and his lips immediately pressed against mine; his hands hoisted me up onto the kitchen counter. Standing between my legs, he began rubbing my clit softly as his lip grazed mine.

My body had not felt this sense of pleasure in ages. Along my skin, there were goosebumps, but there was such warmth that stretched inside of me. I wanted nothing more than to bathe in the feeling as his lips traced the side of my neck. I whimpered as his fingertips stopped, and they began to peel off my thong.

Jackson shoved my dress out of the way and softly blew on my clit, making me shiver. I was then greeted with his warm mouth, and I let out a cry, and my hands immediately dug into his hair. I let myself soak in the warmth as his tongue moved in the perfect motion.

It didn't take long for me to finish, as the sense of this intense pleasure hadn't been felt in months. He slowly made his way back up to my lips, and I could taste the sweetness on his lips. My hands traced down to the hem of his shirt and pulled it off.

Gently, Jackson pulled down the straps of my dress, exposing my breasts. I shivered as he slowly took in one of my breasts. I gasped as his tongue brushed against my nipple.

Pulling his face back up to me, I heard the thud of his pants hitting the floor. My heart raced at the thought of him inside me; it had been too long, and my body was begging for it. Sensing this, Jackson slowly inserted himself, groaning into my neck.

My cheeks flushed, embarrassed by how wet I was. "Sorry," I gasped.

He thrust into me, "Why are you sorry?"

"I," he tilted my chin up, "It's just been a while, so I," he pushed himself deeper into me. "I'm sorry that I am soaking," I finally whispered.

Jackson smirked at me, "This just shows how much you missed me."

Before any other words could be exchanged, he began to make slow and steady movements into me. I moaned as he kissed my neck, and his hands cradled my neck, molding me into him. His movements became more rapid, making me cry out his name before he finished.

Looking down at me, his fingers brushed my cheek. You could clearly feel the heat on them. Carefully, he kissed me on the forehead before pulling out of me. I whimpered, already craving for him to be back in me.

I slid off the counter and began to make my way towards the stairs. Before I had reached it, Jackson grabbed my wrist and pulled me back close to him into a hug. Squeezing me gently, I closed my eyes and embraced having the warmth back inside me. A warmth I had not realized I needed all these months.

Chapter Five

Sun Always Rises and Sets

Maggie

There was such a mixed feeling when it came to my birthday; it had been this way since I was a kid. I didn't like the attention on me. It meant everything that I did that day was in the spotlight. Also, it meant that I was one year closer to death and one more year I had survived death's grip.

Usually, my birthday was around the time school was ending, so my students and I would play games and color, no work. However, I had not seen or heard from any of my students or their families since the shooting. My principal informed me that all the students had been granted the opportunity to move up to the next grade level, even though they missed half of the instructional year.

I had already agreed to return to the school next year. I would resume my position as a Kindergarten teacher. I was offered the choice to move classrooms, but I opted to stay. I knew that a lot of people were puzzled by this decision, but I hoped staying in that room would remind me of the happiness that I once had.

My decision to stay shocked everyone but Skyla. Jackson was upset because he couldn't understand why I would want to relive such a painful moment. Calvin just feared for the same shit to happen again, along with my mother, who just wanted me out of the field of teaching completely. Kelly and Dr. Loggins were more intrigued by my choice than turned off. Skyla knew that teaching was a piece that couldn't be damaged, plus she knew the real reason why I chose to stay.

We were lying in her bedroom; it was dark like usual, and she had a few candles lit. It had been a few days since I had my breakthrough with Jackson, and things were slowly going back to being okay again.

"I think you should tell him," Skyla said with her eyes closed and hair sprawled out. "It isn't something you should be ashamed of."

Unfortunately, I was ashamed of it. "He won't understand it; if anything, it will piss him off."

Skyla scoffed, "Babes, he understands you more than you think. He has stuck around through this dark shit; most people who didn't understand would not still be here."

"Jackson will think differently of me."

"So what? If he does, then fuck him. Wanting to go back because you think you deserve to suffer is just your way of coping." She sighed and rolled over to look at me. "The real people who love you will understand that it is a very small group, but at least there is a group."

I laid my head back, "You are the only one in that group."

"I am the proud founder and leader of the I Love Maggie Kensinger Club."

We were silent for a moment, before we broke out into laughter from how dumb we sounded. It felt good to laugh, because this wasn't just a quick laugh. No, this was a laugh that had us cackling for five minutes, plus with tears in our eyes.

"I know you think you deserve to suffer, and I cannot change that, but Maggie, I think your staying is the most brave thing I have seen you do." She smiled at me as we embraced in a hug. "I know that you going back is going to heal you."

I squeezed my eyes shut, "I am not banking on healing; at this point, I am here to survive."

Skyla laid her head on top of mine, "You can survive and heal at the same time," she whispered, "I know because it is what I have been doing since he left."

Wiping my eyes, I looked up at her, "Life's a bitch, isn't it?" She cracked a sad smile and nodded. "Fuck the world," I shouted.

Laughing, Skyla shouted, "Fuck the world!"

We lay there in the dark, flipping the world off for everything it had thrown at us. I kept thinking about going back to that classroom, to school. I wanted to relive the nightmare, as I deserved it. I needed to hear the gunshots, see the blood, see Maxwell's face twisted in pain. I had taken a life, and I needed to face that—over and over again. I was meant to carry this scar. The only choice I had was whether to let it bleed or try to heal.

In the years past, Skyla treated my birthday as lowkey as I treated hers. We were never fans of the day, and we decided not to make it a big deal. Usually, we went to dinner and got each other a card, but that was it. It also didn't help that Skyla's birthday happened to be on September 11, so the day was already a traumatic reminder.

With all that being said, it was the week before my big twenty-ninth birthday, when Skyla informed me of her plans for this year's celebration. We were down by the lake, near the college campus, taking a walk, enjoying the Vitamin D.

"I have a plan," Skyla smirked at me, "and you're going to hate it."

I rolled my eyes, "Whatever, I highly doubt it."

Skyla pulled out an envelope and handed it to me as we continued to walk. It felt too light to be a card and didn't have the right shape to be one. I gave her a side eye as I delicately ripped the envelope open. In my hands were two plane tickets, two plane tickets to the city of Miami.

My walking came to a sudden stop; Skyla paused ahead of me, grinning as she made her way back to me. It was hard to focus because my eyes kept bouncing back to the tickets and to her intense eyes.

"No."

Rolling her eyes, "Come on, do something crazy." I narrowed my eyes at her. "You nearly died; come on, please?"

"No."

Skyla laughed, "Maggie, seriously, I am asking because you are not the only one who needs to get away." I felt an immediate sense of guilt washing over me. "It's not all your fault; trust me, I know that's where your brain is going. I think it would be nice to just be able to get away."

I groaned, "This isn't a birthday trip; it's just a trip. And no one else is going, right?"

She scoffed, "You really thought I was going to have guys, who I can't stand most of the time, come with? Come on, you know me better."

We started walking again, and I slipped the tickets back into the envelope, then tucked it into my sports bra for safekeeping. The weather was nice—probably in the high sixties—with the sun shining brightly. Not that I loved this kind of weather, but a little change was always a nice surprise.

"You going to explain that finally?" I asked as a couple of college kids walked pass. "You and the boy?"

Skyla's cheeks went red, "He's an ass, and I can't stand him ninety percent of the time. But God, that ten percent of the good can outweigh the ninety any day."

I scrunched up my face, "Ew, the sex is actually good?"

"Shut the fuck up, you asked for this." I rolled my eyes as we turned down a path to go down by the water. "It isn't about sex; you know me and how I feel. The way he gets me and lets me be a bitch and stand on my own, he admires it."

Kicking a rock in front of me, I sighed, "He has to let you be who you are; it wouldn't be fair."

"I wasn't who I was when I was with Bentley." She fired back at me. "I molded myself to be able to fit into his life. I am not saying that I wasn't happy, but I just felt like I had to be careful not to fuck up."

"He wouldn't have cared; you and I both know he loved you for who you were."

Skyla stopped and snapped her fingers, "Ah! You said you were! You said who you were before. Let's be real, if Bentley could see me now, you really think he would love me?"

I now stopped in my tracks, "Skyla, part of who you are now is what he did to you!"

"What if this was always how I was supposed to turn out to be?" She struggled to look away from her shoes. "What if we did everything we planned, and I still was cold and bitchy?"

"You're not cold and bitchy; you're real." Skyla was then finally able to meet my eyes. "You state everything how it is because you don't want the bullshit or sugarcoat it. You've always been that way, and I've always loved that about you."

"I never hated the world as much as I do now. Not even when I was a little kid, Maggie."

"That's not because of you; it is because whoever the fuck is writing our lives, has decided to make it shittier."

"Here is the thing," Skyla plopped down on a big stone near the water, "why do I hate myself and life? I have the dream job that I always pushed myself for. I have you; you're still in one piece. I am not being sexually assaulted. I am not eating ramen noodles for every meal." She ran her hand through her long ponytail. "Yet, I hate everything more than ever."

I crouched down in front of her, "You already know the answer, and it's an answer I know you don't want to hear."

She shook her head, "What the hell did I do in a past life to earn me the position of a broken soul?"

Grabbing her hand, I squeezed it, "We are both broken souls meant to heal each other."

Skyla laughed as tears fell from her eyes, "Fuck you, Maggie Kensinger."

"I love you too, Skyla James."

His house. Jackson's house. Well, I guess, our future house. It had been hard for me to be around the house. I think it had to come back to childhood memories and painful reminders that my dad was gone and that I had killed someone's child. So, when Jackson took me to the house, I would shut down; it was better than sobbing like a child.

After Skyla left to go to work, I decided to go to the house. I hadn't really been there alone, so I had never been able to explore it on my own. Jackson worked until later in the night, so I was on my own anyway. I figured I could overcome the overwhelming feeling of guilt on my own better than with someone watching, well, Jackson watching.

The grass was very green, and the garden was beginning to bloom out front. The previous owner, his wife, loved to garden, so she had planted flowers all around the house, and took much pride in the greenery around the house. Jackson had been watering and mowing the grass, wanting to maintain the beauty.

Walking around to the front of the house, I took a moment to close my eyes and breathe. It was quiet; you could hear the wind tickling the trees and the birds flying around. There were no sounds of cars or lawnmowers, just this peaceful silence.

The house was protected by loads of Jack Pine and different sizes of Evergreen trees. The driveway had been freshly paved as it had been gravel before. As for the exterior, Jackson had the house repainted with a fresh coat of white and the garage a dark green. I knew why he picked that green; it had been for me. I remember that moment very clearly.

Jackson had taken me to the house, about a few months after the shooting. He told me that there was a surprise, and I would really want to see it. I gave a nod of approval as we drove in silence, which had become so normal. When we got there, I noticed the house had fresh paint, and the garage door had a different color, green on it.

"Do you like it?" He asked as his eyes were searching for some kind of emotion. "I thought, since your favorite color is that green and it matched the tones of the woods, you might like it."

I just stared at the garage, "It's nice." I mumbled.

You could hear the air escape Jackson as he looked defeated. I just focused on that damn door because, in all reality: I was touched by the fact he did that. But there was no way the emotion of gratitude or happiness was going to surface. They were buried so deep in me, that I wasn't sure if I even understood those emotions anymore.

It didn't take long for him to just drive away. He couldn't look at me and could barely speak to me for the rest of that day. It hurt me to see him hurt, but I was drowning in my own sorrows that I had lost the compassion and love within me. It wasn't fair to anyone around me, the way I acted, the way I shut down, and the way I refused to let anyone help.

I remember this quote; it was on the wall in the copier room at my old school. *"Asking for help isn't giving up; it's refusing to give up."* I learned that it was from this book: *The Boy, the Mole, the Fox and the Horse* by Charlie Mackesy.

Fascinated by the quote, I went ahead and purchased the book. I spent the entire night reading it, rereading it, and letting the words soak in. The book made me realize a different view of things. I read that book every day before I went to bed for a year. Skyla thought I was crazy. But then, one day, I didn't read it. Then that one day turned into days, then weeks, and then months.

That day, when Jackson and I got back from the house, I was sitting on my bed staring at my bookshelf. It had been a while since I had gotten myself to pick up a book. My mind didn't want me to escape the poison inside me; it wanted me to remember that I deserved this never-ending pain.

It was then my eye caught that damn book. I am positive I had a staring contest with it for hours. Finally, I slid off my bed and grabbed the book. I sank to the floor and read it. I kept reading and rereading it, letting the words sting in my brain, hot tears forming in my eyes, and finally, I slept.

I slept on the floor in my room, that book pressed tightly to my chest with my green blanket wrapped around me. That was the first night I was able to sleep with no nightmares. I had been able to sleep through the night because of that damn book.

As I stood, staring at the green garage, I felt a twinge of guilt stab me. I didn't want to believe I had been selfish; no one wanted to, but when it hits you, it makes you sick with self-hatred. It makes you wonder: what other pain can I cause the ones who love me? I knew the pain I caused; it just sucked having it presented in front of me.

I finally walked up to the small front porch, which needed to be replaced, and turned the key to unlock the door. The floors were done: soft carpet in the living room and bedrooms, sleek hardwood in the other rooms.

Taking my shoes off, I let myself take in the gutted house. The kitchen had nothing left, just the wires and shit. All the walls were screaming for paint, and the cabinets in the bathrooms begged to be replaced. The house needed love; it needed to be taken care of; it needed a purpose to keep standing.

The purple bedroom is where I stopped. The only thing new here was the carpet, but the same delicate flowers were painted with a subtle purple background. I let my fingertips trace the flowers; they all had been hand-painted.

When Jackson purchased the house, he told me early on the information that had been given to him. The couple had to be placed in assisted living closer to their son, so that was why they were selling. The blue room had been for their son, but the purple room had a deeper story, one I did more research on last fall.

This family had a daughter, who was ten years older than me. I didn't know her or the family name at all. The daughter, Laken Danner, was picture perfect: homecoming queen, captain of the hockey team, and president of the student council. She was essentially the girl everyone wanted to be.

It was the winter of her senior year; she had told her parents that she was going to her boyfriend's house. She snuck back into her house and slit her own throat in her bed. It was about a day before the parents finally discovered their only daughter. It was heartbreaking to understand why someone like Laken Danner would take her own life.

Well, the parents kept Laken's room the same it had been since the day she died; all the pictures, books, makeup, DVDs, CDs, and shit still there. It was all untouched, waiting for her to return home.

People struggle to try and figure out why someone would take their life. However, there is no clear-cut answer, never has been. I have a few theories on why

Laken Danner took her life, but only one person knows the truth. And she is dead. Sometimes, that is how people want it to be.

With all the therapy, medication, and hospitals, I have heard all the same quotes and reasons to stay. There had only ever been one that struck a chord with me. 'Taking your own life is the most selfish thing you can do.' Why it struck a chord with me was because it sort of pissed me off.

I tried to be a good person; I had tried since I was little. Picked up trash if I saw it on the ground, played with the kid who was alone, gave change to a homeless person, and even saved a damn turtle on the road. I did everything that a good person should do because that was what I felt I had to do.

Since I can only speak from my experience, it isn't like I want to take my life. I know the pain and destruction it can cause everyone. I understand the logic behind the quote; it even makes my stomach go in knots, knowing how selfish I am being. But no matter how good of a person you can be, you still can make a selfish choice.

My selfish choice was to eliminate myself from the world so I could stop dealing with the pain inside. There was only so much fighting I could do. Everyone had a breaking point, and mine had been reached far too many times. This selfish choice weighs heavily on me; every time I attempt, I have crushing emotions of guilt. I can see it and feel it every time I close my eyes. Yet, when I have reached that breaking point, selfishness within wins.

If I had to guess, Laken Danner had been struggling. She was around at a time when mental illness still wasn't something people liked to talk about. This had happened twenty-some years ago, and even now, people still hush and whisper about mental illness.

I plopped myself down on the carpet in the middle of the room and laid back. Instead of feeling like this room was a grave, I was embraced by such warmth. This room didn't want to be untouched and waiting; it wanted life, a redo. I closed my eyes, took a deep breath, and exhaled. Life it wanted, life it would get.

The peace and warmth I had gotten from that room had aided me in falling asleep. I had no idea when I fell asleep or when I woke up. That was the funny thing with naps; time doesn't exist, and it was quite relaxing that way.

"Kensinger, you really do have the worst bedhead." Jackson was sitting up against the wall. "Well, floorhead at this point."

I didn't sit up, "How long have you been creepily watching me sleep?"

He smirked, "I got here like ten minutes ago, but I spent most of the ten minutes looking for you." Jackson lay back on the floor next to me. "I was too dumb to even look in here."

"I am sorry if I freaked you out," I mumbled, eyes focused on the ceiling. "I meant to just look around; sorry if I overstepped."

"Kensinger, this house is your house as much as it is mine, so don't apologize." I bit the inside of my cheek hard. "I am curious; what made you come here?"

I shrugged, "Just wanted to walk through it alone."

Jackson rolled over and looked down at me, "What's going on in your head, Maggie?"

My eyes met his, "Right now? Food."

He grinned, "I like where your head is at. Come on, let's go get some food."

When I got to my feet, the sun glazed over me, as if it was vanishing in the west. I knew I would feel the warmth again because the sun always reappears.

Chapter Six

Steps Forward, Jumps Back

Jackson

Maggie's birthday was just a few days away, and I still didn't know what to get her, or if I should get her anything at all. Skyla already got the ultimate gift: taking her away for a trip with her favorite person. How the fuck was I supposed to top that?

Calvin was no help; he just said dinner and a good fuck. I had to remind him that this was the sister we were talking about. His answer quickly turned to jewelry. There was no way in hell I would ask Skyla, as she would be pissed off. I had waited this long to get her something.

With my head scrambling for ideas, I didn't even notice Calvin had sat down next to me in the cafeteria.

"You know it's polite to say good afternoon back, right?" He said as he stole a fry from my tray.

I rolled my eyes, "Good afternoon, jackass, what have I done to earn this pleasure?"

Calvin smirked, "Well, the chief has some big announcement he wants to make, and I am spreading the word."

"What announcement could he possibly have?"

Calvin shrugged and grabbed another fry, "It probably is the annual ratings or some shit, probably wanting to remind us how much better we are than Sanford."

"You haven't heard anything about Daniel, have you?"

He froze as he was halfway in for another fry. "Mom hasn't said anything, so my guess is there is no news."

"How can we even work with him?" I grumbled.

"We don't have a choice."

"There's always a choice." I fired back.

"Not with Maggie," Calvin smacked his fist on the table, "there isn't a choice for her."

I shook my head, "She should just turn him in and press charges. You and I both know that if he comes back, he's going to do everything he can to get to her."

"Jackson, she is not strong enough to open that wound," Calvin said as he sunk back into the chair. "We can't do that to her, not when she's taken steps forward."

I knew he was right, and fuck did I hate it when he was. She was slowly starting to come back to herself. Maggie Kensinger was finally returning and fighting back. If Daniel did return, she would vanish again. That wound she had with him was too deep and had been hastily closed.

"If I had to guess, he's not coming back." Calvin interrupted my thoughts. "He's got the fear pumping into her, and something tells me that's enough to keep him away."

"Or that would be the exact kind of thing to bring him back." Skyla plopped down next to me. "You guys don't understand sick, twisted men. They like mind games, keeping that fear going."

Calvin made a face, "You look like shit."

She flipped him off; she did look rough, "You look like you've sat on your ass all day." Skyla turned to look at me, "She's going to be okay."

I scoffed, "You can't guarantee that."

"Excuse me?"

"Oh fuck," Calvin said, "I'm out."

He walked away as Skyla glared at me. "You don't think she's going to be okay? What do you think? She's just going to crumble and not fight? Because if that's the case, you don't know her at all. I was there when she went through it."

"Yeah? Remind me, how long did she keep you in the dark?" I spat back.

Skyla sat back and shook her head, "You think she's weak. You think she's fragile."

"Skyla, she's fucking broken. She's broken and trying to heal, and if he returns, all the pieces she's picking up will be shattered again." I clutched my fist. "I never said she was weak; don't put words into my mouth."

She sat there, staring at me in disbelief, "Reminding a broken person they're broken is another way of calling someone weak." Her words burned as they slapped my face. "Thinking that one obstacle will make her lose progress is another way of calling her weak." I felt my stomach drop; everything I had eaten was ready to come up. "You may not have said the exact words, but you sure as fuck meant it."

Skyla shook her head, a disappointed look in her eyes as she turned and headed back down towards the direction of the pit. It was then I noticed how many eyes were on me; nurses, doctors, and families were looking at me. There was still a buzz of noise; I am sure not everyone heard all the words exchanged, but enough had as they were all staring.

Grabbing my tray, I dumped it and, headed up to an on-call room and slammed it behind me. I pounded my fists on the wall, not pissed off at Skyla, pissed off at myself.

Everything she said was true. I was broken, and if someone thought that setting pills in front of me would cause me to crash down, they would be calling me weak. I pressed my back and, slid down and buried my hands into my face. Maggie wasn't weak, fuck, she was the farthest thing from weak. But thinking that Daniel would make her lose everything she's fought for, I made her sound weak.

If there is anything I have learned about Skyla and Maggie's relationship, it is that they tell each other everything. Especially when it came to shit Calvin or I did. I knew better than to go and tell Maggie I didn't mean what I implied. Skyla would tell her, and I would have to deal with the wrath that followed.

Or I could hope Skyla would keep the exchange to us, which was lunatic thinking. But I was desperate and needed to grasp onto whatever hope I could.

My day continued with two more surgeries before Calvin paged me to meet him in the conference room across from the chief's office. My stomach sank; what the hell could I be needed for? Did it have to do with Maggie? Was there a report that I caused a disturbance in the cafeteria? My mind was coming up with the most pathetic ideas on why I could be finding myself in the conference room.

Taking a deep breath, I opened the door to find loads of doctors from every department in there. Obviously, not all of them were here, but a huge chunk. My eyes scanned and noted that Julia Kensinger was here, standing next to the chief. I took note of Dr. Loggins being here, but I could not find Skyla or Calvin. Julia smiled at me, as she was in conversation with the chief.

What kind of meeting is this? All the department heads were here except Calvin. All of the general was here, and most of the other departments had a good showing. I was puzzled by the absence of Skyla, who probably was stuck in the pit, and Calvin, who was the one who paged me here.

"Okay," Chief Kensinger yelled, "I have called you all here because I have some information regarding the hospital." There was a hushed whisper that fell over us. "First, I would like to introduce Dr. Julia Kensinger. I know many of you know her, but she worked at this hospital for many years and was married to my brother."

Julia's face crumpled a little at the sound of her marriage. In the months since her husband's passing, she had lost weight, her eyes were sunken in, and she lost all warmth to her. From what Maggie and Calvin had told me about their parents, they had been married forever and were happy. It wasn't until dementia that things took a turn, leaving Julia divorced and eventually her spouse dead.

"As many of you have been wondering," Julia began; she stood next to the chief with perfect posture. "Dr. Loggins is retiring coming in July. We are happy to have had him as the head of the psychiatric floor all these years." People clapped and said congrats to Dr. Loggins. "He will be able to enjoy his retirement in warmer weather down in Texas."

The chief gave a nod as Julia sat back down. "We have decided who will be taking Dr. Loggins's place." I felt my veins turn cold. "I am happy to say that Dr. Daniel Dobson will be joining us. He is a world-renowned psychiatrist and good friend to the Kensinger family all these years." My fists were clutched at my sides; sweat was dripping down from my back. "He will officially begin in a few weeks, and I am asking everyone to be welcoming and show the Minnesotan kind we are known for."

There was a chuckle from a few people and a hand motion from the chief that this was over. I bolted out of the room, headed down the stairs, nearly falling, and into the locker room. I hastily changed into shorts and a T-shirt and made my way to my car. My head was filled with white noise.

The weather outside had turned cloudy, and there was a sharp breeze. I drove without thought or care; my mind focused on the fact that I would not be able to protect her. That the nightmare was coming true again. I was washed with the looming thought: I couldn't do anything.

I parked my car in the driveway, without even taking notes of whose cars were there. I slammed my door shut and busted them in the door to the garage. Calvin was the only one in my sight, otherwise the house was empty.

He grabbed my shoulders and gripped them tightly. My eyes were scanning for her, waiting for her to come running down the stairs and into my arms. I wanted to smell the comforting scent of lavender and vanilla. I wanted the calmness of her voice. The mystery of her eyes. I needed to see that she was okay.

"Jackson," Calvin's voice cut through my longing thoughts, "Hey, dude, look at me."

"Where is she?" I growled as I shrugged off Calvin's hands off me.

He shook his head, "You need to calm your ass down."

I glared at him, "CALM DOWN? You're joking? He's back, and he's back soon."

"You don't think I know that?" Calvin snapped back. "You don't think Skyla knows that? The last thing Maggie needs is for everyone around her to come crumbling down."

"Where is she?" I repeated. "Calvin, where the fuck is she?"

He sighed and stepped back, "Skyla and she are together somewhere. She's not here."

"Does she know?"

Calvin nodded, "When I saw Mom at the hospital, she told me, and I went running to Skyla." He squeezed his eyes shut in pain. "I didn't know what to do, so I yelled at my mother for bringing him here."

"Skyla told her, didn't she?" I asked.

"She is the only one that deserves to tell her. You should have seen the pain in Skyla's eyes when I told her. It was like someone had stabbed her abdomen."

I took a deep breath, "What are we going to do?"

Calvin shrugged, "She's taken steps forward; even if this sets her up for a few steps back, she's still taken steps forward."

I wanted to believe that this would only set her back a few steps. But in my pathetic heart, I knew this was going to be a bigger setback than we all assumed.

Chapter Seven

Coping 101

Maggie

I had grabbed the first bottles of liquor I could at the liquor store off the main drive. I had a tight hold on the bag as Skyla and I drove in silence. It had been silence since she came rushing into my room at four o'clock in the afternoon. The look of sheer helplessness indicated what she had to say.

Ever since I saw Daniel, I knew it was only a matter of time before he would come back into my life. He had seen the damage and power he still held. He wasn't going to let that go to waste; he was going to take every minute of it.

In my session with Dr. Loggins weeks ago, he informed me that he was retiring. It was then that I knew Daniel's return was coming. I knew if Mom learned Daniel was looking for a job, she would help him at all costs. He was someone my dad loved and trusted. They had known each other for decades, even before my mom had been in the picture.

Having suspected Daniel coming back, I took my time reminding myself what I had now that I didn't when I was eighteen. I knew that I held an upper hand because not only of the protection I had, but my strength and knowledge of how he worked.

Before I turned to education, I had taken a load of psych classes, and Dr. Kathleen Fauller taught one. She had worked with criminals, meeting with them, trying to grasp what their minds held. She was well respected, but after a criminal was able to physically attack her, she stepped away and became a professor.

Dr. Fauller talked about how serial killers or rapists tend to follow the same footprint every time. A lot of the time, they would take a token for their accomplishment, or they would repeat the same pattern every time. They wanted to be known and feared; that was what they fed on.

There was so much I learned from that class, but taking in those key points of using the same footprint, I was able to figure out how Daniel would get to me. I was able to unleash the painful memories of the assaults. But I knew going through this torture of reliving was only going to help me.

In conclusion, I figured out that I had the upper hand. He wasn't surrounded by those who had worked with him for years. The last time, I was naive and kept everyone in the dark; this time, others knew. Daniel also didn't have the luxury of interacting with me daily like last time. So, this time, he was going to have to seek me out, which was more of a challenge because of the people around me.

I knew he was smart; he wouldn't dare try anything in the first months he was here. I am sure he was going to present himself as not a threat. Daniel was going to work his way to get people around him to trust him, that would be including my uncle and mother.

However, because he still wanted to use me, he was going to try everything to get to me. It was going to be like playing a game, and people like him loved games. What he didn't know now was I had adapted to playing these cruel games.

Skyla drove us to the ski resort, and we sat at the top of the hill while we sipped the different liquor bottles back and forth. She didn't ask questions, and I didn't offer conversation starters. We just took in silence and view.

"You have every right to be scared." She finally said, taking a swig from the tequila, I had grabbed. "You have every right to feel what you want."

I turned to look at her, "I am scared; only a fool wouldn't be."

She gave a sad smile, "You already suspected this, didn't you?"

Nodding, I took a drink from the vodka bottle. "When Dr. Loggins told me he was retiring, I knew." I closed my eyes and laid back. "I am sorry I didn't say something sooner."

"There is no need to apologize for how you processed the information. I just wish I had a heads up."

"It isn't going to be like last time." I opened my eyes and looked at her. "This time, it is a whole different playing field with more players in this game. Just this time, more are aware of the game."

Skyla shook her head, "You always find a way to make things poetic, don't you?"

I smiled, "You know that poetry is my forte."

She laughed and laid back with me, "Life is a cruel game."

Life is a cruel game.

***

The following days, Jackson didn't bring up the elephant in the room. We avoided any conversation about it. I wasn't ready to hear the anger and protests of turning Daniel in. Most of all, I didn't want to start a fight when things were finally getting back to some sense of normal.

It wasn't until we had landed in Atlanta that Jackson texted me that he was going to support me however I needed. I ignored the text and focused on getting off the plane and to our next gate.

I had traveled more times than I could count with Skyla. We both liked to be overly prepared and on time. We also both had a slight problem with motion sickness on the plane. It also didn't help that Skyla had a fear of heights, so that she couldn't sit near the window. She usually put a sleeping mask on, took a fuck load of Dramamine, and slept. Which left me to be the one who was awake and sluggish.

The window seat had always been my favorite seat. I loved to look down at the squares roads formed or the veins of cities at night time. I enjoyed the peace of being in the clouds; it felt like the real world was just a dream and that this was reality. Being high up in the clouds meant you had no idea what was going down below, which, for me, meant no stress. I could just enjoy being removed from reality.

As always, the landing part of the plane ride was always the worst. I had to close the window, squeeze Skyla's hand, and count in my head until it was over. In the meantime, she would be gripping my hand just as tight, fearing for her life.

In the airports, Skyla and I loved walking around. It was interesting to see how much people didn't care in airports. As I have stated before, everyone is focused on just getting there, and everyone has that in common. What I have also noticed is that people just don't give a shit about anything else. Skyla and I found such peace that, for once, no one bothered to look at us because they were too busy worrying about themselves. We could finally live without an audience.

When we finally landed in Miami, the heat slapped us across the face. Skyla sighed happily; she lived for this shit, the heat. As for me, no. I could already feel my hair expanding from the humidity.

"You and me, babes." She wrapped her around me. "We are going to let go."

Let go, we did. We put our phones in airplane mode and stayed focused on just us. Alcohol, sun, delicious food, sunburn, nightclubs. We ended up drunk riding on an electric scooter together and fell off a fair share of times. Then we went night swimming in the ocean, well only me. Skyla was deathly afraid of sharks, and as she reminded me, lying on the sand while I floated:

"SHARKS FEED AT NIGHT BITCH, I AM NOT SAVING YOU!"

I just laughed and let the warm feeling spread through my body in the cold water. After the scooter ride and swim, we jumped on the king bed with an expensive bottle of tequila. I don't know how late we were up, laughing and giggling about random shit.

The hangover was deathly, but it was worth it to let go. A place where there was no chance of seeing someone we knew. We were able to do a spa day, perfect for recovering from the hangover. We ate pizza in fancy hotel room robes, drank wine, and watched *Forensic Files* on the big flat screen. It had been a while since I felt this overwhelming joy and relief, so I savored every minute. Most of all, I got to let go of my better half. Best birthday, hands down.

Jackson

She was in Florida. She was safe. That was what I had to keep telling myself. It had been choking me alive that we hadn't discussed Daniel. I wanted to know what she was thinking, what her plan was, and if she was scared. For once, I can say, I envied that Skyla was the only one she had talked to.

I knew better than to be jealous of the bond they had. In fact, it was kind of remarkable. They held each other accountable, yet they defended and protected each other, even when one might have been in the wrong. Their bond wasn't something you saw every day; it was rare.

Yet, this pissed me off. Maggie went to her instead of me. Maggie trusted her instead of me. Maggie loved her instead of me. Maggie would always choose Skyla.

"You realize that you are overthinking it," Calvin said as we were in his high rise. "The reason she went to Skyla wasn't because of you; it is because they understand each other better than them own selves."

I kept my eyes focused on the stupid NBA game on the TV. "I still can't help but be offended by it."

"Bentley used to say the same shit," Calvin chuckled, "it would take something serious for him to get to that point."

I glanced over at Calvin, "You make it sound like you were best friends, when I know for a fact, you weren't."

"Correct, but Skyla and I do more than fight and fuck." I made a face as Calvin smiled. "Bentley used to get offended when Skyla would have nightmares, and she went running to Maggie. Or when Skyla and her mom would fight, take a guess who she went running to."

It made sense, but selfishness inside was winning. "I get it, but there's got to be a point when they realize they can love someone just as much."

Calvin shook his head, "There is no doubt Maggie loves you more than you seem to think. But you must realize they have gone through shit, and they were the only ones there to help each other. I know it is frustrating, but you've got to understand it isn't because she doesn't love you; it's because Skyla is her everything." I looked over at Calvin, who was dressed in shorts and a baggy T-shirt. "Carlsen, you better get used to it if you want to stay around."

***

Maggie and Skyla had been gone for three days, and in the three days, I had managed to work a forty-eight-hour shift and spend the last day sleeping and lounging at Calvin's. I didn't want to be at the townhouse; it didn't feel right without either of them there. I also wasn't up to sleeping in my house, which had no water or electricity running.

On the day they were set to return, I was on call for the night shift. I knew they wouldn't be getting in until later, so I found myself in an on-call room alone. It didn't take much for me to drift off into a sleep. In the years of medical school and residency, you learn how to sleep when you can. You also get used to sleeping where you can as well.

I don't know how much sleep I had managed to sleep before getting woken up, not by my pager, but by the door slamming shut and the twist of the lock. It took my eyes a minute to adjust to who was in the room with me.

"You know, Kensinger, a simple nudge would've been fine to wake me up."

Maggie rolled her eyes and stood over the bed, "Yeah, Calsen? I have been nudging you for the last five minutes, and that clearly worked."

I sat up, "What time is it?"

"One o'clock. Our plane got in a few hours ago, and Skyla went to sleep because she works in the morning. Calvin said you were on call, so I figured I would slip in and see you."

She had clearly gotten a lot of sun in the days she had been gone. You could see parts of her shoulders had been burned, along with her cheeks. However, her skin had a little more color to it instead of the milky pale skin I was used to seeing. She was dressed in track shorts and a tight-fitting tank top; I could tell she wasn't wearing a bra.

I pulled her in between my legs; I could smell the lavender and vanilla. "I am going to assume you had fun?"

My fingertips brushed the inside of her leg, sending immediate warmth throughout my body. "Minus being hungover on the second day, I would love to stay there forever." She paused and smirked, "The heat could vanish, and then it would be perfect."

Maggie then slowly lowered herself on top of me, wrapping her legs around my waist. She wore a small smile as I carefully brushed a strand of her hair from her face. I then placed my hands on her waist as she raised an eyebrow at me.

"You're really going to fuck me in an on-call room?"

I felt my heart pounding, "Is there a problem? I want to fuck you right now?"

She shook her head as a joyous laugh escaped her. I took off her tank top and immediately began teasing her breasts. Maggie's hands took off my top, and then my mouth collided with hers. I laid her back down on the bed, kissing her neck and pulling off her shorts.

I pushed one finger inside of her, fuck, she was wet. She whimpered as I lowered my mouth right to her clit. Maggie took a sharp breath as I slowly began tasting her. In perfect circular motions, my tongue began making her legs shake, and fingers rake through my hair. She gasped and whispered my name, indicating that she was close. Fuck. I gently sucked on her clit as her sweet cum hit my lips.

Without another thought, I took my cock out and thrust into her. I groaned into her neck as her nails dug into my back. Fuck she was tight. I really didn't know if I could last long, making me pissed at myself, but she was just too irresistible. It wasn't long until I finished, after she growled my name in my ear.

We lay there in that on-call room, as she smiled up at me. I cupped her face and kissed her forehead and then lips. Despite being sunburned, her skin was still smooth. Her hair even seemed to be lighter from the Florida sunlight.

"What are you thinking about?" She asked, eyes searching my face.

I smiled, "Just admiring."

She rolled her eyes, "Whatever, Calsen."

I pulled her close to me. "Are you scared?"

Maggie didn't react; she simply mumbled, "Of course."

"I don't know what to do," I admitted as I smoothed her hair down. "I don't know what you want me to do."

Maggie remained silent for a moment as she pondered my statements. She looked at me, "Don't underestimate me."

This caught me off guard, "What?"

"Don't underestimate me. I know you think that you must do all the protecting. I am stronger than you assume." I opened my mouth to argue, but she pressed her finger on my lips to silence me. "I know you've seen a weak part of me these last months, but don't let that fool you."

There was so much I could say, so much I wanted to say. But the best thing I could do was pull her to my chest and whisper: "Okay."

Chapter Eight

Face Your Fears, Child

Maggie

My first biggest fear as a child was squirrels. I was like four years old when Calvin told me if you looked squirrels dead in the eyes, they would come and attack you. I went and got close to one and looked it in the eyes, and sure enough, it started to run towards me. I was then terrified for years. Mom got me a stuffed animal that was a squirrel, and I screamed and had nightmares.

It wasn't until I was nine that my fear of being stung by an insect won over. That still holds true to this day; I fear I will go into encephalitic shock and die. I had yet to be stung to this day, but you can bet your ass I go running when I see something with a stinger.

It didn't matter about all the fears before; what mattered was facing the ones now. Being attacked by a squirrel or stung by a wasp seemed pointless. I had to walk back into the place where not only was I nearly killed, but the place where I killed someone. A fear that I could've never imagined in my wildest dreams.

I had attempted to go to the school, but my heart started racing at the sight. My head then filled with the sounds of gunshots, and then I would have to leave because I couldn't. Then I would be upset with myself for not being stronger, that this made me weak and broken.

Growing up, mom and dad would never let us say we can't. And if we did, we got things like CDs or magazines or even TV time taken away. Their reasoning was: What if we all said I can't? Then, it would go down some lecture about not getting anywhere if you had that attitude and mindset. However, in these last months, I haven't become part of my daily vocabulary.

I wasn't a strong believer in God or some higher power. The hand I had been dealt with and Skyla's hand she had been dealt, it seemed impossible there was some good. I had been raised Catholic by my parents, but it was never something that I used to identify myself.

When Bentley died, I figured he was just up in the clouds watching the horrors of the world. Then, I liked to think he was selective about what he saw, the same with my grandparents and my aunt, whom I never knew. It was better to think they saw only the good parts of my life. That same mindset stood for my dad, but somehow, I knew he saw it all. Me being weak. I'm trying to kill myself. I'm pushing everyone away. I am in all the worst situations.

Because of this sick feeling that he was watching my every move, I figured I needed to face my fears, because I couldn't wasn't something I could keep saying. It also didn't help that August would be here in the blink of an eye, and I wouldn't have a choice to face this fear.

Facing it by choice felt better than facing it forced; that was what finally convinced me.

I knew there would be only one person I would want there: Skyla. I couldn't have Jackson see any more part of me become weak. I needed him to believe in me, and seeing me face this fear would not help.

The weather was eerily like that day, making my stomach do flips as Skyla drove. I couldn't think about the day; I needed to think of all the good that had come from my job. The happiness and joy I had, like my first day of student teaching or getting my own classroom. I needed to train my body to believe I was safe.

When we turned into the parking lot, I took a sharp breath. Joy in the job. First day of student teaching. Seeing a child succeed. Seeing a child killed. Killing a child. I bit down hard on my lip, thinking of the first moments of walking into your classroom. Remember the hugs, the smiles, and how devoted you were. I had my hands clutched into balls. Joy. Happiness. Devotion.

Skyla parked and watched me carefully as I unbuckled my seatbelt, eyes fixed on the front doors. They had replaced and fixed the glass that had been shattered. How much would look different for the fixes? How much would it still look the same?

"Are you ready?" She asked as her hand lingered on the door handle of her car. "You've made it further than you have before." She reminded me.

Think of the laughter that filled your classroom. Think of the pictures they would make you. Think, focus, think happy. My mind was spinning like a lunatic, repeating phrases and shoving memories into my brain. Focus, breathe, and think happily.

Without a thought in the world, I opened the car door, closed it, and made my wall up to the front of the school. I pressed my hand onto the new glass; echoes of screams filled my head. I hit my fist hard against the glass, pausing all the sounds. I must go in. I must.

I scanned my key card, and it turned green, making a dinging sound. Skyla opened the door, and I stepped inside; the little girl crying out my name screeched in my head. Think of all the books you bought for your classroom and how much joy it was. Focus. Breath. I am a lunatic.

Stepping into the commons and lunchroom, nothing seemed different. My eyes were scanning for the differences, and there was nothing. It was then I remembered that footprint and timeline they had played out on the news. Maxwell had entered from the front, shooting through the glass. He then fatally shot Ms. Kelly (the secretary) and fired at Nurse Dana, who was only hit in the shoulder.

Luckily, there was no one in the cafeteria or the commons, which seemed odd, but maybe it was a stroke of luck. Maxwell proceeded down the third-grade hallway to the right, finding all doors locked. Quickly made my way to the second-grade hallway and was able to get a few shots at students who were up against the door screaming. Their teacher had to run to the restroom, so the teacher next door was trying to watch both rooms. When she heard the announcement, she barricaded her room, leaving the others to fend for themselves.

Mrs. Jenkins, the teacher who had been in the restroom, came running out, and he shot her quickly in the stomach. Her students were pressed up on the window, and the door saw her go down. Little did anyone know she was thirteen weeks pregnant with her second child. So technically, another life was taken, just no one knew right away.

Maxwell must've heard kids evacuating in other hallways and decided that they were easier targets than busting down that second-grade door. The assumption was that he knew his time was short, so he went down the Kindergarten wing, and that's where a good chunk of the fatalities were. Ms. Ashton, a girl I went to high school with, decided it was worth the risk of evacuating. Fourteen of her nineteen were killed, the others fatally wounded. Ms. Ashton was hit four times in various places.

My room was the next closest one, and he had to know his time was running out. Then, everything happened: the swing of the bat, screams, gunshots, and blood. It was then the shooting ended, but also the life of Maxwell Fath.

I know most people see him as a villain, and I normally would, too. But I knew that he had been in pain, and a sick part of me felt bad that he had been experiencing this. Where I drew the line of sympathy was the moment he decided to take his pain out on others.

Slowly, I took a step forward towards the kindergarten hallway, taking a deep breath. Gunshots echoed in my head as I entered the hallway, and images of six-year-olds dead on the ground. When they were carrying me away from my classroom, I saw all the bodies. I saw the damage. I saw it all. Seeing Ms. Ashton lifeless, a girl who I did not like, but grew up with, stung. The students were running for their lives, and seeing them felt like I got shot all over again.

The hallway I stood in now looked nothing like the scene I had experienced the last time. The floors were shiny because they had been waxed. The bulletin boards were bare, and the flags and hanging lights were gone. It looked like the inside of an operating room, not touched.

My door had been replaced; it didn't even look the same. I stood staring, flashes of the gun coming into view and Maxwell Fath. The screams from my students filled my ears, and I could feel my feet rooting into the ground. My name being called by that poor student, Abbie Ashland, the youngest of four and only daughter. Her mother was a general surgeon at Stanford Hospital; her dad was a stay-at-home. Abbie loved coming to see me; she would always hug me every morning.

I wished I could've opened the door. It ate me alive every night, her voice echoing the halls of my dreams. I remember in my first year of teaching, we did a live active shooter drill, just the staff. We had a meeting informing us of what we were going into. I was placed into a room with three other teachers and prepared for the drill. I didn't know what I was getting into.

During the drill, they fired blanks in the hallway. Then, they had people pounding on the door, begging to let them in. It was their pleading voices and slamming fists that made me swallow back vomit as the teacher next to me had a panic attack. The gunshots didn't phase me; it was the pleas and then shots that happened right outside the door that struck a chord with me.

You can't open the door to save one life when you put multiple people in danger. The person stuck in the hallway must find their way out or somewhere to hide. Normally, some trainings have you barricade the door, and there is no way you can open the door for someone anyway. You were left to fend for yourself.

"Maggie," Skyla's voice cut through my thoughts, "you don't have to go in. You've gotten this far, and I am proud."

My hand was hovering over the new door handle, "I have made it this far; I am not backing down."

The cold handle met my hand as I walked into the place that had been my peace. I didn't know what they all had kept in my room; I don't remember the mess or what had to be removed. I was expecting a cold and empty room, like nothing had happened, but that was not what I got.

The lights and decor that I had hanging were gone, and the ceiling looked brand new. My class carpet was gone; a new carpet had been ordered and was on the floor beside my rocking chair. My classroom library was still there, and my storage was untouched. My tables were all pushed to the back of the room as the floor had been waxed and cleaned. My walls had been painted a gray tone, and there was nothing on any bulletin boards.

The only thing that seemed untouched and unbothered was the back corner where my desk was. Without glancing at anything else, I made my way to it. My black coat was still on my chair. My handwritten lesson plans opened up on that day in January. My computer was still plugged in and on the stand. My purple bag was open; you could see a few notebooks peeking out. All the pictures I had were still there. My can of Red Bull still sat there, with dust and mold. No one had touched this. Right in front of me was the last piece of my old life I had left.

My fingertips brushed my lesson plans; I had everything set and planned for the rest of the month. I grabbed my coat and closed my eyes as the sudden screams and gunshots filled my head. Throbbing flashes of Maxwell's body appeared. If only I had barricaded the door. If only I had just knocked him out. If only I had been in a car accident that day. If only I had a fever or threw up that day. If only. If only I could stop it all.

If I had not been here, what damage would have happened to my students? What kind of guilt would I bear? If only it was a mind trap; they didn't comfort you; they made you relive your intrusive thoughts.

Skyla was watching me as she sat at one of the tables and crossed her legs. "Eerie, isn't it? They change everything but leave your area the same."

I shrugged; she had a point. The fact that almost everything else was cleaned, but my personal space wasn't. Maybe it was supposed to be a reminder of the purpose I had agreed to. Or a symbol that there still was life here. Either way, Skyla was right: eerie.

"I never thought there would be a day where the place I found peace and comfort, would become the place I feared," I said as I picked up the can of Red Bull and threw it into the trash.

Skyla frowned, "I wouldn't say you fear this place as much as it is a place you grieve."

"I killed someone in here. Who's to say I won't become a killer again?" I snapped back.

"You killed that boy because he was going to kill those damn kids you love and yourself." She stood up and walked up to me. "You're not a murderer; you aren't killing people for the thrill or some fucked reason."

I squeezed my hand around my jacket. "That's not what I am saying; who's to say I won't be put in the same situation."

Skyla sighed, "The chance that a public-school student will be shot is 1 in 614,000,000, according to the internet. The statistics of it happening again is even lower; there have been maybe like four school shootings that have happened in the same place twice, but they were high schools and colleges."

"You did research," I said dryly.

"Maggie, what you have to ask yourself is this: what would you change if you could?"

I sat down in my chair, "I would still hit him, get the gun out of his reach, and hold him down until help arrived."

Skyla smiled, "Then, in the rare case it happens again, you know what you would do differently."

"Sometimes it pisses me off that you are wise."

"Yeah, sometimes it pisses me off how little you think of yourself." She fired back.

I looked up at her, "It pisses me off how little you think of yourself; it goes both ways."

Skyla kneeled in front of me, "I would give anything to see how you see me." She whispered and squeezed my hand. "I know you think the same thing."

We stayed frozen like that for a few moments. Funny how you could see someone you loved through a different lens from what they see of themselves. It was more cruel than funny. However, I know that I feared seeing myself through a different lens. A fear that remained buried deep, a fear that I refuse to face.

Chapter Nine

The Devil Has Many Forms

Jackson

Growing up, my mother would do her best to drag us to church. It was her peace, especially after my father died. I never liked going to church, neither did my sisters. For me, it all logically didn't make sense to me, and it definitely didn't bring me comfort. I still went because I knew it made my mom happy. I didn't complain because being in that church was the only time I saw my mom relax. It was a rare sight, and that was what brought me comfort.

Church was difficult for me; I had too many questions. There seemed to be too many unrealistic events. Not to mention the whole water turning into wine shit. But I will say, I do believe there is a devil. I have seen the devil.

The image that was always in my head was this little man with a pointed tail and ears dressed in all red. I always pictured him with black eyes, beard, and nails. The fire wasn't what I saw in my mind. Instead, it was this black fog that hung around. It was a fog that seemed to cling to you, something that couldn't be shed.

The devil has many forms. It wasn't just that cliché little man; it was different for each person. For some, it was gambling or guns. My father's devil had to have been the bottle of liquor. My devil was pills. Maggie's devil wasn't an object; it was a person.

Daniel was set to return this coming week, but no one knew any details about it. I just know there were a lot of people who were excited to have him on staff, talking about all the good he had done overseas and in the Denver area alone. They seemed to always be praising the papers he wrote.

When I was working a night shift, I sat down in the pit with Skyla after doing my rounds. I used the computer down there to read these papers. As sick as it made me, Daniel was very smart, and they were written very well, at least better than what I could ever do. Instead of using his knowledge to protect, he used it on Maggie; he used it on someone who was forced to keep their mouth shut. He knew Maggie wouldn't be able to convince anyone, and she knew herself. Sexual offenders usually liked holding that power, something that was a drive for some.

Reading those papers put me in a sickening mood that I had to force myself to drink ginger ale, so I wouldn't throw up. The devil was returning, and I knew he was going to have that black fog around him, suffocating Maggie and taking her down.

It wasn't like I viewed Maggie as weak; she sure as hell could hold her own, but there is something different about the devil. A person's greatest weakness is the devil. In my mind, that black fog penetrates the body, taking whatever strength there is and killing it. That is how it clung to you, taking the place of your strength.

I know the concept seemed silly, but it was the concept I stuck to, one that I believed. And I had no problem if others didn't see it that way. As I said, the devil has many forms.

***

Wednesday morning, I woke up to Maggie tossing a variety of clothes out of her closet. She was clearly on the hunt for something. I sat up and threw back a shirt she had tossed out. It landed beside her, and she glared at me as she threw it back.

"I had it over there for a reason."

I smiled, "And good morning to you, too."

Maggie's eyes softened, "Sorry," she sighed, "Mom is asking me to wear something nice when I go over and it's freaking me out."

"Why do you need to wear something nice?"

She shrugged, "Who knows? Maybe she has reservations for lunch at Tutto Bene."

"Where?"

"A nice Italian restaurant here in town. It is my mother's favorite place, always has been." Maggie pulled out a pink dress and made a face. "Either way, you have to put your name in for a reservation weeks in advance since Covid.”

Ah, good old Covid. “I don't think I have ever seen it. Where the hell is it at?”

“Downtown, I am sure if I showed you the building, you would recognize it.” Maggie threw a pair of heeled boots out. “Whatever Mom wants me to dress up for doesn't matter.”

“Why are you so stressed about it?”

She paused and looked back at me, “Anika is back in town because of Daniel returning.”

“And because you two don't get along.”

Maggie gave me a frown before coming over and sitting right next to me on the bed. “Anika blames me for Dad dying.”

“What the fuck?” I blurted.

“Anika believes if I had never come back, Dad wouldn't have gone downhill so quickly. She thinks I caused too much stress.”

“She's a doctor! Anika had to have known how bad your dad was getting; there was nothing that could be done.” I fired back, pissed off now at Anika.

Maggie placed her hands around mine, “It is easier to blame someone for death than dealing with it.”

Without another word, she went back into her closet and began to pull out more clothes as I sat back on the bed. My mom blamed herself for my dad's death. My sisters blamed me for Dad's death. Calvin had to blame Kara for Heather's death. Blame. Blame was the common word used. It was also easier to blame people for fucking up or why something didn't go the right way.

I threw on a t-shirt and headed downstairs to the kitchen to get some coffee brewing. To my surprise, Skyla was passed out face-first in her book at the kitchen table. Calvin was brewing coffee as he was scrolling through his phone; he glanced up and motioned for me to be quiet.

Obeying his motion, I grabbed a coffee mug, filled it up, and headed back upstairs to shower. By the time I had showered and dressed, Maggie had been able to finally decide on something to wear. I kissed her goodbye and told her I would see her tonight. And just like that, what seemed to have a normal start would turn to hell.

Maggie

I knew why Mom wanted me to dress up; I had known for a few days. Daniel was to start at the hospital today, and the Kensinger family had to be front and center welcoming him. I knew it was going to happen. Mom had told me last week, but I didn't want to tell Jackson. I have known Daniel returning was stressing him out, fuck, it was stressing Calvin and Skyla. So, telling Jackson the exact date it was going to happen was only going to ruin his week, and he didn't deserve to have a fucked week.

Anika had flown in late last night and was flying out this evening, so she didn't miss anything at school. The good news about that was I didn't have to talk or deal with her. I knew she blamed me. I knew she was pissed that I was the one to find our father. Anika was also equally pissed because I had attempted again. Anika was bitter, just like she always was.

The bright side to this was that she had never said it to my face; she only whined to Calvin, who told Skyla, who then told me. There was no way in hell Anika would say this shit to my face now. She probably was too scared to see my reaction, especially after our last interaction.

The plan for the day was to meet at the hospital at noon; there would be an announcement and lunch catered. All I had to do was stick close to Calvin and smile. As long as I remained close to him, Daniel wouldn't dare touch or talk to me. If he did, that would be enough for Calvin alone to punch him.

I knew I was asking a lot of Skyla, Jackson, and Calvin. I knew it wasn't going to be easy working with the very man who destroyed everything in me. But there was no way I could handle exposing Daniel right now. In my mind, there would be no good that would come from it. All there would be is sadness and anger; Lord knows we already have enough of that going on.

The outfit I settled on was a lilac-colored long-sleeve romper with black heels. My hair was naturally wavy, and I wore the basics of makeup; I didn't need to draw attention. I just needed to remain in the shadows.

The drive to the hospital was silent as I sat in the front seat of Calvin's car. It was pouring down rain with an endless supply of gray clouds in the sky. It was a bit chillier than normal, mid-fifties out, and a light breeze. The weather seemed to match my mood perfectly; better yet, it mirrored how I felt daily. I think that is why I have always enjoyed these kinds of days.

"You think he's going to try anything?"

I shook my head, "He's smarter than that, plus he's not going to give himself away like that."

"When are you going to tell Mom? Or even just our uncle?"

"Not anytime soon." I shot back at him. "They are still grieving because of Dad; the last thing they need to find out."

Calvin clenched his jaw as he focused on the road. I know it seemed selfish to put the people I loved most in this position, but I couldn't deal with Daniel. I had so much other fucking shit that I needed to patch up first before getting to that open wound.

When we got to the hospital, we parked on the first level ramp in Calvin's precious spot. He hung close to me as we made our way through the side door and down the hall. I kept my head down, the way I usually always was, as we proceeded onto the elevator.

"It's okay if you're not okay," Calvin stated as he swiped his card and pressed the button to my uncle's office.

I shook my head, "It will be okay." I said unconvincingly. "All I have to do is smile and pretend."

The elevator chimed, and we stepped off and walked into my uncle's office. No surprise, my mother and Anika were there drinking coffee from the coffee shop across the street from the hospital. They both had always had a coffee addiction, and yet, neither of them owned a coffee maker.

Anika frowned at me; her hair was pulled up in a tight bun, and she had dark makeup on. I ignored her as my mother embraced me in a hug, going on about how beautiful I looked. I just gave her a weak smile as I saw Anika's eyes dart down to the scar on my leg. She looked back at me and rolled her eyes.

I watched Calvin give Mom a huge hug and give a slight nod to Anika. There was a loud silence that hung in the air. I could tell Mom was uneasy; she knew Anika hated everything to do with me. Growing up, we always fought over ridiculous things like clothes and makeup, but once my father decided to disown me, Anika had no issue jumping ship. She was a suck-up and got what she wanted because she was the baby.

"Julia!" Chills went down my spine as the door opened, and his voice filled the silence. "My God, you look amazing."

Calvin's eyes were on me as I remained frozen and tense. Anika bounced up from her seat and went to greet him. The sounds of sirens filled my head, drowning everything else out. I closed my eyes and let the sirens take over as I saw the flashing colors.

"And, my dear, Maggie." His voice cut through my calm as I flashed my eyes open to see him standing there. "You look beautiful as always," he reached out to squeeze my shoulder, and Calvin butted in by hugging him.

I took a few steps back and let the pain of his voice grace my body, and the image of him smiling at me burned in my head. Even during the hug, his dark eyes focused on me. He was searching me, taking in the sight of my body that had changed. Daniel was savoring every aspect there was to me, and there was not a damn thing I could do but remain frozen, letting him. He loved every second of it.

"Daniel, you look good." Calvin patted him on the shoulder. "Old age hasn't hit yet."

From a person who was good at reading people, but voices as well, he was clearly sarcastic. Mom's eyes narrowed at him, clearly picking up on the dig, but everyone else seemed oblivious to it. My uncle began talking to everyone about positions and where to stand, and where to look for the damn cameras.

Without really listening, I followed Calvin out the door with my head down; Anika was behind me. Taking a glance back at her, my eyes met Daniel's as he was talking with my mother. I snapped my head back and focused on my steps; it had been a while since I walked in heels. I kept listening to the click and click of my heels on the floor, letting that echo in my brain instead of the nagging fear.

Jackson

When I finished with my only surgery of the day, to my shock, Skyla was waiting in the scrub room. Her long dark red hair was down, falling below her waist, and she wore light traces of mascara. Skyla, for once, did not look like death or have dark circles under her eyes.

"I would quit staring perv," she snapped, "hurry up and scrub out."

"Why?"

Skyla snapped her fingers, "Let's go; I need someone to stand by at this stupid event thing, so hurry the fuck up."

"What event?" I asked as I began the process of scrubbing out. "And why aren't you begging Calvin to be your side bitch?"

"Careful, Calsen," she shook her head and pulled out her phone to check the time. "And because he's with Maggie at this stupid event."

I snapped my head in her direction, "What is this event?"

She sighed, "Introducing Daniel to the hospital and the community, all of them are on stage."

"Why didn't she tell me?" I growled as I threw my scrub cap off. "I even asked her what she was doing."

Kicking the laundry bin, I pressed my hands to my eyes. Why had she kept that from me? It wasn't like a secret that Daniel was returning; we were past that, but a little heads up would've been nice.

"This is why," Skyla said softly, "she knew you would react like this."

"LIKE WHAT?" I yelled at her. "Like a concerned boyfriend?"

She shook her head, "Your anger. Ever since Daniel was confirmed to come back, you've been angry, but your anger isn't directed towards the right person."

"I am not angry with her! I am pissed she's putting herself in the situation."

"SEE?" Skyla finally yelled and got close to my face, even though she was way shorter than me. "You're pissed at her because he's back, don't lie; you're angry with her because you think this whole situation can be solved. Guess what? It cannot be solved with a simple confrontation or police report! Don't you think she's tried? For fuck's sake, you don't think I have tried to solve this?

"That's why she didn't tell you. You are convinced it can be solved so easily, but it can't. Take your anger out on the right person, not the one you love. Trust me, you keep going at this rate, and she will shut you out completely, and there is no chance of opening that door." Skyla shook her head and began walking to the door. "Let's go and support her through this hell."

Feeling like the smallest man who ever walked this earth, I followed her down the hall. My mind couldn't decide what it wanted to focus on, so endless muffled chatter filled it. My eyes were glued to Skyla's black tennis shoes; I was terrified to look around because I knew what my face read: pathetic.

When we walked out into the front entrance, the windows were floor-to-ceiling that showed the grey sky. The rain streaks brushed them as well, as it was coming down fast. This weather was a perfect representation of how Daniel's return felt.

There was a decent gathering of doctors, nurses, and people in street clothes. More cameras than I expected. However, I suppose this was big news in this area, especially since hockey season was done and everyone was tired of politics. It also didn't help that the pro basketball team lost in the playoffs, and the pro baseball team sucked; people needed something, I suppose.

"Crazy, isn't it?" Skyla whispered as we settled towards the back. "He is like a celebrity in the medical community, not to mention the donation he made to this hospital."

Afraid to speak to her, I focused my eyes on the staircase where Julia Kensinger and the Chief were standing. Both were smiling and waving to a few people as the Kensinger children descended the stairs. Anika was smiling and waving, enjoying the eyes on her, whereas Calvin and Maggie kept their heads down.

Maggie was wearing a beautiful lilac-colored romper that covered her scarred arms. Her heels had her standing nearly as tall as Calvin, who did not wear his cocky smile or presence. Maggie had a bare minimum of makeup on, and her hair was still stunning in its natural state. I was blown away to see her exposing her bullet scar, but it hardly stood out because her presence and beauty demanded your attention.

As I was left breathless by her power, I realized Daniel would see her. He was here. He would be within reaching distance. I couldn't protect her. Skyla must have sensed my discomfort because she squeezed my shoulder.

"He's not going to do anything," she whispered, "he's smart and cunning. Trust me, I know these kinds of men. This is part of the game, and I would know because I was a piece in the game."

I took a deep breath. Skyla had lived a life I would've never guessed for someone like her, and I didn't even know half of the story. Whatever it is, it explains who she is.

"Good afternoon," the Chief said into a microphone, "I am so glad we could come to gather to celebrate a monumental change for Kensinger Memorial. And I am honored to stand here with my sister-in-law and my beautiful nieces and nephew. I will turn it over to Dr. Julia Kensinger."

There was a round of applause as Julia stepped up and took the mic. This is when Maggie's eyes scanned the crowd and locked in on Skyla and me. I gave her a nod, and she gave a half-assed smile as Calvin glanced our way.

"As many of you know, my late husband, Mitch Kensinger, passed away from dementia this past January. Losing a husband, father, son, friend, and brother so painfully," she paused and took a deep breath, "we have decided to put more money and research towards mental illness." There was a round of applause as Anika and the Chief smiled, while Calvin and Maggie wore emotionless faces. "This could not be done alone; longtime friend and colleague Dr. Daniel Dobson donated three million dollars to research and funding for mental illness." My stomach sank as people cheered a little louder. "Not only did he generously donate to this hospital, but he has also even agreed to take over the Psychiatry department. Now, please, give a warm welcome to my friend, Dr. Daniel Dobson."

Daniel had a very charming smile, pearly white, and straight teeth. His hair was dark, with no hints of grey or white, and longer shaggy. He had light brown eyes that had hints of gold in them. He was taller than me and was built, especially for a man his age. As sickening as it was to say, Daniel was handsome.

Maggie kept her face emotionless as he appeared. Calvin looked pale as everyone else was beaming and cheering. Skyla had her eyes narrowed at Daniel. The devil in the flesh.

Chapter Ten

Sweet Like Honey

Maggie

Here was the thing: the body is an amazing thing. The body is built to protect you, every part of you. When a traumatic event occurs, your body adjusts to save you, and what's crazy, you don't even know? It isn't like something that you must turn on yourself; it does it on its own.

Trauma is a complex thing because people react to events differently. It took me a long time to realize that trauma doesn't have a definite definition. It isn't just deaths, different abuses, or poverty situations; it can be the way you were raised, how someone speaks and treats you, and many more things. It is different for everyone, but it doesn't matter because the body doesn't recognize anything different; trauma is trauma, and the body is kicked into survival mode.

I've seen many ways the body protects you. Reliving memories from traumatic events can freeze the body. Here, I was frozen.

When my mother and uncle were talking, it all sounded muffled, like you were underwater. I knew they probably said something about the donation Daniel made and how much of a great guy he was. I didn't want to hear it, and my body made sure that happened. Protection. I couldn't bear to look at him, so my body blurred my vision, and nothing was clear. Even with all of this said, Daniel's voice alone was able to cut my protection off.

"Thank you, thank you." His face had his wicked smile painted on. "I have to give it to you guys; you have not failed the saying of Minnesota nice." There were a few laughs, a loud one from Anika. "I am pleased to have this opportunity to be reunited with my close friends, the Kensingers." Those eyes flashed at me, and I felt exposed. "I cannot wait for my journey here, thank you."

Everything drowned out; he was hyper-focused on me, like a lion hunting his prey. I was out in the open, ready to be murdered. My vision was blurred; only Daniel was clear, and he was smiling at me. I felt the suffocation filling my throat, the same smile he had every time I was pinned down helplessly.

"Maggie," Calvin's voice was muffled, "Maggie?"

I snapped my head towards Calvin, "Yeah?"

"You okay?"

Nodding my head, I glanced over to Skyla and Jackson. Both were watching me, Jackson worried, Skyla ready to fight. I gave her a nod and a small smile, something we both did to signal the other if we were good or not when words weren't an option. She responded with a nod and a small smile.

My mom and Daniel went on to talk for a few minutes and wished farewell to Dr. Loggins. His last day was coming up, and I had one more appointment, which I was dreading. He was pushing me to start seeing Daniel, but I declined harshly each time. Dr. Loggins was a psychiatrist; he knew there was something up there, but he was smart and didn't want to push it and lose my trust.

When everyone gave one last round of applause, Daniel made his way to me. Calvin began to step in front of me, but I grabbed his arm to stop him. There were too many eyes for a scene to be caused, plus somehow, getting a rise out of Calvin would be exactly what Daniel was gunning for. It was all a game, a sick, twisted game.

"Maggie," he held out his arms for a hug, "it is so good to finally see you."

It burned, burned my fucking skin, as he wrapped his arms around me. I felt like I was sitting in boiling water on the stove; my skin was probably turning red. I remember when I was drunk and cooked dinner, I woke up with burns on my arms. They blistered and ached for weeks on end. Daniel touching my body was burning me, and I could feel the marks forming on my skin.

"Tempting you are," he whispered in my ear, "teasing me with your perfect body and full lips." I could smell the sharp scent of cologne. "I know you think you're safe, but don't forget what I am capable of."

Daniel backed away and squeezed my arm. His breath lingered on my ear, and his scent stung my nose. I gave him a small nod before sinking back into my position next to Calvin, who was glaring at Daniel. I gave a painful smile, nodded, and focused my attention on finding Skyla and Jackson.

They were both frozen, waiting for a signal to attack. I gave a slight nod; there was no need to alarm anyone. This was a battle that I had been fighting myself, and I knew if anyone else got involved, they would get hurt. I had already done my damage to people; this was on me. I was older, stronger, and prepared. At least, that was what I was hoping for.

"Hey," I turned and looked at Calvin, "I am going to the restroom, be back in five."

Before he could respond, I made my way up the stairs and towards the bathrooms. I glanced back behind my shoulder; there was no one following me. Quickly, I slid off my heels and took off running to the stairwell.

In high school, I ran track; I wasn't bad, but not great. I was fast but used all my energy way too quickly. My high school coach told me I was untrainable, so I quit track before my junior year started. Ever since the shooting, I was running faster than ever, and I never seemed to use up all my energy.

Running now, I felt my chest seizing up, my energy fading. My mind was filled with white noise as images flashed from my abuse. A weak sob escaped my mouth, and I quickly turned around to see if anyone was following me, no one.

Once I reached the roof of the hospital, I slammed open the door and raced out. My body, which still was burning from Daniel's touch, was greeted with a heavy downpour of cold rain. I fell slowly to my knees and closed my eyes as I tilted my head toward the gray sky.

As a kid, I hated rainy days, because it usually meant we couldn't go outside. I swear all I wanted to do was be outside when I was little; it didn't matter what time of year it was. My dad used to joke about how it was a pain in the ass to get me back inside, especially with the snow. I now long for rainy days because it was how I felt on the inside. Plus, it gave me good reasons to not have to leave my bed.

In the rain now, I slowly lay down on my back and threw my heels to the side. I wanted to burn this romper. I wanted to peel my skin off. I wanted to get out of my body. The body he had touched, scarred, and violated. I squeezed my eyes shut, and tears came out, blending into the rain.

Bottling up emotions was a good and a bad thing. In my thought process, it was a way to control your emotions. The bad thing was you never dealt with them, and when something snapped, all hell broke loose. Everything that has happened with Daniel, I had done a good job of suppressing heavy emotions. I was able to talk and address what happened without feeling a damn thing. But now, hearing his words, and feeling his touch finally snapped me.

"Why," I whispered, more tears spilling out, "why?" I screamed as thunder erupted. "Why me?" I cried as I sobbed.

The rain kept coming down, and my tears kept coming. This is why I ran. This is why I raced to be somewhere alone because I knew something I had snapped. I didn't want anyone to see me like this; too many people had already seen me like this. Plus, I didn't want anyone to be alarmed. Was I afraid of Daniel? Only a fool would say no. Was I afraid to admit I was scared? Yes. Why? Because everything was starting to get back to some form of normal.

Maybe being alone was what I was meant for. I was a grenade, and anytime anyone touched me, I blew their life into pieces. I caused pain and heartache. I did the damage a grenade would do, just only damage that was invisible to the naked eye. Maybe being locked away alone is what I deserve.

"You know it's okay to not be okay." I opened my eyes to find Calvin standing above me. "You pretending only makes it worse."

"I just need a minute, and I'll be fine," I grumbled, wiping my face and sitting up.

Calvin sat down next to me, "I said that so many times when Kara and Heather died that I almost believed it."

I looked over at him; I can't remember a time when he said that they were dead. When I think back to that time, I just think of the drugs and the constant fear he was dead.

"Maybe that's what we need, to convince ourselves we're fine." I sat up and crossed my legs.

He smiled and looked up at the sky, "I used to think that too, but there are only so many times you can say you're fine when you're not."

"I am fine." I snapped at him.

"Bottling shit up is only going to do damage. I know this better than anyone." He took a deep breath. "Kara and I had issues; everyone knew that. Instead of talking to each other, we bottled it up with the aid of whatever drug we could get our hands on. And because we bottled it up and all the hell broke loose, Kara did what she did because she didn't know what to do or how to deal with it.

"If we had learned how to deal with emotions and be honest, life would've been different. Maybe there would've never been a fight because we had already said and dealt with it. What I am saying is—bottling up emotions can be the thing that kills you."

I stared at him; he never talked about this. Not even in the years after his rehab. I figured I wouldn't push the issue because I didn't want to know the truth, and who wants to relive their pain?

"I can't keep not being okay," I whispered.

"You have no reason to be okay right now," he fired back, "in these last months alone, you've dealt with shit people only dream of. Truthfully, I would be more alarmed if you were okay right now, but you aren't."

"I am just tired of everyone being worried."

Calvin shook his head and put his arm around me. "I understand wanting to be left alone and breaking down in the shadows. It was all I ever wanted."

I rested my head on his shoulder, "I am not okay."

He squeezed my hand, "I know."

***

When Jackson came home, I had successfully showered, thrown the wet clothes in the trash, and eaten a healthy meal of blueberry *Pop Tarts*. I was up in my room, reading a new book that Skyla had suggested, when he came in.

As always, he took my breath away. His hair was getting shaggy, and his eyes were still so comforting to get lost in. The smell of fresh mint reminded me of the day on the plane when we met. That seemed so long ago, considering everything that has happened.

"Hey," he said as he dropped his bag on the floor next to the suitcase of clothes he had been living out of. "How are you feeling?"

That was not the response I was expecting from him. I was ready for the demands and accusations of why

I kept him in the dark. I also was expecting anger to radiate off him, but instead, he remained calm and his body at ease.

"I'm good, how are you?"

He smiled and sat down next to me, "I'm all good, Kensinger, as long as you're good."

I rolled my eyes, "Whatever."

Jackson leaned in and kissed the top of my head. It was nice for us to get back to normal. I didn't realize how much I missed it until it had been taken from me. However, the world likes to do that: take away things to make you realize how good you had it.

"Mom called me," Jackson started, "she wants to know when she can meet you."

Closing my book, I looked at him, "What did you tell her?"

"She knows about the shooting and your father, but as for anything else, she doesn't know." I let out a deep breath of air I didn't realize I was holding in. "And obviously, she knows the basics."

I scoffed, "I am surprised she hasn't told you to run as far away from me as you can."

"Maggie, you realize that I'm not perfect, and my mom is surprised you haven't run away from me."

I ignored his statement, "Well, what did you answer with?"

"That I would check with you, but we could probably come out next weekend. I surprisingly got a full weekend off and was hoping you would want to do something anyway."

"Next weekend works. I just want to make sure your mom likes me, and I am assuming I will meet your sisters, too."

He laughed, "My mom already likes you, so you don't need to worry about that."

I moved my body so that I was on top and straddling him. His fingertips traced the edges of my body. I could feel how hard he was for me. I leaned in and kissed his lips softly as he cupped my face. I flashed my eyes open to meet his intense eyes, hungry for me. I gave a small smile and began to yank off his T-shirt.

Jackson's hands quickly moved under my hoodie and cupped my breasts. I let out a moan as he pulled the hoodie over my head and began to slowly move his tongue around my nipple in perfect motion, feeling the orgasm building up.

It was then his fingertips dug past the waistband of my shorts and met my wetness. I made a moaning sound as he gently brushed past my clit and down to my hole. He slid one finger in as I snapped my head back, groaning.

"Look at me," he commanded as he thrust another finger in, "I want to see you come for me."

Holy fuck. The movement of his fingers inside me combined with his mouth teasing my nipples; there was no way I was going to last long, not with him. I let out a cry, I was so close, and he knew it. I did what I was told and kept my eyes on him as he was taking me in.

"Come on, baby, come for me." He whispered, and that was enough to send my body shaking. "Fuuuucccckkk." He groaned as I squeezed his fingers tight inside me.

In one swift motion, Jackson placed me on the bed and yanked off my shorts. He then pulled down his pants, took himself out, and guided himself into me. I gasped, still experiencing the aftereffects of my orgasm. He smirked at me as he thrust deep inside me, making me arch my back.

Everything that happened next was a blur. He would go slow before pounding me, then ease back into a slower pace. Time seemed nonexistent when he was inside me. All that mattered at that moment was I and him. This addictive feeling reminded me of being high, which Skyla and I tried once and didn't like. But fuck, this was different; this is what was crave-able.

When it was over and he finished, he kissed my forehead and pulled me close to him. Being with Jackson brought a whole different set of feelings I had never expected to experience before. I had missed him; all these months that I had shut everyone out, I had been depriving my body of all these happy emotions, the ones that were sweet like honey, the emotions that made life just a little more bearable.

Chapter Eleven

The Plane All Over Again

Jackson

Thankfully, since it was the summer season, we were able to score a flight out of Bemidji instead of driving to Minneapolis. Maggie was still sluggish as Skyla drove us to the airport; early mornings were still a struggle.

The last time we were at the airport was when we met. So much has happened since that day, so much good, so much bad. In my mind, the good outweighed the bad. Maggie had been worth every struggle, every tear, and every emotion. The way she made me feel was unmatched by anything, so I would go through whatever I needed to keep that feeling.

Maggie was dressed in black biker shorts and a cropped tank top that was dark green. Her hair was in two braids, and she wore little to no make-up. She effortlessly was able to take my breath away, even if she struggled to keep her eyes open. Clearly, the two cans of the yellow edition Red Bull had not kicked in.

We had a 7 am flight from Bemidji to Minneapolis, then a flight to Phoenix, and then the last one to LAX. We were due to arrive on the West Coast at about 2 in the afternoon Pacific time. Since my mom had to work, we would be taking an Uber from the airport to our hotel out towards my neck of the woods.

I had essentially planned the whole trip; we were arriving on a Friday and having dinner with my mom. Saturday, we were to see both of my sisters, and then we had the night to ourselves as my mom was working the night shift. I promised my mom we would see her on her break Saturday. And then, on Sunday, we were set to have brunch with my whole family, and then our flight left in the late afternoon. It was going to be a quick trip, especially since my mom didn't have the luxury of taking a whole weekend off.

There was a deep part of me that was nervous to show Maggie my life here. It wasn't like this place had very many happy memories for me to relive, plus Maggie was really going to see how poor I had grown up. I knew she understood, but it was still intimidating when she had grown up with such wealth.

When we got to the airport, Maggie hugged Skyla goodbye. I gave Skyla a nod goodbye as she drove off. Thankfully, Maggie knew how to pack light, so we both just had carry-ons. We walked into the very quiet airport, with maybe a handful of other people.

"Funny to think how much time has passed," Maggie said, smiling up at me.

"Still seems like a dream sometimes."

She rolled her eyes, "Don't get soft on me, Calsen. Come on, and let's get to our gate."

Shaking my head at her and smiling, I followed like a lost puppy. I knew that Maggie was a very punctual person, so it was no shock that we were at our gate an hour before our flight took off. She explained her reasoning a few days ago, while we were in her kitchen.

"You get there an hour before your flight takes off." She said while pulling out bread from the oven.

"And she doesn't mean just getting to the airport," Skyla said, mixing the salad in the bowl. "She means to the gate an hour before the flight leaves."

I looked over at Maggie, "What the fuck?"

"I have a good reason!" She fired back, throwing a glare at Skyla, who was smirking. "Calvin, you know why."

Calvin leaned back in his chair beside me, "Mags, it was one time, Mom and you freaked out."

Maggie rolled her eyes, "The day before Christmas, when I was in fourth grade, we were going to go to New York City. We were at the airport about an hour before our flight, and we were stuck in line for over thirty minutes because some woman didn't have a ticket.

"Long story short, we got to the counter, and the lady told us that we were too late and needed to rebook our flight. Mom was furious and swearing; Dad was trying to argue with the lady, and we three kids were clueless as to what was going on. After being on hold for three hours, we were able to get on a different flight, but not until Christmas Day, cutting our trip from five days to three. It was a disaster I never wanted to experience again."

Calvin shook his head, laughing, "It wasn't that big of a deal; we learned our lesson."

"You also were flying during the busier times of the year, plus you were in the Minneapolis airport. Way the fuck bigger than Bemidji." Skyla chimed in as she set the salad bowl on the table. "Not to mention that was like seventeen some years ago; there's now online check-in."

Maggie glared at them both, "Making sure we get to our gate and staying put there is important. Flights can change times or even gates. Sorry for wanting to be prepared."

I smiled at her, "Okay, I get it. Be prepared for Maggie being over-prepared."

She frowned at me while Skyla and Calvin laughed. Needless to say, Maggie was not very happy with me. She glared at me the entire time we ate dinner.

Now, I followed her, smiling as she handed her ticket and ID to the security guard. I did the same and followed her through the long and intrusive process of security. This was my third time flying a round trip, and I could understand how this was the worst part of flying. Sadly, I understood why we had to do it. When 9/11 happened, I was just shy of being seven years old. All I remember is sitting on the classroom carpet, watching the news on the TV all day.

Once we passed through security, got our shoes back on, and our bags from the rack, we made our way into the tiny airport. There was barely anyone in here, minus the few men in business suits. Maggie and I went to our gate and settled into the uncomfortable chairs.

"I get your reasoning for being here early, but this seems a bit extreme," I said as she pulled out her book and frowned at me. "Is there even a place where I can get something to eat?"

She shook her head, "Sit back and take a snooze; we can eat in Minneapolis."

Rolling my eyes, I leaned back and did my best to try to nap. It was a sigh of relief when we were able to board the plane. For this flight, I had opted out of first class since it was a short flight. We ended up sitting in the middle section of the smaller aircraft, with maybe seven other people in total on the flight.

Maggie took the window seat and laid her head back. I can remember every detail of how she looked that day, the crazy mane of hair she had and blue shirt and leggings. Her face was cleaned of makeup like it was today, and her eyes were as stunning as they had been that day. She still smelled of lavender and vanilla, and her smile brought that warmth to me.

"What are you looking at?" She asked with that smile on her face.

"Just reminiscing is all," I said as I laid my head back.

She rolled her eyes and looked out the window; it wasn't long before she passed out.

It felt like it was forever, but we finally landed at LAX. It was a 180 change from Bemidji's airport. People were everywhere, shoving past each other. It was like a madhouse, just like what everyone would say. Not to mention, if there were any celebrities, it was even more chaotic. Maggie didn't seem phased by any of this; she simply just followed me, keeping her head down.

Finding an Uber was not as hard as I thought it was going to be, but as expected, it was going to cost an arm and a leg. Maggie sat with her legs crossed, staring out the window. I noticed the driver kept looking back at Maggie; he couldn't be more than twenty-one years old. I frowned when he looked over at me finally.

After an hour of silence, the driver didn't even turn on the radio or music, and we finally arrived at the hotel. I paid the kid, who gave me a nod and smiled widely at Maggie as she politely smiled and said thank you.

I checked in, thankful that the receptionist was a woman, who smiled at me. When I glanced over to Maggie, she was shooting daggers at the woman. It was kind of sexy to see her jealous, but she had to know deep down no one would ever compare to her.

When we got to the fourth floor and room 421, Maggie let out a sigh of relief and fell back onto the bed.

The room was spacious and had a large fridge, a 60-inch TV, a couch, and a king-size bed. The bathroom had all newer finishes and a lot of storage space. Our view was hideous, just buildings and the smog, typically.

"Why were you glaring at the receptionist?" I asked when I set my bag down on the couch.

She narrowed her eyes, "Clearly, she wanted more than just your credit card."

"Kensinger, she was just doing her job and being nice."

"Oh yeah, with looking you up and down, admiring you. Trying to use the oh come fuck me voice."

I laughed, "You're jealous."

"I don't want someone else looking and trying to steal you." Her cheeks then flushed. "What's mine is mine."

"You act as if I am interested in anyone else."

Maggie sat up, "You aren't going to acknowledge how beautiful she was?"

"What?" I said, confused. "I was more preoccupied getting checked in and forgetting about the Uber driver who clearly was checking you out the whole drive."

She frowned, "No, he wasn't; why the hell would he find me attractive? I practically have crazy branded on both my arms, not to mention the bullet wound scar."

I stared at her in disbelief, "Maggie, do you not realize the value you have? I mean fuck, just looking at you makes me stop breathing for a second. Not to mention everything else there is to you."

We looked at each other in silence; she was picking her thumb and biting the inside of her gum. How could she not see what I see? How could she not see what everyone else does? How?

She blinked back a few tears before grabbing her carry-on and taking out her cosmetics bag. I watched her place out a green lace thong and strapless bra to match, and then black ripped jeans and a cropped light blue off-the-shoulder shirt. Maggie grabbed these things and the bag, went into the bathroom, and closed the door. I heard the shower turn on and the door lock.

I let out a deep breath and took out my gray cosmetic bag and the clothes I had picked out for dinner. I turned the TV onto ESPN, which had *SportsCenter* playing. I focused on the announcers discussing some trade that had happened for the NFL; it was easier to think about that than replaying Maggie's face a few seconds ago.

Listening without really listening to the TV, I dressed in jeans and a jet-black V-neck. I ran my hand through my hair; it was getting a bit longer than I liked; maybe I could beg Skyla to cut it. I knew it was a long shot since she refused to even do Calvin's hair.

When Maggie came out of the bathroom, she avoided looking at me and went to dry her hair. I knew better than to push a conversation out of her. I didn't want to upset her, and I wanted her to take some time for herself. If there was anything I learned from growing up with all women, it is that when they want to talk, they will talk. If they don't, then don't push it because the outcome would be brutal.

Checking my phone; we had about an hour before we were due to meet my mom at the new apartment she lived in. Thankfully, she was on the nicer side of town and not terribly far from both of my sisters. The only downfall was her commute to work was an extra thirty minutes, but this place was smaller and safer.

Maggie walked over to the side of the bed closest to the window and sat down. I finally let myself look at her. The jeans hugged her hips perfectly, and the blue in the shirt brought out her eyes. Her hair was dry and in natural waves, and she wore mascara and some lip gloss; otherwise, her skin was smooth and natural.

It was then I realized she was covering up her scars, jeans, and long sleeves. It was like eighty degrees out; there was no need for her to be wearing that. Then I thought back to what she had said earlier: she had crazy brands on her arms. Her scars were the last thing anyone would notice; they were thin white lines with faded purple around them. They were still healing, and yes, it was something your eyes would be drawn to, but there was so much more to look at. I knew damn well the Uber driver wasn't looking at those; he was admiring her full lips and stunning eyes.

"I'm sorry for shutting down," she finally said, "I am just tired and got insecure when I saw that woman looking at you, and I am sorry for that."

I walked over to her and stood in front of her, "It's okay," I tilted her chin back up to me. "Do you want to take a nap? I can see if we can just meet my mom at the restaurant."

"No, I'll be fine. I am just sorry."

"It's okay. How much longer do you need to get ready?"

"I am ready whenever you are," she gave me a small smile that sent chills up my spine.

I swallowed, "Yeah, give me a second."

I made my way to the bathroom and closed the door. Fuck I was hard, and I figured fucking my girlfriend right before seeing my mom would not be the way to go. I splashed some water on my face; the things this woman does to me. Every day I woke up, she got more beautiful and breathless.

When I came back out, she was putting on open-toe heels, making her forehead fall right to my chin. I took a deep breath and grabbed my wallet. Maggie followed as I held the door open. While we were in the elevator, I was able to score an Uber that would take us to the apartment and get us there in about thirty-five minutes.

Maggie walked in front of me, and my eyes couldn't help but focus on the sway of her hips. As many times as she said she didn't have an ass, she sure as fuck did, it may not be Beyonce standard, but it was big enough for me to grab.

She must've sensed I was watching because she glanced back at me and gave me a frown. Smiling, I wrapped my arm around her shoulders as we stepped outside and waited for the white Honda Civic to arrive. It was windy out, cooling the actual temperature down, but it was hotter than it had ever been in Bemidji yet.

"Please tell me you gave your mom enough time after her shift to get ready and be relaxed."

I smiled, "Trust me, I did," she smiled at me as the car pulled up, "You know Kensinger, you do know how to clean up nicely."

She shook her head and smiled as I opened the door for her, and she slid in. I followed right behind her and greeted the old man driver, who thankfully had the radio on. Unfortunately, he was playing like seventies disco music. I glanced over at Maggie, who was holding in a giggle.

The drive was quick and silent as she stared out the window, taking in the boring view of buildings and people panhandling on the sidewalks. It was so different here, and I wasn't just talking about the weather. There were just people everywhere, and garbage littered on the sides as well.

In the parking lot, I was able to spot my mom's beat-up Ford Fusion, so I knew she was home. I held the door open for Maggie, who took in the sight of the apartment building. They looked older, but they at least weren't crumbling or had mold growing on the outside. My mom's apartment before was a house of horrors: cockroaches, leaks, unknown smells, and no AC.

Before the Uber driver had driven away, my mother came running out of the side stairwell. She was a tall woman, nearly six feet tall, with long brown hair streaks of gray, and light hazel eyes. Besides my hair and height, I looked nothing like my mom. Both of my sisters were spitting images of my mom, but they were not nearly as tall.

My mom jumped into my arms like a little kid. She still smelled of cherry blossoms, the same smell of comfort. She squeezed me tightly and pulled away, wiping tears from her eyes. It had been too long since I had seen her, and there was a twinge of guilt in my chest. My sisters were never big fans of seeing my mom, so it had been up to me. I was her favorite person; she always reassured me of this.

My mom's eyes went to Maggie, and she smiled, "It's about damn time I met the girl who puts up with my son." Maggie broke into a wide smile. "Elizabeth Calsen, but please call me Liz."

"I am so glad to meet you; Jackson has told me a lot about you," Maggie said, her voice steady.

"He's told me about you, but I think we should talk about all the embarrassing things about Jackson." My mom laughed and shot a warm smile at me. "Let me grab my purse, and we can be on our way."

When my mom vanished back up the stairs, my eyes met Maggie's. Her face was unreadable; there was a sparkle in her eye, but her face was stoic.

"What are you thinking, Kensinger?"

Maggie shook her head, "I can't believe you haven't booked us a plane earlier." She turned and looked at me. "She's absolutely wonderful, and I am pissed you've robbed me of time with her."

I let out a sigh of relief that I didn't know that was there.

Chapter Twelve

Insecurities Surface

Maggie

We ate at a nice Mexican restaurant, his mother's favorite place. It was not far from the apartment complex; we truthfully could've walked the three blocks. During the short five-minute drive, I kept quiet to let Jackson and his mom get caught up and have their time. Our driver was a younger female who remained quiet the entire time.

It was a shame that we were only getting a night with her. Her extreme warmth and easy attitude had blown me away. It made me smile to see how much she missed Jackson; he clearly meant the world to her, and I couldn't imagine how hard this had been for her. I wished there was a way we could extend our time here, but Jackson was due back at work Monday night.

Elizabeth focused on telling embarrassing stories of Jackson's childhood, making him red in the face. I found myself smiling and laughing a lot more than I thought I would. She was intrigued by my job and wanted to know what Colorado and Minnesota were like. I asked about her job and her life; Jackson was basically an afterthought for both of us.

During dinner, I realized that Jackson didn't talk much about his mom or sisters. In fact, I knew the bare minimum when it came to their lives. Yet, somehow, Jackson was involved and knew everything there could be to my fucked-up family. Did I not let him talk enough? Did I act uninterested in his life? Was I just too focused on myself that I didn't care about my boyfriend's life? My stomach sat in knots, but by the grace of God, Elizabeth was able to distract me from my realization of how shitty I was as a girlfriend.

I learned that Elizabeth's upbringing had parallels to my mom's. They both had alcoholic fathers who abused them and deceased mothers. However, Elizabeth did not get the same fortune my mom did. She had no siblings and was stuck providing rent and bills, so she and her drunk father had a roof. She never finished high school; she had to drop out before she even finished her sophomore year.

She met Jackson's dad at the restaurant where she worked; he came in and ordered just chicken tenders and water. It took about a week when she figured out, he was coming to just see her. He smiled and said about damn time, and from that day, they were inseparable. Kris Calsen was a mechanic at his uncle's shop; he was a few years older than her. They dated for about a year before they tied the knot at the courthouse, and she moved into the tiny one-bedroom apartment he had.

Everything seemed great; they had Jessica and Julissa, both healthy babies and two years apart. However, when Kris's parents were killed, his brother, and then Elizabeth's father finally died in one year, everything changed drastically. Kris lost his job, sat at home, and drank, unable to leave the couch. It was then they found out they were pregnant with Jackson. That was when the fights started, and then the accident happened; she did not go into much detail there.

"My Kris had demons," she said as she took a sip from her wine glass, "he had grown up a family man, and losing everyone just shook up his world. The demons took over him, and now, he is in a better place without having to deal with the pain." She gave a sad smile and squeezed my shoulder. "Remember the person and not the monster that destroyed them."

Jackson remained quiet, clearly very uncomfortable to talk. Elizabeth remained calm and at ease. It was as if she was at peace with all of this, something I was inspired to reach one day.

"I always felt bad," she said, smiling at him, "he was always stuck playing dress up and dolls. He never got to throw a ball around or learn how to play a sport. I will give him this: he never complained. He always wanted what everyone else wanted."

I smiled, "A people pleaser, he still is."

"I wouldn't put it past him."

Jackson rolled his eyes, "You know I am still here." We both smiled at him. "And as delightful as I am that you two are getting along, it is getting late."

Elizabeth looked at her phone and gave a sad smile to me. "I am afraid he's right; I do have to open tomorrow. I can't believe how fast time has flown by."

"I am so glad to have finally met you," I said as Jackson pushed into our chairs.

Once we were outside of the restaurant, she asked me to speak alone, which made my stomach drop. Jackson didn't seem phased by this and stepped away to get an Uber headed our way.

She squeezed my shoulder, "I know all the shit you've had to deal with this year, and something tells me you understand the dark side of life. I am sorry that you've been chosen to deal with this. Don't give up on life; please don't give up on my son."

I curled my lip, refusing to let myself shed a tear. Jackson had so many of his mother's features, high cheekbones, and almond-shaped eyes. She was beautiful naturally, and even though life had been cruel to her, age had been kind to her. It made me wonder why she never tried to remarry or be with someone, but I think I knew the answer: Kris had been her love, and her heart couldn't bear the weight of loving someone the way she did, Kris.

"Thank you," I managed out as she wrapped her arm around my shoulder and walked towards Jackson. "Thank you," I whispered one more time.

I let Jackson and his mom say goodbye alone, while I sat in the car with another Uber driver. I knew we would get to see her briefly tomorrow and a little bit on Sunday, but this was the last chance he got with her to himself. I smiled as I watched her hug him again, tears in her eyes. She loved him.

The drive back to the hotel was silent; Jackson stared out the window, lost in thought. It made me wonder if he missed living here or regretted leaving his mother. They were obviously close and meant the world to each other. It made me curious as to why she would be so kind to me. I would've assumed she resented me because I was keeping her son away from her.

When we got back to the room, Jackson immediately went to shower while I scrubbed my face and put on a baggy t-shirt. Finally, the time difference was hitting me. I don't even know if Jackson was out of the shower when I fell asleep on the bed. Sleep welcomed me.

***

I had never been a morning person, ever since I was a kid. It used to make both my parents laugh because of how cranky I would be. I would always wear this scowl on my face while I would sip my milk at the breakfast table. I would snap at anyone who tried to talk to me, and it remained that way until I was in high school. Then I would just sleep to the last possible minute, ignore everyone, and suffer through the first period on a Red Bull that I would slip into my water bottle.

College was brutal, but somehow, I had managed to never have an 8 am class. Once again, Red Bull came to save the day. Everyone would bitch at me for drinking this many energy drinks, saying that I was bound to have heart problems and shit. If I could drink coffee, I would, but I couldn't. It was one of those shitty things that went straight through me and fucked my entire digestive system.

Mornings were just never my thing. And it still held true as I was an adult. Jackson, on the other hand, was a morning person. He loved getting up and working out right away, and he never snoozed on his alarm. At the same time, I would press snooze like twenty times because getting up would be painful.

While Jackson went to work out at five in the morning, I groaned and forced myself up. I dressed in sweats, took my meds, walked across the street, got three cans of Red Bull, the yellow edition, and walked back. The air was already warm, and there was smog in the air. It was like a whole different world compared to Bemidji. There were already so many people out and about, and the constant noise of the highway and other things I couldn't fathom. I had traveled a lot in my life; it just always shocked me how quiet and reserved Bemidji really was.

Back inside the hotel, I flipped on the news, and sipped on my Red Bull, trying to get myself awake. I was nervous about meeting Jackson's sisters; from what I gathered, they were stuck up and, to put it nicely: bitchy.

"This is a wonderful sight," Jackson said, laughing. "Your scowl is adorable."

I narrowed my eyes, "Fuck off, I am only up because of you."

He laughed and shook his head, "I will say the baggy hoodie, scowl, and Red Bull is a sexy combination."

I flipped him off, and he went to rinse off in the shower, still laughing. I leaned my head back and closed my eyes; all I wanted to do was sleep. It also didn't help that the medication I was on made me even more groggy. I flipped off my pill case that was lying on top of my backpack.

When Jackson finished getting ready, dressed in joggers and black short sleeves, I got myself presentable. Even though he wasn't close to his sisters, I knew getting along with them would mean a lot to him. I brushed my teeth, straightened my hair, put on some mascara, and eyeliner, and did my eyebrows. Then, as I was about to put on my long-sleeved purple V-neck and black ripped jeans, I stopped.

For as long as I could remember, I hated looking in the mirror at myself. I would gladly stare directly at the sun than at myself, just as Taylor Swift stated in a song. There was so much to me that I hated, but there were some things I could speak positively about. Now, fuck, I couldn't name a single thing, and all I saw was everything there was to be hated about me.

My body had stretch marks, particularly around my stomach, but in my thighs and arms. I was not skinny; I was heavier around my stomach, and that was always where my eyes went first. My boobs were two different sizes and bigger than I wanted. I had no ass to save my life, I was like flat Stanley back there, and I would say that was one of my biggest insecurities. My hair was always frizzy, my eyes were too far apart, and I had faded freckles on my face. I could keep going, but there was no point In rehashing every disgusting detail of my body; I had done enough of that in the last months.

Turning away from the mirror, I got dressed, cringing at how these jeans gripped my stomach tightly. I opened the door and threw my dirty clothes next to my suitcase. Jackson was watching me with a smile on his face.

"What?" I asked, probably too harshly.

"You're beautiful."

I rolled my eyes, "No need to be romantic."

"I am serious."

"So am I; romance is not my thing."

"It's a fact, Maggie; take the compliment." I stared at him for a second before focusing on making sure everything was in my purse. "I see the Red Bull hasn't fully kicked in."

I closed my eyes; I needed to push my negative thoughts aside and focus on making sure Jessica and Julissa liked me. "It will; I just need one more."

Jackson stood up and walked to me. "What's wrong?"

"Nothing," I said, probably too defensively, "the time change is still fucking with me."

I knew he didn't fully believe me, but he also knew better than to push for details. That was something I always appreciated about him. He never pushed, and he was okay with waiting until you were ready to talk. I always found myself baffled that he could deal with my moods. I could barely deal with them.

"We are going to be at Jessica's house for lunch, and then we can come back here, and you can take a nap. I can go see my mom. I know that you're tired; thank you for coming."

I looked up at him, "You don't need to thank me. I am just glad you wanted me to come."

"Of course I wanted you to come," he smiled and pulled me close to him. "My family is important to me, just like you are. Plus, I needed my mom to stop chewing my ass about meeting you."

"Well, I am glad I got to finally meet her."

"Now, I cannot promise what the hell is going to happen with my sisters, but know we don't have to be there terribly long."

I smiled, "I am sure we will survive."

***

Wealth looked different everywhere; however, if there was a stereotype of wealth, Jessica's house was it. Her house was huge and gated; we had to be let in by someone. She had beautiful flowers and landscaping in the front with a vibrant green yard. The house had a Mediterranean feel with the roof. Jessica was on the front porch waiting for us to walk in. She had a spitting image of her mom, minus the fact she was a lot shorter.

Jessica wore leggings and a tank top, looking like she had just come from a yoga class. She greeted Jackson with a huge hug and me with the fakest smile you could get. When we entered the home, I was floored by the high ceilings and natural light. It was an open concept, with a large kitchen, and grand staircase. In the backyard, you could see the large patio and pool.

In the kitchen is where Julissa, who looked just like Jessica, could be fucking twins. She wore a nice pink sundress that complemented her deep tan. Julissa greeted me with a more genuine smile than her sister, which made me feel a little better.

His niece and nephews tackled Jackson. Julissa had two boys: Max, who was five, and Griffin, who was three. Jessica had a girl, Kate, who was eight, and a set of twin boys, Patrick and Samuel, who were four. They were all dressed in some sort of name-brand clothes, and their hair was all done fancy.

A slew of people served lunch, and we ate out on the back patio. All the kids wanted Jackson's attention, so his sisters were left to me to make conversation. It was quick to discover that we had nothing in common, not one thing. They didn't work; I did. I went to college; they barely made it out of high school. They were married and had kids; I had neither. I was not interested in celebrities or high-end fashion; they were. They enjoyed the hot weather and beaches, but I did not. They had little interest in anything but their lives; I cared too much for everyone else.

It seemed like we couldn't have been more opposites. They had loads of friends, and they seemed to just gossip about them. Both disclosed to me the maintenance they did to keep their husbands interested in them. They sadly seemed to have no true mind of their own, and did everything a housewife should do, well, a housewife with a lot of money.

Julissa was more friendly than Jessica, who just seemed to have already made her mind up about me. Neither of them bothered to ask questions about me or my life, which was fine. They barely seemed interested in talking to their brother.

I did the best I could, smiled, and asked questions. I pretended to be interested in the shit they had to say. Deep down, all I could think about was how much Skyla would hate these two. It wasn't about the fact they were rich; it was more about how they had no sense of empathy for anyone, even for their kids. When any of the kids wanted their mom's attention, they met with one of the nannies instead. I felt bad, thankful that I didn't grow up with nannies and shit.

When we left Jessica's house, I had never felt more relaxed. I didn't realize how tense I had been the entire time. Jackson also seemed to be comfortable with leaving as well. It was obvious his sisters didn't want much to do with him; it made me feel bad. On a very aggressive level, I understood discomforting sibling relationships, and it would make me sad to see anyone go through it.

"I am glad that is done and over with," Jackson said as we got into the Uber to head home. "Those kids don't get enough attention from the right adults."

"Do you think either of them will have any more?"

He shook his head, "No, they both got boys, and that's all that mattered to Henry and Joel. Plus, they are getting to the end of childbearing years."

"What matters to you when it comes to kids?"

Jackson was caught off guard, but smiled and said, "Just as long as they are healthy and you're okay."

"My body will change."

"So what? Maggie, I love you not just because of how beautiful you are. Your body, no matter what changes, will be sexy as fuck to me."

My cheeks turned red; thankfully, the Uber driver had the music loud enough. Having kids was the last thing on my mind, but the chilling thought of how much my body would change hit me. You always hear these horrible stories of couples whose relationships changed because the husband didn't find the woman attractive or the woman was just too different. Now, I am sure there are other reasons why a relationship doesn't last, but these are just what you hear.

"How often does your mom get to see them?"

Jackson let out a sigh, "Maybe once a week, and if anything, it is for my mom to babysit, and the nannies can have a break."

I made a face, "I am glad nannies didn't raise us. My mom took a dip in her career to make sure we were raised right."

"Yeah, well, Jessica and Julissa are what they are. They are still my sisters, and I just love them."

I nodded; I understood that all too well. Calvin and I were back on good terms, but there was no telling if Anika would ever. I knew she was stubborn and wouldn't believe anything I would say. Deep down, I just knew that I would never have a proper relationship with my sister.

Jackson told me to get some sleep and would be back; he was going to see his mom. I wanted to protest, but he said he knew I needed sleep. Sure enough, he was right. I passed out not long after he left and didn't wake back up for a few hours. None of my dreams were clear, so thankfully, I had no nightmares. They were slowly going away.

By the time I was able to keep my eyes open, Jackson was lying next to me, reading a book. The sun was still up, and the digital clock said that it was not long after five.

"Hey, sleepyhead."

I sat up and stretched, "You should've woken me up sooner, and we could've gone and done something."

"Maggie, you've been sleep-deprived these last months, so seeing you take a nap is refreshing."

I laid my head back, "What's the plans this evening?"

Jackson traced his fingers down my back, sending shivers. "Well, I was thinking we could eat and go out to a bar or club. If none of that pleases you, I am open to suggestions."

"I am fine with that, but I am going to need to change and look a bit better for going to a bar."

Jackson laughed and pulled me close to him, "I think what you have on is fine."

I smiled up at him, "Okay, Calsen, you seem to think that everything I wear is fine."

"Kensinger, you could wear the ugliest thing in the world, and I would still think you looked fine and would still happily claim you."

"I'll hold you to that," I said as I got out of bed and crouched over my suitcase. "How fancy are we talking?"

"Nothing that requires formal dress; seriously, you can wear what you're wearing."

I rolled my eyes and grabbed the clothes I was going to change into. "Give me fifteen minutes, and I will be ready."

The clothes I picked out were a slim-fitting red dress that was sleeveless and fell mid-thigh. I had low black heels and a black jacket to cover my scars. I brushed through my hair and washed any mascara that had been under my eyes. I applied some lip gloss and decided that was enough; the longer I looked, the worse everything began to look.

When I stepped out of the bathroom, Jackson's eyes took me in. I gave a small smile before throwing my dirty clothes in my bag and grabbing my small crossbody purse.

"Jesus Kensinger," he said as I spun around, "you amaze me every time."

I smiled, "Well, get a few drinks in me, and you might get lucky."

He tilted my chin up, "Is that so?"

"I guess you'll have to find out."

He groaned as his phone chimed. "Fucking Uber will be here in a few minutes."

"Shame, because I've got nothing underneath this dress."

Jackson, in one smooth motion, laid me down on the bed and pressed my dress up. I groaned as he traced his fingers around my clit. He carefully teased me, kissing the sides of my legs, before meeting me in the sweet spot. He knew it wasn't going to take me long, especially since my legs were already shaking. I let out a gasp and growl as I let myself feel the euphoric sensation.

"Trust me, we're just getting started." He whispered in my ear before helping me up.

There was heat on my cheeks as we made our way down to the lobby. He held the door open for me to get in the car and greeted the driver. I kept my eyes out the window while Jackson and the driver talked about some major trade that had happened in the NFL. I was happy not to be included because my body was still coming off that high.

We had dinner at a nice Italian restaurant. Jackson ordered us a bottle of chilled white wine. The waitress struggled to look at me as she was all about Jackson. I put my jacket on even though I was nowhere near cold; if anything, I was sweating.

I let Jackson control most of the talking, sipping my wine, and pushing my food around. Ever since I had looked at myself earlier in the mirror, I had lost my appetite. Growing up as a female at this age, it was all about looks. In high school, I played sports and always was in shape. In college, I was so depressed I barely ate. As an adult, I struggled to find balance with everything. Did I eat the way I should? No. I could benefit from trying to take care of myself. Yes. All that mattered was if you had the body; stretch marks and scars were frowned upon—a curvy figure, full ass, flat stomach, and a good set of boobs were what you strived for.

Over the last months, I have probably been the most active I have ever been. I had more muscle than I did before; however, since taking my medication on a regular basis, there had been weight gain despite how active I was. Weight had never been an issue for me, but since the shooting and my attempt, everything about myself had been heightened.

"Are you sure you're, okay?" Jackson cut through my thoughts.

I blinked a few times, "Yeah, why?"

"You're a terrible liar," Jackson said, amused at my response. "You haven't been acting like yourself."

"A lot is going through my mind." I truthfully answered. "Also, the time change is affecting me."

Jackson hesitated before he finally spoke, "You need to eat; you've barely eaten anything since we've been in California."

My stomach took a few turns, and I decided to change the subject quickly. "Do you ever miss it here?"

"I miss my mom, but I would say that's about it. There isn't a lot for me here." He then smiled at me. "You wouldn't be able to last here; it's too hot."

Shaking my head, I smiled. "This is true, not one of the few states I could last in."

The rest of the dinner conversation was smooth. Jackson couldn't keep his eyes off me, making me blush, but making me happy that the waitress wasn't getting any of his attention. We paid and walked along the street, which had a few other restaurants and bars. Jackson held my hand and let me talk nonsense about the book I had been reading.

He finally was able to pick a bar, thankfully not a club where we would have to stand in line. It was dark with multiple color lights that brought a seductive mood. There was already a decent number of people in the bar, and it was barely nine.

I told Jackson I was going to use the bathroom and that I would be right back out. As usual, there was a line, about four girls ahead of me, who all looked identical. They each wore various colors of the same style of clothes, and their hair was bleach blonde.

Ignoring all of them, I was able to get in, pee, and back out in under six minutes. This was impressive because, in college, Skyla and I were always stuck in the bathroom for ten minutes or just to pee. It became a game to see which time would be the shortest or what would be the longest.

When I got back out, I took a deep breath and straightened out my dress. My eyes zeroed in on Jackson, who, as usual, took my breath away, but he was talking to another woman. She was tall, had a very flat stomach, and a huge ass. Her face was naturally beautiful, and she surprisingly wore little makeup. Her long jet-black hair looked silky and was straight.

This woman was smiling at Jackson as she talked; her hand grazed his arm, and that was enough to send my body into full shutdown mode. I took a deep breath, watched as he caught my eye, and turned and headed out the door. I could feel the tears forming in the corners of my eyes, so I kept my head down. I didn't need strangers to see me in the vulnerable state I was in.

Insecurities and fears were flooding my mind. Why was I like this? I was being overdramatic. It wasn't like he was going to kiss the woman or anything, but I then realized why I was so upset. It wasn't because she was talking to him; it was the fact that she was everything I wasn't, which was perfect. She probably had a nice family, didn't have depression, and didn't take medication. This woman probably had a well-paying job and worked out at five in the morning.

She was who he deserved. Someone who didn't cause worry or stress. Someone who would never bring him to the point of wanting to relapse. And she was probably someone who was good in bed and did all the right things. She was everything I wanted to be.

I knew there was never such a thing as a perfect person. I knew that everyone had shit and demons. I knew these things, but insecurities beat the logic within me. And I let it devour me.

Chapter Thirteen

How Could You Not?

Jackson

I had a bad feeling the moment that woman walked up to me. The first thing I noticed was the open scabs on her forearm: meth. In her eyes, you could see she was high, and her movements were very sluggish. There was no denying that, at one point, this woman had been naturally beautiful, but meth takes a hard toll on the body.

Hanging with the crowd I did, you saw several things. Some of the guys I used to buy from sold a variety of other drugs. Also, being a doctor, you understand the signs of drug use. It pained me to see this woman, who was maybe of age to be in the bar, be addicted to a deathly substance.

The woman greeted me with a smile, a smile that didn't send my heart racing. Her eyes didn't bring the same warmth as Maggie's, and most of all, she didn't make my blood run. The world's color faded just a bit, looking at this woman. She wasn't Maggie.

"You look lonely," she said, fingers tracing my arm, "let me buy you a drink."

Her touch didn't do anything for me; if anything, it made me tense up and flinch like a repulsive reaction to someone other than Maggie touching me.

Being the polite man my mom raised, I said: "I am good, thank you." And that's when I felt her eyes on me.

The heat went through my body, and I knew Maggie was back. It all happened so quickly; her face shattered as I turned to look at her. My stomach dropped, and the air around me felt hot and thick. Ignoring the woman around me, I immediately went racing after her. I know what she probably thought, but I didn't think she'd crumble right then and there.

How could she think that anyone could replace her? Everything about her was tattooed on my skin; her touch controlled me. How could I ever want someone else when she made me see the color in this world and the possibility of love? There was no replacing her; she had become my everything, and I had no problem with that.

Shoving my way past a few people and going out the door was when I finally was close to reaching her. Maggie had pulled her black jacket tightly around herself, and those eyes were focused on the ground. You could see her shoulders shake as she was clearly crying.

"Maggie," I said, and she kept walking, "Maggie, please stop walking, please." I pleaded.

She hesitated before she stopped, turned around, and kept her head down. You could see that she was bleeding from her thumb, something she did when she was nervous or upset. It took her a moment, but she looked up at me. Maggie had also chewed hard enough to cause it to bleed. Those eyes looked lost; at this point, Maggie Kensinger looked absolutely defeated.

"I don't know what-" I began, and she held her hand up to stop me from going on.

"That's not why I am upset," she managed, but there was no emotion. "I trust you."

Even though that should bring relief to me, it didn't. There was something else that was bothering her, something about the interaction that ticked it off.

"Maggie-" I began again, but she held her hand up again.

The people around us seemed uninterested in anything but themselves. They were all too busy looking at and talking on their phones. We were nothing more than two people taking up space on the sidewalk outside the bar.

"You deserve someone like her."

I had to blink a few times and pause for a moment to make sure I heard her right. I deserve someone like who?

"What?"

She finally snapped her head back, and the tears came trailing down from the corners of her eyes. "You deserve someone who isn't fucked up in the head. You deserve someone with no stretch marks or scars, who's got a flat stomach and motivation to workout with you at five in the morning. You deserve to have someone who can build you up and not bring you down." Maggie took a long, shaky breath. "You deserve someone who isn't broken, someone who has it together."

My jaw dropped, what the fuck? Stretch marks? Flat stomach? My mind was swimming, trying to catch up with everything that had been said. Someone to build me up? Scars? Someone who isn't broken? What the hell is going on, Maggie Kensinger?

"What do you mean?" I finally managed out. "You think that there is someone else out there for me that can make me feel the way you do?"

She avoided eye contact, "I am just saying you deserve more than what I can give you."

I scoffed, "You give me everything! You give me more than I thought I would ever get in my fucked life!" I shook my head, feeling my heart race. "If anything, I should be concerned I am not enough for you."

"You could have anyone you want, and they would be lucky to have you." She fired back, clearly pissed at my comment. "I am nothing but a ticking time bomb ready to implode."

I shook my head, "Before you, there was nothing but gray, gloom, and emptiness. I had gotten to the point where I accepted it was what I deserved." Maggie's lip was quivering. "Then there you came, pulling me up and back into a world with color, emotions, and love. I never thought I was capable of loving someone; I always assumed no one could ever love me. But you came into my life, and love was suddenly something I felt.

"You saved me from a life of nothing. In return, you have given me a life of everything. Just looking at you makes me feel all these things that I have struggled to put into words. You are like the damn sun pulling me to you." I took a deep breath and shook my head. "So no, I don't deserve anyone else but you."

I stepped forward and brushed a piece of hair from her face. She was biting down, hard, on her bottom lip. I wiped away a tear that fell from her left eye, staring down at the woman who had left her mark everywhere there was to me. Even through the tough times, everything about Maggie Kensinger was worth fighting for.

"I'm sorry," she whispered, "I'm so sorry."

This is when I pulled her into a tight hug; she still smelled of lavender and vanilla. I smiled and kissed the top of her head, while she pressed her face into my chest; she was still crying.

"Come on," I pressed her chin to look up at me, "let's go back and watch some *Friends* reruns or whatever baseball game is on."

She scrunched her nose, "Baseball is horrible to watch on TV."

I laughed, "So *Friends* reruns it is." I pressed my lights gently to hers, which were still bleeding. "And we grab some antibiotic cream at the convenience store a block away from the hotel."

Maggie curled her lip and then smiled, sending my heart rate skyrocketing. I grabbed her hand, got us an Uber, and watched the spark and life return to her eyes. My Maggie's eyes.

*****

I couldn't keep my eyes off her the entire night. Instead of watching the TV, I focused on her and what she laughed at and tried to see everything through her. Tried to understand why she laughed at one joke, but not the other. I was curious to see what would bring a smile to her face. I just wanted to know how the world looked to her after all that she had been through.

If she knew that I was watching, she didn't say anything. We happily ordered a pizza from a local place, just a simple pepperoni and a side of cheese sticks. Maggie hesitated at first, but her stomach was growling, and I knew she was starving. We managed to stay up watching reruns of *Friends* and then *Big Bang Theory* until about one in the morning.

Maggie fell asleep quickly and in the same position she always slept in: on her right side. I would never tell her, but she was a constant mover from the left and right sides. The thing that always made me laugh was how she would end up in the same position where she started.

In the morning, I was able to sneak glances at her while she changed. Who gave a fuck if she had scars? Besides the ones on her arm, between her legs, and the bullet scar, there was maybe one other scar she had that she got when she was a kid on her face. I sure as fuck didn't notice her stretch marks, and so what? If anything, they were beautiful. There was nothing to her that I could hate, nothing about her body. So, what if the medication had caused some weight gain, she still was Maggie?

Throughout brunch, it was hard to look away from her. She was wearing jeans and a black lace top with little to no makeup on. Her hair was down and wavy, and she had black flats. To me, she looked effortlessly breathtaking. I wasn't oblivious to the guys who took a second look at her, but I didn't care; I knew she was mine. I also knew Maggie didn't even know people were looking at her.

My mom did her best not to cry when we said goodbye. I promised I would see her soon, knowing that it was killing her that I wasn't minutes away. It had been an adjustment being so far from her, but I knew Bemidji was for the better, not to mention what I was able to find in the tundra.

Maggie slept most of the flights, resting her head on my shoulder. I took advantage of being able to study her face. The smoothness of her skin, the way her lips were full and parted as she slept, and the small faces that she would make as she dreamed. What I have noticed since the summer took over: her freckles were more predominant, there were flecks of green in her eyes, and she had more color in her skin.

When the plane finally landed in Bemidji, it was closer to midnight. Skyla picked us up; she was waiting at the front doors. Maggie embraced her, and Skyla hugged her back; it was as if they had been apart for weeks. I couldn't imagine if they had been separated for weeks what the embrace would've been like.

The whole drive was quiet; I watched her focus on the world outside, her world. There were a few people out by Babe and Paul and one or two boats on the lake. You could see the line of hotels, the gleaming lights with people on the back patios, and the millions of stars in the sky.

As soon as her head hit the pillow, she fell back into a steady sleep as she had no caffeine for the entire day. I didn't ask why, but it was a relief to see Maggie sleep without thrashing around and screaming from the nightmares. I kissed her forehead and headed down the stairs to grab some water from the fridge. Skyla was out on the back patio, the door open, and she had the string lights on.

I hesitated before walking out on the back patio. Skyla ignored me as she focused on her book. The view of the lake and the sounds of bugs were still such an unfamiliar sound, but I was starting to understand the peacefulness of it.

"You learn that there is a comfort in the silence." I looked down at her; she was watching me. "Growing up, there was always noise; it never was silent, and I just assumed that was life."

"Why was it never silent?" I asked as I sat down in the chair beside her.

Skyla closed her book and set it down on the outside coffee table in front of us. "Why do you care?"

I rolled my eyes, "You mean more to Maggie than anyone; in the end, she will always pick you. I want to understand."

"I am glad you know your place," she teased, smiling. "Well, I was born to a single mother; my dad apparently didn't believe her. They were both in high school, so she had to drop out. My mom did her best; she had been raised by a single mom, too.

"When I was three, my mom began to use meth. Since she didn't have the money to pay, she would do other favors for the dealers. I grew up with different men in our small apartment every day. There were always fights and screams, but I remained in the bathroom like my mom told me. Once the men would leave, she would come and open the door. Bruises, blood, sweat, and open scabs. My mother always looked destroyed." Skyla's face remained stoic as she spoke. "My grandma viewed my mom as weak and refused to be a part of our lives, so it truly was just her and me."

"Shouldn't your grandma understand how hard it had to have been for your mom?" I asked.

Skyla gave a sad smile, "She didn't have my mom until she graduated from high school and apparently had her shit together. I know my mom was in love with my dad, but he clearly didn't feel the same, and I think that took a toll on her."

"Have you ever tried to talk to your dad?"

She shook her head, "Last I heard, he was in jail for murder, so his life ended up great. Lucky for me, he isn't on my birth certificate, and I have my mom's last name."

"What about your grandma? Have you been able to get in contact with her?"

"She died when I was ten; we didn't know until my mom was diagnosed with cancer a few years back. Basically, my life consisted of me and my mom. Even though the drugs were taking away the woman who loved me, I still loved her, and that ended up being the thing that broke me.

"When I was five, that was when everything changed. Instead of staying in the bathroom, whenever there were screams, I would run to the bedroom. There would be my mom, naked, and some man smacking her. I would scream for him to get away from her, which led to the shit getting smacked out of me. A few years later, everything changed.

"Mom finally had a turn in her life: her boyfriend Bill would always be there. Bill had been one of the dealers she had been buying from, and he finally wanted her to be his. He supplied her with addiction and made her feel shit for being weak and dependent on meth. They always fought with each other, and I learned to let her fight the battle. But then she finally got a job, and being left alone with Bill led to him pleasuring himself with me. It started with just touching, then it was full-blown sex."

My stomach churned, "How old were you?"

"Eight. I kept my mouth shut, just like Bill told me. No teacher at school would say anything about my bruises or appearance. I knew that I was on my own, and others refused to help. When I was thirteen, I tried to overdose on sleeping pills, and it really alarmed my mom, and she realized everything that had been going on.

"Once the doctors released me, we packed up and moved here to Bemidji. My mom remained clean ever since, and life was not as fucked."

"Life still has to be fucked because you just can't forget." I thought out loud.

Skyla smiled, "Yeah, I refused therapy and medication. I adapted to the night terrors and never really being able to sleep. My mother had to live with being a recovering drug addict and knowing what happened to me. I think that was why she was overprotective of me and why Bently could never be trusted." She sighed and laid her head back. "She died of breast cancer; she had stage four. It was not a very long battle, but I think it brought peace for her knowing the pain would be over with."

"Was she proud of you?"

She nodded, "Mom was speechless when I got into college and even more stunned when I was accepted into med school. She was happy I made something of my life, instead of crashing and burning like she did."

"Did she like Maggie?"

"Please, my mother loved Maggie, happy to see me finally have a friend. It was a relief for her."

We sat in silence as the bugs made humming sounds. I couldn't imagine living with those memories in my head. Truthfully, I would've probably killed myself a lot sooner. I also had a feeling that there would be no way I could forgive my mom. However, Skyla was not me, and she fought her way out and still loved her mom.

"Did you ever resent your mom?" I asked.

She shrugged, "There were moments that I did, but I remembered that life had been equally brutal to her. When someone resorts to drugs, they must be in a lot of pain, or they are running from their demons. I knew my mother loved me; she did her best to keep me full and hydrated. The safety part, not so much, but my basic needs were met, and she always hugged and kissed me goodnight."

"So, the silence is comforting?"

"Yeah, for once, I don't have to be worried about what's going on in the other room."

I looked at her and gave her a sad smile, "I'm sorry for the shit you've been dealt."

Skyla leaned over and squeezed my hand, "Everyone has something, Calsen; you just have to learn how to exist. Because that is what everyone in this world is doing: existing."

There was no arguing with her there.

Chapter Fourteen

The Touch That Burns

Maggie

Life was slowly back on track; it wouldn't be long until I would have to go back to contracted hours and school started. No one dared to say anything about how it was going with Daniel taking over. Dr. Loggins had officially retired and passed on his patients to Daniel. I refused to go and see him, even though my mom begged me. My argument with her made me sick to my stomach, but it worked. I told her that he was family, so it would be a conflict of interest for him to treat me. Thankfully, that was enough to convince her, even though I found myself in the bathroom a minute later, throwing up.

I was able to get in, with the help of my therapist Kelly, at Sanford and see a psychiatrist there. I was still going to go monthly, and the medicine dosages were not going to change. There were no questions to my face about why I, a Kensinger myself, was being treated at Sanford. As with every juicy piece of information, I am sure there were plenty of people talking.

It was a few weeks out of me going back to school and getting my room put together. The weather was warm, in the upper eighties, and the tourists were slowly dwindling. Before long, college kids would be back, and the town would be back to being Bemidji and not a summer destination.

Jackson had a morning shift, so I was woken up to him getting dressed. I struggled with going back to sleep, so I eventually got up myself. Skyla was passed out on the couch with her book pressed into her face. I quietly grabbed my tennis shoes and gently closed the door behind me. It wasn't overly hot yet, and if I was going to do any form of exercise, now would be the time to do it.

I decided to walk around the lake, instead of running. I was still too tired to even think about running. I pulled my hair up into a ratty bun and headed down a path from our backyard that led to the walking trail around the lake. I had walked the trail more times than days I had been alive. Growing up, mom and I would walk it almost every day, and then Skyla and I would go running in high school on it. At this point, I could tell you every detail about the ground and greenery that surrounded each part.

It was still early enough that there weren't too many people out and about. Something about walking or running with strangers around made me uncomfortable. Hence why, going to a public gym was something I refused to do. Even growing up and playing sports, I hated having people watch me work out.

There was a slight breeze in the air, bringing the temperature down a bit. I had on a baggy sweatshirt and biker shorts, something that was easy to grab from my closet. I didn't bring my headphones because I wanted to take in the sounds of animals and the lake. Lucky, I didn't wear headphones, because I probably would've died of a heart attack right then and there when he spoke.

"Maggie," his voice cut through the air, "why isn't this a pleasant surprise."

I felt my hands turn to fists and my blood go cold as his burning hand grasped my upper arm. My feet had rooted into place, and my eyes were darting around, trying to find someone, anyone, who could be a witness as to what would happen to me. As per usual, with my luck, there was not a soul in sight.

"What do you want?" I said, yanking my arm away.

He flashed his wicked smile, "You know what I want."

"No." I managed to say.

"Oh, Maggie, you and I both know that's not how this works." He stepped close to me; I could smell the sting of cologne. "You're filled with such fear that you can't fight back, and you are weak-minded, so you believe this is what you deserve."

I bit down, hard on my lip, already tasting the saltiness of my blood. I tried to turn away, but his hands grasped my neck to force me to look at him. In my nightmares, I could always see his face so clearly and smell that sharp cologne. Standing here now, the searing burn of his hands on me, I felt as if I had fallen into my nightmare. I squeezed my eyes shut, willing my body to wake up.

"You can beg all you want, Maggie, but you're still mine." I locked my knees. "You know what I am capable of, don't you?" I felt my stomach drop. "Answer me." He growled.

I was starting to feel the effects of locking my knees, but his growl sent alarms off in my brain. "Yes, I am," I whispered.

When I opened my eyes, he was so close to my face, I could feel his hot breath on my face. "I am always watching; I am always two steps ahead of you. No amount of protection will help you. You'll be a good girl and speak nothing of this."

He gripped my neck tighter, waiting for an answer that I didn't want to give because I knew I wouldn't hold to my word. "I will not speak of this."

Daniel took a deep breath, inhaling my smell. "You smell the same, peaceful lavender." He smiled, kissed my forehead, and walked away. "Have a good day, princess."

As soon as he appeared, he was gone. I snapped my head in all my directions, waiting to see him watching for my reaction. In his sick, twisted mind, seeing me break would just get him off. Focus. I needed to get home, take a shower, and burn this sweatshirt. I couldn't run; I had to walk, not giving him the satisfaction of seeing me run away.

I focused my eyes down on my feet, taking one step at a time, and letting some stupid song about taking a step at a time rerun in my head as I made my way home. There was still stinging around my neck and my upper arm, the points where he touched me. I felt tears spring to my eyes as I tried not to let my mind think, just keep replaying that ridiculous song.

Once I hit the trail that led back to the backyard, I broke out in a dead sprint. I could hear my heart pumping blood inside my head; it echoed in my head. I swung open the back door, not even considering that Skyla was sleeping. I slammed it shut, deadbolted it, and kicked off my shoes, ignoring Skyla's yelling. I closed the bathroom door, leaned over the toilet, and let myself feel.

"FUCK!" I screamed and slammed my hand on the toilet. "JESUS FUCK."

I began stripping my sweatshirt off, tears pouring down my face. I knew there was nothing I could do to stop him, because something told me that it would take one wrong move from me, and Skyla or Jackson could be hurt. I let out another scream as I leaned over the toilet and let the tears pour out.

Skyla pushed open the door and kneeled beside me; anger was not there; usually, when you woke her up, that's what you got. Her eyes were filled with fear as she searched my face and body for some kind of harm. When her eyes met mine again, I crumpled into her arms and let out a sob as the stinging of Daniel's touch eased with

Skyla hugging me tightly. He was back. I was his. Nothing could stop him.

"Maggie," she whispered as she squeezed me tightly, "what happened?"

I took a long, shaky breath. "I went for a walk."

"No shit, what happened?"

I curled my hands into fists, finally letting everything replay in my head. "He's watching me."

Skyla's whole body tensed up, "What happened, Maggie?"

I turned my head into her chest, letting a flood of emotions fill me up. "He's not going to stop; he's back for what he started."

She was silent for a second before she rubbed my back. "There's no way he can get to you."

"Well, he just did," I snapped back, "all I did was go for a walk alone, and then he ambushed me."

"Maggie," she sighed, "I know you don't want to go to the police, but just putting a restraining order on him would be better than nothing."

I shook my head, "You and I both know we need more evidence than one encounter. There was no rape kit ever done, so no history of sexual assault. Plus, that would be the move he'd want me to make in this game; it's a sign that I am scared."

"And that's what he gets off on," Skyla finished my thought; she knew all too well the dark side of men. "What can I do, since you won't let me kill him."

"There's nothing we can do. If he even has the slightest idea, you know, something, he'll find a way to hurt you."

"I am the last person we need to be worrying about in this situation," she said coolly. "The only way he could hurt me is by hurting you."

I looked at her sadly, "That's the problem; if he hurts you, then it will hurt me. I can take everything else, the rape and stalking, but him doing anything to you will be the thing that does me in."

Skyla thought for a moment before she spoke. "Damn you, Maggie Kensinger." She wiped away a tear from her left eye.

"We play the game, and we won't get hurt," I whispered.

"And when you get hurt, there will be nothing that can stop me from killing him."

Closing my eyes, "How am I supposed to let you do that?"

"How am I supposed to let you get hurt? How am I supposed to let myself live with that?"

I rested my head on her chest again, "We'll be okay." I said, it was very unconvincing.

"We will be okay," Skyla replied with no confidence.

It took me thirty minutes to shower, and I couldn't stop scrubbing my body. I started a fire outside and threw my clothes in; I stood there and watched them burn. Once it was all gone, I put out the fire and went back into my room. I gathered all my dirty clothes and took them to do some laundry, something normal.

Skyla was able to drift back into a sleep on the couch, but not for long. She ended up just sitting and watching *Rick and Morty* mindlessly on the couch. I joined her for a few episodes, but there was too much going on in my brain to sit still. I cleaned the kitchen and even took it upon myself to reorganize the pantry.

Around seven, Skyla had to go to work, and that was when Jackson was due home. I had been debating if it was worth saying anything to him because I knew he would lose it. He already was terrified for me; this encounter most likely would send him over the edge. Jackson didn't understand how dangerous Daniel was, and he also didn't realize there was no evidence to go to the police with. It wasn't so simple to solve this problem. Honestly, there was no way I could think that I could fix it. As I had told Skyla, we played the game; it was the best chance we had.

It took me a few days, but I finally got out of the house and went to my classroom. I just played off these last days as if I was sick, and Skyla went along with it. Jackson didn't seem to buy it, but he also knew better than to push for information, especially information he didn't want to hear.

This was going to be the first time I was going in alone. It was nearly ninety degrees out, making me already feel agitated and uncomfortable. I had on track shorts and a cropped white tee with a black baseball cap on. There was no one in the parking lot, making me the only one. I took a deep breath and scanned the playground and trees around, making sure that Daniel wasn't around. From what I could see, I was in the clear, so I kept my head down and jogged to the front door.

When I entered, it was still a shock to see the differences all over again. In my head, there were faint sounds of gunshots and screams. I balled my hands into fists and charged my way through the halls. Focus on the shoes and taking a step at a time, that damn sound overriding the horrors in my head.

I was able to make it to my room and take in the sterile outside; I wonder how many times they had to wax and clean the hall. Who could have the stomach to come in and remove the bodies? Who would've been able to clean? I know Jackson and Skyla have seen some gruesome injuries, but something about seeing these kids come in with gunshots did not sit right. I can't imagine who could have the stomach to clean up after murders and shootings.

Shaking my head, I entered my classroom and locked the door behind me. There was stabbing pain that entered my heart seeing this room all over again. My eyes were drawn back to my desk area that was untouched from that day. I needed to start setting up somewhere, might as well start where there was no damage.

My goal for today was to just clear out any junk and get the bare-bone layout. I wasn't due back until next week, but a lot of that time will be spent on meetings and active shooter drills. I had done so many in my years of teaching, but I don't think I could do it again, knowing what it felt like. No amount of training could prepare you for what would happen.

I tuned out my thoughts and blasted some *Twenty-One Pilots* songs in my headphones. It took me maybe an hour to get shit cleared and set up; all that really needed to be done was the decor and preparing paperwork and crap for the open house. Something that I wasn't worried about now, because that is when I got the call.

Chapter Fifteen

Roles Reversed

Jackson

Maggie was not telling me something; she was a terrible liar, but the fact Skyla backed her up told me not to worry about it. I went about at the hospital, avoiding the Psych floor. I hadn't actually run into Daniel, but Skyla had. She ignored him, even when he would be flat-out talking to her. It wouldn't be long before she would page a different trauma fellow to deal with him. Calvin avoided Daniel like the plague as well, but his interactions with him mimicked what Skyla was doing. Now, granted, this is what I had been told and whispered about in my OR.

I was on hour twenty of a forty-eight-hour shift. I was covering for the other fellow, Greg, who had to go home for a family emergency. I wasn't happy to do it, but Maggie assured me that she would be busy getting her classroom ready. It still amazed me that she wanted to go back, but to go back to the very same room concerned me. I had to have some faith in her; she had slowly gotten back on her feet and was living again. Seeing the amount of progress she had made in these last few months gave me hope that we were over the biggest hill.

My lower right abdomen had been hurting for the last day; I figured that I had eaten something bad from the cafeteria. But as my day went about, the pain worsened, and I started to get a raging headache. I took some aspirin and went into my gastric bypass surgery, the last one of the day before I was due to help down in trauma.

I scrubbed in with Dr. Kellog, a general resident I had been stuck with. He was new, and from Florida, so he thought since I was from California that, we would automatically be friends. He was wrong, of course. Just because we came from warm places didn't mean we were the same person and had the same interests. That was far from the damn truth; he was the opposite of me. It didn't take long for him to realize I was not a fan of his, so now, any conversation that was had was professional.

"Jackson, you look like shit." Dr. Kellog stated plainly. "I think you should sit this out."

I rolled my eyes, "I only look like shit because I am tired. I am fine, now let's go."

I stepped into the OR and got a gown slid on. General surgeries weren't usually popular ones people wanted to watch; that was more neuro or cardio. I was fine not to have a bunch of people watching from the observation deck. The fewer people that are in my OR, the better; it was less stressful for me not to have to worry about others getting in my way.

"Dr. Calsen," one of the scrub nurses had a worried look in her eyes. "Are you okay? You look, well, awful."

There was another shooting pain in my abdomen, and I shook my head, "I'm fine. Are we ready?"

Fuck, my stomach felt like it was on fire. I stepped up to the operating table to begin when the shooting pain hit me hard enough that I stumbled back. I crouched over and moaned in agony, fuck this hurt. The scrub nurse who had talked to me, rushed over and felt my head.

She frowned, "You're warm; someone goes get a wheelchair." And Dr. Kellog rushed out. "Symptoms go."

I moaned, "Lower right abdomen."

She began talking again, and my vision blurred, and her voice drowned out. She began feeling my stomach, and I let out a pathetic cry from the pain. My brain was searching for answers, symptoms suddenly occurring and lower right abdomen pain. Fuck. My appendix ruptured, but when and how? I moaned as a few more faces came in front of me, and I slowly let myself close my eyes.

Going under any kind of anesthetic was not a comfortable experience for me. I felt heavy, and everything was dark. I also was smart enough to know shit was being done to me, and there was no way I could control anything. Which just left me in this panic state, not something I prefer experiencing.

When I began to slowly feel myself getting out, I had never felt happier at that moment. Blinking my eyes a few times, finally, everything was slowly taking shape. I could hear the beeps of machines and the TV. Finally, my eyes fixated on the person leaning up against the doorframe. She wore a smirk on her face and had her arms crossed over her chest.

"You know, I kind of like being on this side of the bed," Maggie said, walking over to me. "Nice not to be the center of attention."

I moaned as she sat down on the edge of the bed. "What happened?"

She smiled, sending warmth through my body, and my heart rate sped up. "Your appendix burst; they think it was from some bacteria. So, you collapsed in the OR, and they had to rush you into surgery."

"Great," I moaned as I grabbed her hand and squeezed it, "that means I am out for three weeks at least."

Maggie laughed, "Hey, now it just means that I get to take care of you."

"You go back to work," I pointed out as she squeezed my hand. "I also will be fine, just can't lift anything heavy or make sure the incision site doesn't get infected."

She shook her head, "Anyways, depending on how you do tonight, you might be able to go home tomorrow."

"How long was I out?" I asked.

"Not even twenty-four yet, but my uncle says everything looks good. He was the one who did your surgery."

I narrowed my eyes, "Your uncle?"

"Yes, he viewed it as something he should handle so it wouldn't get fucked up. Don't worry; Skyla and Calvin were both watching to make sure you didn't get murdered by him." Maggie joked.

"Just don't like the thought that my boss was the one who operated on me." Maggie rolled her eyes. "I am sorry if I scared you."

She shook her head, "When Skyla called me and told me you had been rushed into emergency surgery, I was freaked out. But when I got to the hospital, Mom was there to tell me what happened."

"Your mom was here?"

"Jackson, you are basically family, so yes, my mom and uncle were concerned. Calvin left mid-surgery to let some fellow finish so he could be there. Skyla was able to get someone to cover the pit and rushed to get to you." She smiled and crawled into the bed with me. "I am just glad you're okay."

She rested her head on my shoulder. I smiled and kissed the top of her head before we both drifted off into a deep sleep.

Chapter Sixteen

Safe Space

Maggie

Jackson was losing his mind, being stuck at home for three weeks, but he listened to everything my uncle told him. He also pretty much had no other choice because either Calvin, Skyla, or I would be with him, watching him like a hawk. Out of the three of us, Calvin was the meanest one.

While he was recovering, I ended up going back to work. Skyla helped me in my room: hanging the lights and putting shit up. I was able to skip the active shooter training; they were only making new teachers go through it. Thank God. My class list was twenty, more girls than boys. My new grade partner was a brand new first-year teacher, and it was a shocker that Courtney (my other grade partner I had gone to school with) got along with her so that I was the odd one out again.

The open house had been a little intimidating because there were police in the parking lot, not to mention the metal detectors. Someone must've complained because by the first day of school, they were gone, and only one police officer was in the building. My kids were sweet; some of them were very nervous, but they all slowly seemed to get the hang of coming to school and knowing that they would get to see their parents soon.

The thing that had been frustrating for Jackson was that I refused to have sex with him. I told him not until he was cleared to go back to work, and he took that as forever. He had also been over the top nice: sending me flowers every day and meeting me outside when I would get home. He even packed lunches for me to make sure I would actually eat, and then he would make dinner. I didn't mind it; it was just a little over the top because he had nothing else to do. It was driving him crazy being home.

When Jackson was finally able to go back to work, I was expecting these little things to stop. But they didn't: flowers, Red Bull, food deliveries from *Subway*, and he even made dinner the nights we had off together.

"Can I ask something?" I was lying down on my bed.

He smiled, "I know you're going to ask anyway."

I rolled my eyes, "Why all of a sudden this change?"

Jackson looked confused, "What?"

"Why the flowers and shit? You never did that before. What has changed?"

Instead of being upset, he laughed, sending a confused look to my face. "I realized I wasn't doing enough of the boyfriend shit while I was losing my mind and because you deserve it."

"Yuck, don't get sappy." He laughed and laid down next to me. "I am serious; you don't need to do all of that."

He brushed a piece of hair out of my face, "What if I want to do it?"

"Then find a better reason than boyfriend shit, and I deserve it."

"You can never let me be romantic."

"I don't need you to be romantic; I just need you to be you."

Jackson lay on his side and cocked his head. "And what do you define as me being me?"

"Being a doctor, my brother's best friend, and giving good head when I want it."

There was a sparkle in his eyes, "Would you say that you are in need of said head?"

I smiled and shook my head, "I always need it."

He carefully kissed my lips as his fingers slowly pulled down my leggings, along with my thong. I felt my body relaxed. I already knew I was going to be soaking; the way Jackson just looked at me was enough to make me wet. He groaned as his fingers met my wetness; I felt my cheeks flush red.

"Fuck," Jackson whispered, "are you always this wet?"

My eyes met his, "Only with you."

Jackson kissed my forehead, and lips, and then he lifted my shirt off and snapped my bra off. I felt goosebumps form along my skin as I watched him take in my body. He kissed both of my nipples, then my stomach, and finally my sweet spot. I let out a gasp of air as his tongue moved slowly, making me arch my back and legs shake. I knew it would not take long for me to come.

Jackson's eyes met mine as I let myself relish the feeling. It felt like weed-high on steroids that made me gasp, wishing it would never end. Jackson came up and kissed my lips; I could taste my sweetness. He smiled down at me as I sat up, tugged off his shirt, and pulled down his pants. My eyes hungrily took him, admiring every inch. I pushed Jackson back down on the bed and licked my lips before my mouth met him.

He ran his finger through my hair as I watched him enjoy the power I held. I licked him the full length before taking it all in, making me gag, just what he liked. Jackson pulled me by my hair back to his lips, and I took this as my chance to lower myself on his cock. He groaned, gripping the sides of my lips, and I began moving, using him to pleasure myself.

"Fuck," he mumbled, watching me. "Don't stop, come for me, baby."

I smirked down at him as I did what he asked. I moved myself in such a sweet and smooth motion that drove him crazy. It wasn't long before he finally took control, wanting me at his pace. Everything that followed was a blur; I let myself get lost in all the feeling, riding the high.

Right then and there, I was safe. A place I wanted to stay in.

Chapter Seventeen

Thin Line of Lies and Truths

Maggie

I knew my paradise wouldn't last long. A few days later, Skyla wanted me to come and visit her at work. I was never going to pass up a chance to see my best friend, especially since our schedules had been opposites for the last week. When she got home, I was leaving; we both were too tired to exchange more than just a morning grunt.

The sun was on the cusp of being set when I began to walk into the front doors of the hospital. The air was finally starting to feel like the fall weather, my second favorite time of the year, winter being the first and summer being the worst. One of the best things about Bemidji was you got all four seasons, anymore I felt like everywhere else in the Midwest had hot summers and then cold winters.

While walking through the parking lot, I felt the unsettling feeling of being watched. I took a deep breath and picked up my pace to walk to the door, thinking that I would be safer there; yeah, right. I could hear footsteps from behind me; I didn't look back. I could smell the stinging cologne from feet away, probably miles away; I had the nose of a bloodhound.

"It would be smart if you stopped," Daniel stated.

I stopped and turned around, "Leave me alone."

He laughed, and in a few strides, he closed the space between us. I could see his hospital badge hanging off his hip. Daniel was dressed in slacks and a button-up, the same outfit he wore in my nightmares. I quickly turned back around before I would be frozen.

"You know, Maggie, ignoring people isn't polite."

Snapping around, "You know, Daniel, raping your best friend's daughter isn't polite."

A smile spread across his face, reminding me of the Grinch from that damn Dr. Suess book. "That's what you think? Oh," he clucked his tongue as he brushed my hair to the side, "that's not what it is. You are mine, will always be mine."

"If I was yours, why did you go running like a pussy when I finally broke?"

"Be careful," he seethed through his teeth.

I shook my head, "Leave me alone, Daniel."

Before I had even fully turned around, his hand locked around my hair, and he yanked me back. His hand was over my mouth before I could make a noise. Daniel dragged me out of anyone's sight and shoved me up against the hospital wall. My whole body froze as my mind went blank, not prepared for my nightmare to be sparked alive. I closed my eyes, hoping this would help in some pathetic way.

"Look at me," he smacked me across the face, "listen to me," it felt like dozens of needles had pierced my cheek. "I don't know what makes you think you can talk to me like that, but most of all, you are not allowed to walk away from me like that."

Tears wanted to come pouring out, but I was too scared. "Okay," I whimpered out.

"Tell me you understand," he growled into my ear.

"I understand," I managed out as I watched him grin at me.

"You're pathetic, but you're mine." He gripped my face and turned it to make sure there were no markings. "You won't have a mark; maybe next time you'll think twice before talking to me like that." Daniel backed away from me. "See you soon, princess."

Daniel vanished into the shadows while I slid down against the wall until I met the ground. I gripped my cheek, still burning from his touch and force. He was hellbound and determined to make sure I understood that there was no escaping him. I covered my mouth and sobbed into my hand; how silly of me to think that I could escape. How pathetic I was to believe I deserved a happy life.

Shaking my head, I grabbed my phone and called Skyla. She picked up on the first ring: "Where are you?"

"Outside to the right," I squeaked out as tears fell down my face.

Without asking any more questions, she came running out to me; her eyes had a wild look in them. She scanned the area before kneeling in front of me. It always amazed me at how breath-taking Skyla really was. She had very intense eyes, such a piercing dark mixed with light blue that were cat-shaped. Her hair always had red undertones and had been longer than her waist since I had known her. Skyla was beautiful on the outside, but what I found the most beautiful was her soul.

"Maggie, what happened?" She cut through my thoughts.

I shook my head, "I can't, I can't do this, Skyla."

She grabbed both sides of my face, "Yes, you can. You don't give up now."

"Why did I think he would never come back?"

"That doesn't matter. What matters is getting through this." There were tears in her eyes. "I can't lose you, not after everything we've been through."

I let out a shaky breath and nodded. Skyla pressed her forehead to mine, and a quiet sob escaped her. "Jackson needs to know."

Skyla nodded, "Let's not worry about that now. Come on and eat a pathetic dinner of chicken strips with me."

That was exactly what we did: sit in the mostly empty cafeteria and pick at one serving of chicken tenders that Skyla had brought from the house. I didn't want to think, right at this moment, it was easier to just sit and stare into space. Because as soon as Skyla had left, I would have to face the gut-retching truth: I was in danger. To top it off, I was going to have to officially rope Jackson in.

Skyla stood up, squeezed my shoulder, and met Jackson a few steps ahead. Calvin was following behind him, eyes were locked on me. I ignored him and diverted my eyes to the windows that overlooked the lake. The moon was almost full, which meant my kids were going to be crazy at school. I could never understand how the moon phases affected elementary kids, but it was a true thing.

"Mags," Calvin said, "walk out with us. I had surgery that ran late, and Calsen took too long on night rounds."

I gave a slight nod, before being engulfed in Skyla's arms. I felt relaxed, fatigue finally hitting me. I just wanted to curl up in my bed and let the nightmares take me. However, I wanted the nightmares of Maxwell Fath trying to shoot up my classroom and being shot. I knew better; Daniel would be lingering in the dreams.

Both Jackson and Calvin walked on either side of me, shielding me from danger. Instead of feeling safe, I felt like I was drawing attention. I knew he would see and both Calvin and Jackson protecting me, making them threats, and threats were meant to be eliminated. I swallowed and kept my head down.

When I was finally ready for bed, the words were able to form. Jackson sat there the entire time, expressionless. I was prepared for him to lash out, saying he was going to murder him. I also thought he was going to demand I go to the police. I didn't expect him to just reach out and hold me. And because it was so unexpected, I cried onto his chest and fell asleep in his arms.

Jackson

The crazy thing was, as Maggie spoke about what happened, it wasn't a surprise. I knew it was bound to happen, especially the way he looked at her at his introduction. I had never asked what he said to her, but it affected Maggie as she went running. She didn't deserve to relive that moment.

Letting her break down in my arms, broke a part of me, because her nightmare was coming back. I still remember her explaining what had happened when she was a freshman in college, waves of hell for me, but all of this seemed like I was living in hell with no way to escape.

You could tell that Maggie was afraid; her eyes scanned everywhere we went. The rest of us didn't let her go anywhere alone; we would follow her work and back. Skyla had made it clear at work that if they sent Daniel down to the pit when she requested a psych evaluation, she would go out of her way personally to ruin their career. Everyone was already scared shitless of her, now they were even more terrified. Calvin luckily didn't have much interaction with psych, because I don't think he would be able to stop himself from killing him. I couldn't blame him; I felt the same way.

It wouldn't be before long that the chief would catch wind of what was going on, and I don't think the three of us could stop ourselves from divulging the truth, no matter how much Maggie begged us all. I knew it would be something she could never forgive us for, but the selfish thing was I hoped the chief would ask.

I've never really asked Maggie about her relationship with her uncle; my only guess would be not great. Something told me the chief would take matters into his own hands; she was still his niece, and family had to mean something to him, especially since he had no one.

The only thing I knew about Chief Kensinger was he had been a cardiac surgeon before he took over the hospital when he was in his forties. He had never been married and had no kids. The rumor was he was gay, but Calvin denied that really quickly. Making some comment about how you should see the number of prostitutes he had on speed dial, not anything I wanted to think about.

It was a rare Friday morning when I was called down to the pit to help. Apparently, some sickness was going around, and Skyla begged me. Dr. Kellog had no worries looking out for my patients and had my only surgery for the day. Not that I was all that thrilled to be Skyla's bitch boy, but I knew it would earn me brownie points for her. I knew she was always waiting for me to fuck up because she didn't trust men, and knowing her past: rightfully so.

I was wrapping up in treatment one when I heard a commotion coming from the pit. When I went to check, I saw Skyla examining a patient on a gurney with police standing behind her.

"Twenty-three-year-old female, found by the lake. Apparent head trauma, unconscious in the field, heart rate low at 49 beats per minute." The female paramedic informed Skyla.

"Alright, we've got it from here." The paramedic nodded and led the patient into trauma bay 3. "Calsen page neuro, and" she hesitated, "also page psych."

Without questioning her, I did both. Hopefully, psych knew not to send Daniel down. Saying a silent prayer in my head, I headed into the bay to help Skyla.

The patient was dressed in running clothes, but her shorts were put on backward. Her head was gashed open, and clear defensive wounds on her hands. There was bruising around her thighs, like someone had been holding her down; my stomach twisted.

"You think she was sexually assaulted?" I said, and Skyla met my eyes and nodded. "What do you want me to brief to psych?"

Skyla looked sadly down at the patient and said, "Just what you said and how they found her."

Brushing past the police, the last people I wanted to talk to, I met Calvin, who was making his way through the pit. "Trauma bay 3."

He eyed the police, "And?"

"Dr. James called for psych, suspected sexual assault."

Calvin moaned, "Just who I want to talk to: the police."

"I know," I was thinking the same thing.

The police were right there; I could go and end everything with Daniel right now. But Maggie would never forgive me, and something told me there was more reason behind why we hadn't gone to the police; I just wasn't in the loop.

Following Calvin back into the bay, he immediately got to work. Skyla was finishing x-rays and scans, clearing for any signs of fluid in the lungs or belly, and no broken bones. Skyla wore a blank expression while she worked; her eyes had a fogged look; it was like she was fighting any emotion from surfacing. Calvin wore the same look; only sadness was clear in his eyes.

"Someone called for a psych consult?"

All three of our heads snapped and met the devil himself. Daniel Dobson was standing at the door, fuck. Skyla shot daggers in my direction, knowing I was the one who called psych. Calvin ignored him and kept his focus on the gash.

"I need an MRI." He said without looking back up. "Her pupils are sluggish, but they are reactive. Heart rate is low, but steady enough for the scan." Calvin looked at the nurse in the corner of the bay. "Let them know I am coming up for a scan."

"Has she regained consciousness?" Daniel asked.

Both Skyla and Calvin ignored him, leaving me to answer. "No, they found her like this."

I felt the heat of Skyla's glare on me as Daniel walked up, taking a look. "Shame, so young to have to go through this."

"Excuse me?" Calvin hissed.

Daniel wore a fake look of confusion: "Dr. Kensinger, you know I worked with victims of sexual assault. I know the lasting impacts it has on them; it's just a shame every time to see someone so young."

I felt anger bubbling inside me. Skyla's fist was clenched, and Calvin was glaring at him. There was no way Daniel just said what I thought I heard. He had to be joking. He had to know that we all knew what happened between Maggie and him. This had to be bait, seeing if any of us would take it. Fuck it was tempting.

"You're fucking joking, right?" Calvin seethed.

"I am not; it makes me want to lock up monsters like this. Once again, I worked a lot of cases and always had a satisfying feeling that we were able to get a predator off the streets." Daniel sighed and looked back down at the patient. "There's a special place in hell for monsters like this."

Calvin was shaking with anger, and Skyla shot me a worried look. We both knew Calvin was taking the bait. Truth was, I didn't want to stop him if he lashed at Daniel. Deep down, I knew Skyla wasn't going to interfere either.

"There's a special place in hell for you." Calvin snapped.

Daniel had that fake look of shock, "What are you talking about? I spent a lifetime helping police get predators off the streets. Why would I deserve to be in hell?"

"Calvin, don't," Skyla warned.

"YOU THINK WE DON'T KNOW?" He finally screamed out. "I can't believe you; I trusted you and looked up to you." Calvin stepped closer to Daniel. "And then you turn around and do the shit you did to Maggie?"

Daniel laughed, sending an alarmed look on Skyla's face and chills down my spine. "What do you think I have done to Maggie? All I have ever done for your sister is mentor her before she changed careers. I would never do anything to Maggie; she's family."

Before anyone could react, Calvin punched him hard in the face. Skyla shoved Calvin back, before he could do anything else. I stepped forward, blocking Daniel from coming any closer. His lip was bleeding; I was pissed there wasn't more damage.

"You're a sick bastard," Calvin growled. "Pretending like we don't know, fuck you."

Police finally stepped in, looking between everyone. This was the moment I could step in and save Maggie. A chance was right there in front of me. Skyla was watching me, shaking her head slightly, as if she had read my thoughts.

"Is everything good here?" The officer asked.

Calvin shrugged off Skyla, "Just peachy," he snapped, "let's get her up for an MRI now."

I stepped aside to let the nurse and Skyla get the patient wheeled out and out to the elevators. Daniel was watching me; his eyes were burning at me, making me uncomfortable. The officers were still watching; Daniel wore a small smirk, wanting to see if I would break. I closed my eyes. Maggie didn't need saving; she needed me to keep my promise.

That is what I did. Hold my promise.

It wasn't a shocker when the three of us were paged up to the chief's office. I had a sick feeling because I didn't know which one of us would break, which one of us would Maggie hate forever. I was hoping Skyla would be the one, because I knew she couldn't hate her. However, I knew I was going to be the weak link between the three of us.

Chief Kensinger didn't look like his brother, more of a tan and lighter eyes. Since the passing of Mitch Kensinger, the chief had dark circles under his eyes, like he had not slept in weeks. He probably wasn't getting a lot of sleep: he ran a damn hospital, his niece nearly died, and his brother died. I wonder if he would run to his addiction: hookers.

I was standing between Skyla and Calvin, who both wore looks of disgust. The chief was darting his eyes back and forth from one end to the other. There was obvious anger, but if you stared long enough into his eyes, you could see the panic.

"One of you better start talking." He said calmly, keeping focused on Calvin. "Particular you."

"There's nothing to talk about," Skyla stated. There was even disgust in her voice. "We disagreed with Dr. Dobson on things and let it get the best of us."

Well fuck, she wasn't going to break Maggie's trust, so it was down to Calvin and me. I looked over at

Skyla, who gave me a slight shake of the head. I knew what it meant, and I knew better than to break the trust.

"So, you're telling me that this disagreement led to my head of neurology and nephew punching Dr. Dobson." His eyes remained locked on Calvin, who didn't speak. "You have nothing to say at all?"

The corners of Calvin's mouth twitched, "I don't think Daniel should've come back."

Skyla shot her head down and stared at her black shoes, while Chief Kensinger raised an eyebrow. "Why is that so?"

I looked at Calvin and shook my head; he couldn't do this, not after building a relationship with his sister. I could not see her forgiving him if he revealed the truth. It was hard to see Maggie hating someone. She didn't even hate Maxwell Fath, the fucker who tried to kill her. Something deep down told me that she didn't even hate Daniel.

"He was the last person who needed to be here." I took a deep breath; Calvin held his eye contact with the chief. "It was the last thing Maggie needed." He stated.

The chief was taken aback by this answer, "What do you mean?"

"Ask Maggie." I blurted, and both Calvin and Skyla looked over at me. "If you want answers, ask Maggie. Otherwise, we will not let personal issues get in the way."

Skyla eagerly nodded, while Calvin remained straight-faced. We were all staring at the chief; I was hoping that he would just take my word for it. I knew better than to hope for anything, because, in my experience, hope led to more heartache and pain.

"Back to work, all three of you." The chief shook his head as if he didn't like his answer. "Another incident, and you all will be suspended, without pay."

Without another word, the three of us exited the office, not breaking Maggie's trust. Instead of feeling relieved, I felt dread and anger. Her trust was the only thing in the way between saving her and losing her.

Maggie

My first memories of life came back to the damn Lake of Bemidji itself. The clearest one was feeding the birds toast but being scared they would bite me. My mom held my hand and never let go. I just remember her reminding me that she was here to keep me safe. Another memory from an early age is trying to skate on the lake with my dad. Funny enough, he was a terrible skater, more brains than brans, but he still tried to get me on the ice.

The lake is a big destination for people to ice fish; strangely, my dad was not into it. Although he did like going fishing, ice fishing was a turnoff. During the wintertime, there would be tons of ice-fishing huts.

Crazy, that will be the scene of what I was looking at now.

Skyla and I were sitting at the edge of a dock near the line of hotels. It was finally cold enough that the bugs were gone. We were only a week or so out from Halloween, something my students hadn't stopped reminding me of.

"You're killing me," Skyla said as she stretched out on the dock, "I was close, Maggie, to losing it."

For the past few days, I have heard about what had happened to all three of them. I knew she was pissed at me, especially when she texted me back with single words and periods at the end. Not to mention the short responses she had given me about the incident, Jackson could barely speak to me about what had happened.

"I know," I whispered, eyes focusing on the ripples in the water. "You and I both know there isn't anything we can do, no evidence, no protection."

Skyla scoffed, "Trust me, something tells me the police here are butt buddies with Daniel, so they wouldn't be any help anyways."

To be fair, with all the shit Skyla had been through, trusting the police was not in the cards. It didn't matter how many lives they saved; they didn't help her when she needed it most. I did not blame her one bit that she resented them; it made sense. Sometimes, I wonder how different her life would've turned out.

"What do you think I should tell my uncle?" I asked, picking at my thumb.

"Depends on the reaction you want to happen."

Telling my uncle would lead to questions, information being shared, and confrontation. The things Daniel could say and do to me left ice in my veins. I could see everything being spun back to me being mentally unstable; that would be how he got away with the accusations.

"How much would you resent me if I kept quiet?" I looked back at her. "Be honest."

Skyla laughed, "Maggie, you've done a lot of questionable shit, and I have never resented you. This would be no different."

I smiled at her, "I don't deserve you."

"Yeah, yeah, don't get weepy."

She sat up, and I rested my head on her shoulder. Life was a bitch, but Skyla at least made it bearable.

Avoiding my uncle like the plague, I was able to do this more than a week before my mother stepped in. She showed up at my house, with a very stern look that used to send me running as a child. Honestly, she scared me more than my dad ever did; that was saying something.

"Maggie Grace," It was never a good sign when my middle name was used. "Get your ass up to the hospital now, or I will be dragging you by your hair."

My mother was beautiful; there was no denying that, even with old age. I was lucky to have her unique golden hair color and eyes. Anika looked more like Dad, with light brown hair and more pale blue eyes. Mom was tall and slender and always had the demands of the room. I know my dad admired her for that. She was someone who could match his demand.

"Gee, Mom, I am happy to see you too." She narrowed her eyes at me. "Okay, okay, I planned on going today anyway."

"Liar." She snapped at me. "I don't know what's going on, but I hope you're okay."

There was a hint of fear in her eyes, which she had every right to feel. I had put my mom in awful situations in these last years, not to mention having two other children giving her a run for her money. There was never a moment she didn't worry about all of us; that was her job and what she signed up for.

I smiled at her, "I'm fine, Mom." I stepped over and hugged her. "Promise."

Mom gave a heavy sigh and hugged me back tightly, an embrace that brought back many warm memories. "I just worry about you."

Closing my eyes, I could smell sweet pea lotion and perfume she had for as long as I could remember. "I know, Mom. I am okay."

She pulled back and smiled, "Get going; I don't want another call from your uncle."

I had always been close to my mom, for as long as I could remember. She would be the person I wanted as a kid when I was upset. Mom also was always around since she was the one who gave up her career to raise us. I know it hurt her that she was the one who had to do it, but I knew she was grateful for that time with us. I think because she was around more often than Dad, that was why I was closer to her, and even Calvin too.

Within the next ten minutes, I was in my car driving to the hospital. There would be very few things I could say no to when it came to my mom. Talking to my uncle to let him get off her back was not one of those things. So, as terrified as I was at the chance of seeing Daniel, there I was going to the very place he'd be at.

My uncle was waiting at the front doors of the hospital, arms crossed and pissed. It was the same stance my dad had when we did something wrong. My uncle and Dad were mirror images of each other; they could've been identical twins for all anyone knew.

I felt heat rise to my cheeks as I stopped a few paces in front of him. He took a deep sigh and motioned me to follow as we walked into the hospital. As usual, there were a decent amount of people walking around, and a low sound of chatter throughout. It always seemed busy to me as a kid, the amounts of faces you would see. The number of conversations that were going on around drowned out your thoughts. Now, there was some comfort in being a speck in this place and not being able to hear your thoughts.

When we were finally in his office, you could hear a pin drop. All the noise and sounds were gone. Separated by walls and a door. I sat down in one of the chairs in front of his desk; there were very few personal items in the office. There wasn't even a picture of the family in here. The only thing that was my uncle's was his diplomas and degrees.

"What's going on, Maggie?" His voice was much deeper than my dad's. "What is the problem with Daniel Dobson and you?"

My fingers began picking at my thumb, "Nothing, he's just family."

"BULLSHIT!" He slammed his fist into the table. "I know you're lying; why are you lying now? To me?"

I narrowed my eyes at him, "Excuse me? Just because we are blood does not mean you care."

"Of course I care, Maggie. I wouldn't be blowing up your phone and your mother's if I didn't."

"Please, you're only wondering because it's directly affecting you. Otherwise, if you did care, you wouldn't have tossed me aside like my dad and siblings did for nine years. So don't play that card; you have no right." I fired back.

My uncle shook his head, "Maggie, what is the deal with Daniel? You refused to be treated by him or anyone in the psych department. Now I have your brother punching him over a patient and your best friend refusing to work with Daniel. This all is connected to you. Especially when the best answer I can get out of anyone is to talk to you."

I bit the inside of my cheek, nervous. "Everything is fine. I can talk to Skyla and Calvin about treating Dr. Dobson with respect."

"LIE!" My uncle screamed. "Why did you stop studying under him all those years ago?"

"I wanted to be a teacher."

He groaned, "Something happened, and I want to know so I can help."

I started to laugh, "You want to help? The only reason you feel like you need to help out is because my pathetic father is dead. So now, you feel the need to have replace him." I shook my head, laughs still escaping me. "News for you, I went almost ten long years without a father; I can gladly do another fifty without one."

Both of my uncle's hands were formed into fists. He was frustrated with me, but everything I had said was true. I had done without a father all these years; I can do without one for the rest of my life. The last thing I wanted or needed was my uncle coming in to save the day.

"Clearly, you and Daniel have some history," he stated calmly, hands still in fists. "I don't understand what could've happened to cause you to lie and the people closest to you protecting this secret."

I took a deep breath, "Daniel and I have never gotten along; we fought like cats and dogs; that was why I stopped studying under him."

My uncle was studying me hard, "Why this built-up anger from your brother and best friend?"

"He said some shitty things."

"We all have said shitty things at one point in our life Maggie. So, tell me, what happened?"

"I can't tell you." I was finally admitted.

"What?" He was clearly taken aback by the answer I gave him. "You can't tell me what?"

"I can't tell you," I said more firmly this time, "you and I both know I am stubborn, and this is the closest answer you're going to get."

It was a good three minutes before my uncle got up and left me in his office, telling me to let myself out. He had gotten the closest thing to answer he would ever get.

Chapter Eighteen

Surprises Can Be Good or Bad

Maggie

There was so much that had happened in my life that sometimes I begged for a different life. One where I hadn't made the mistakes I did. One that didn't involve mental health and abuse. In life, well, we don't get the luxury to start over and wipe the plate clean. We just must push forward and carry everything with us.

I had heard of different motivation books saying that you can start fresh. You can let go of everything bad that happened to you. I wish that it was that simple: letting go, but how can you let go of something that altered everything your brain thought? Depression wasn't something that I could let go of; it was something I had to manage. My abuse couldn't be just let go; it was always going to be there, haunting in the back of my mind.

One night, back in college, I remembered Skyla and I discussing deep shit; we were drunk off some cheap bottle of vodka. We were lying out on the grass in some city park; it was snowing and sticking to the ground.

With everything she had faced, there were moments when she wanted to let go of life itself. What are you supposed to do then? When someone wants to do that, then they are considered weak, selfish, or broken. She said that if you wanted us to let go of our traumas and baggage, maybe for some people, that meant letting go of life. When she had tried to kill herself back when she was thirteen, that was what she was doing: letting go of life.

I had never deemed someone taking their life as a selfish thing to do. Quite honestly, when someone gets to that point, it's a more selfless thing to do. Now, I understand how people see it as a selfish act, but not until you've been in a moment where letting go of life is the best option can you truly understand both sides. Selfishness and selflessness.

Here is what a lot of people don't realize: asking someone with a broken brain to live is like asking a regular person if they would die for them. People like me, Skyla, Jackson, and millions of others live in a constant state of shame. We are the black sheep of society, the banged-up and damaged toy a child doesn't play with. We don't belong because we chemically aren't right. So, asking us to live with knowing that revealing your struggles will be used against you is asking more than you think.

I have firsthand witnessed many people getting their mental health used against them. Shit, I have even been in that situation. The way Skyla eventually told me how she avoided it: don't tell people shit, then they can't use what they don't have. No one really knows of her past, but that is because she kept her mouth shut. I learned quickly to follow suit, especially when it came to talking about what had happened with Daniel. As I stated before, revealing everything would get turned back to me being mentally unstable. That was one of many reasons I had to stay quiet about him.

Another reason was how he would react. Sure enough, as I got home and parked my car, there he was, leaning up against the garage. It was early November, and we had a few snow flurries, but nothing that had stuck. I didn't see any other cars on the street, which told me he had either walked or had some hiding place. Neither sit well with me.

Driving away may have seemed like the better option, but since fear was exactly what he wanted to see, I got out and braced myself for whatever he had in store for me.

"We've got a problem." He started, eyes following me as I walked to the rear of my car. "A problem that started with you disobeying me."

I stopped, "Get away."

There was fire in his eyes, the kind that was there when I had fought back when he raped me. "I told you to keep your mouth shut." He covered the distance between us in three strides. "Yet, you disobeyed me."

It was like I had fallen back in time, "Leave me alone." I said, trying to sound strong.

Daniel laughed and grabbed my throat; the burning instantly began. "What makes you think you can talk to me like that?"

"Get off," I tried to shove him off.

He gripped my throat harder, crushing my windpipe. "I like it when you try to fight back. Shows just how much power I have." Daniel got close to my face, centimeters away. "Just shows how pathetic you are."

Daniel let go of my throat, and I coughed, letting the air fill me up. The edges of my vision got hazy, and my body felt heavy. I steadied myself against my car, looking up at him. He wore that smirk as he got close to me again; the smell of the sharp cologne stung.

"What," I coughed, "do you want from me?" I wheezed out.

"Oh, Maggie," he gently tilted my head up, "you know what I want." I felt tears slipping down my cheeks. "You're mine and mine only."

He pressed his lips to mine, and that's when everything snapped inside me. I kneed him hard in the groin, and he stumbled back. Taking this moment of surprise as my chance to escape, I was able to reach the front door, but he grabbed my shoulder and slammed me to the ground. Finally, finding a voice, I screamed, so loud that my eardrums ached.

As soon as I found that voice, Daniel disappeared. It was like he was smoke, disappearing between your fingers. I sat up and glanced around my surroundings. There were a few clouds in the sky and a light breeze. Our neighbors across the street were out on their front porch; they were an older couple. They wore a look of confusion and were debating if I was okay. I don't know what they saw or if they saw anything at all, so I just waved to them, painting a smile across my face.

I awkwardly stood up and got my keys out; my hands were shaking as I scraped marks from being pushed down on the concrete front stoop. Once inside, I locked the door and went running up the stairs and into the bathroom. Reflecting in the mirror was a wide-eyed Maggie. My throat was red, with very light bruising from where his fingerprints were. There were still tears coming down my face as mascara was running down with them.

Closing my eyes, I let out a small sob as my lips trembled. What was I to do? It all was still my word against his and still the problem of no concrete proof. Even with this light bruising, it wasn't going to be enough. I slammed my fist down on the counter; if I went to the police anyways, who the fuck knows what he would do. Would he hurt Skyla? Calvin? Or Jackson? I couldn't let him get to them, if he wanted to hurt someone, it was just going to be me.

I sat in the shower, crisscrossing applesauce for thirty minutes. The cold water pelted my skin, bringing relief to the skin that Daniel had touched. When I got out,

I wrapped a towel around me and grabbed my long-sleeved shirt and leggings, walked down to the kitchen, and threw them into the trash. Taking a shaky breath, I made my way back into my room, dressed, and crawled into my bed. Laying my head back, I let myself crumble in silence.

Skyla got home later in the evening and came straight into my room. She knew something had to have been up since I didn't respond to anyone who texted me. I turned to look up at her and watched her frown. She sat down on the bed and tilted my face to the side to get a look at my neck. I brushed her hand away, and she gripped my wrist, taking in the scraps.

"Do you need anything from the kitchen?" She asked, gently squeezing my wrist.

"He didn't damage my legs," I said, my voice hoarse.

She gave a sad smile, "Well, I am going to grab some cheesecake; you don't want wine?"

I shook my head, "Skyla, I can't do this."

"Yes, you can, get that damn thought out of your head. You did not survive a shooting, suicide attempts, and sexual assault just to give up because of a man." She shook her head, upset. "You do NOT give him that power, that satisfaction; you're strong, Maggie, even if you don't think so. I know you are; you always have been."

I turned my face away as she slipped out of my room and returned a few minutes later. Skyla slid into my bed and turned on the TV to *Rick and Morty*. I gave her a weak smile before feeling comfortable enough to close my eyes and fall asleep.

Sunday morning, I refused to leave my bed. I had heard her explain to Jackson what had happened; I listened as he yelled and kicked the wall. I pretended to be asleep when he came in, afraid to hear the anger that he would have. Lucky for me, he had to work, so I didn't have to deal with him.

Around mid-afternoon, while still lying in my bed, I realized something that sent my stomach sinking. I sat up, grabbed my phone, and pulled out my calendar. Oh shit. I threw my phone down, awkwardly slid out of my bed, grabbed a hoodie and shoes, and went rushing to Skyla's room. My stomach was now doing flips at the realization of what was happening.

***

Back in high school, when Bently was still around, Skyla used to talk about having a family. Growing up, she had determined not to end up like her mother or even grandmother. She had decided at ten years of age that she was never going to get married and have kids. Skyla did not want to bring life into the cruel world; I didn't blame her. When it came to Bently, that, of course, changed.

It was crazy the effect he had on her. Love at first sight sort of shit for both, so unlike Skyla. He was able to make her blush, smile brightly, and giggle like a kid. Bently was very protective of Skyla but loved to flaunt her around (which she hated and bitched about). I knew all the boys in our high school envied him, but the bond the two of them had was magical. Gaggi, romantic crap.

Once we were in college, Bently finally decided to take her ring shopping. He wanted to have her dream ring for when he would pop the question. They never settled on a ring because his depression hit hard. It was also around this time; Skyla went in to be examined for fertility. Thankfully, I went with her to this appointment; Bently didn't want to be in the room while someone was between her legs. Plus, Skyla wanted me there and not him.

We were sitting in the tiny room, the heat blasting on us, and watching some stupid video on her phone. When the doctor came in with a straight face, we both knew that what was about to be shared was not good. And we were correct.

It was determined that because of all her scar tissue buildup from her abuse, she had less than a one percent chance of getting pregnant. I felt my heart shatter as I turned to look at Skyla, who now wore a straight face. She had gotten her hopes up at having a family with Bently. This was the exact reason she didn't get her hopes up, because the heartbreak was painful.

Bently kept reminding her that it didn't matter; he just wanted her to be healthy and safe. She thought she had failed him. Better yet, her body had failed her. When

Skyla finally talked to me about it, she couldn't understand how she couldn't do the most basic thing a woman was destined to do. It was just a reminder that her past had come back to fuck up her entire life, no matter how far she had come from it.

Over the years, Skyla was able to overcome the pain, and decided that her original decision of bringing life into this world was the better. It also helped that the only person she ever wanted kids with was dead. She also discovered, when visiting my classroom one time, that kids were not her forte. After that, she said that she would only love my kids and my kids.

That was why I went rushing to her room; Calvin kissed her, and demanded we needed to go to the drugstore. Without any hesitation, she hopped up and grabbed her purse on the floor. Calvin groaned and shot me the finger as I was in too much panic to even flip him off.

There were no questions; she just followed me in the store, but when I finally stopped in front of the pregnancy tests, her mouth dropped.

"You're joking." She hissed. "Is it at least Jackson's?"

I rolled my eyes, "Not funny," she laughed lightly, "I don't know what to get and how many."

"How late are you?" Skyla started analyzing the variety of tests. "Do you have any symptoms?"

"Over almost two weeks, and you know I am never late." She nodded, eyes still scanning the shelf. "Just bloated and being late."

She took in my information and grabbed three boxes of some blue tests. The cashier was looking between us, trying to figure out which one of us this was for. Skyla wore an annoyed look, while I kept my eyes down and paid. After that awkward interaction, we drove back to the house in silence, both of us preparing for what could happen next.

I was twenty-nine, and most people that we went to high school with were married and had kids. I had just always assumed that was never going to happen for me, but here I was: possibly pregnant. What would everyone think? Would Jackson even be okay with this? How was I supposed to tell everyone? What was going to happen if Daniel found out? My stomach did a flip, and I took a deep breath when we came back into the house.

Calvin was sitting on the couch, watching something on ESPN. To my disgust, he was shirtless and in basketball shorts, not to mention feet on the coffee table. Skyla scowled as she walked by and up the stairs. I rolled my eyes as Calvin looked at me, wounded.

"Feet off the coffee table," I said, and he quickly moved them off. "One of her biggest pet peeves."

I quickly made my way up the stairs and closed the bathroom door. Skyla was already getting out all the sticks I was going to have to pee on. I locked the door, and there was no chance Calvin could walk in. The last thing I needed was to alarm everyone, when there was still a chance that I was not even pregnant.

"Do you even have to pee?" She looked at me in the mirror.

I nodded and took a deep breath, "Who would've thought this is what we would be doing at twenty-nine?"

She gave a sad smile, "Whatever the result is, I am here to support you." I laughed and nodded my head. "I will pass you as many sticks as I can for you to pee on. Make sure you aim on the tip."

"I am a girl; I cannot aim."

She narrowed her eyes, "You can tell where your piss is coming from."

I shimmed down my pants, sat down on the toilet, and held out my hand. "What is the goal for the number of sticks?"

"As many as we can; if we can get more than three, this round would be good." She handed me the first stick, and I began to pee.

I was able to pee solidly on four sticks. Skyla capped them and placed them on the counter. I flushed, put the lid down, and sat on top. Skyla sank to the floor and set a timer on her phone. Now we were to wait, something two impatient people are not good at.

Most of the time, people would be excited about the idea of having a baby. Some people dreaded it because it was a mistake. Then you had me, not knowing what to feel. I felt excited at this life change, panicking at when it was happening in life, and guilty that I could get pregnant easily, not to mention knowing Skyla couldn't experience this.

"I know what you're thinking; knock that shit off." It was as if she was reading my mind. "I have come to peace that I cannot have kids, and I don't feel like I am missing out on anything. That is why I get to experience it all through you."

I sighed, "I don't even know how this happened."

Skyla smiled, "Well, Maggie, when two people love each other very much," I flipped her off as she burst out laughing.

The timer went off, and I remained frozen, fearing that if I moved, this would all become more real. Skyla shot up and flipped them over; her expression remained neutral while looking at them. I swallowed, becoming uncomfortable; what the hell was the result?

She motioned for me to stand up and look. My hands were shaking; I didn't even know what I wanted it to say. I wondered if I would be sad if it was negative, or would I be pissed if it said positive? My eyes locked on all four screens, which all said the same thing: pregnant.

Chapter Nineteen

Unexpected Turn for the Better

Jackson

It was hard to focus on work; my whole body was on alert. Skyla told me what happened, and something just finally snapped. If I saw Daniel, there was no way I could stop myself from attacking him. I couldn't bear knowing that she was always in danger, so if attacking him would stop him for her, I would. Even if it meant she would never talk to me again, at least she was safe.

Maggie had been through more than she needed to be in one lifetime. If I could just shield her and lock her away from the cruel world, I would have peace of mind. But Maggie Kensinger was not someone who was to be shielded and hidden from everyone. No, she was too kind and pure, something our world needed. I was just being greedy, wanting to keep it all to myself.

When I got back to the house, my eyes were scanning to see if I could possibly spot Daniel lurking somewhere. I didn't see anything; I parked behind Maggie's spot in the garage. I took notice that Skyla and Calvin were both gone; neither of them worked as I knew of. This meant Maggie and I had the house to ourselves.

The house was dark, which already meant Maggie was locked away in her room, sleeping most likely. I was happy to finally see her sleep, right when she finally got discharged; I think she maybe slept four hours the first week. When she had a nightmare, she would be screaming and thrashing around. Once Maggie realized it was a dream, she would remain awake, staring into the darkness. When staring got boring, she would go downstairs and watch *The George Lopez Show* reruns.

I grabbed a bottle of water from the fridge and headed up to her room. I could smell the lavender and vanilla candles burning, and when I walked in, there she was, sitting and reading a book in the minimum light. I smiled when she looked up at me; she hesitated before she returned it.

"I heard reading in the dark ruins your eyes," I said as I threw my backpack where all my crap was in her room.

She rolled her eyes, "My eyes are a perfect 20/20, so no need to worry."

I laid down next to her, and she had a strong smell of vanilla coming from her body. "You okay?"

"Go look in the bathroom."

I raised my eyebrow, "Um, what?"

"Go look on the bathroom counter."

Maggie's hand was in a small fist as I stood up and went to the bathroom. What the hell could be there? I turned on the light, and immediately, my eyes landed on the sticks. I looked at the four screens on the sticks: pregnant was clearly printed on them. I frowned and turned around to see her leaning up against the door. Maggie was wearing baggy track shorts and a form-fitting long-sleeve, hair was down and wet. There were no traces of makeup, and to me, that was when she was the most breath-taking. Who the fuck was I kidding? She always was able to make my heart stop and take my breath away.

"Okay, Mr. Doctor, do you understand what you are seeing?" She had a smirk on her face.

My eyes looked back at the sticks; every single one said pregnant. Holy shit. Maggie was pregnant. I snapped my head back, pure joy filling my chest.

"You're really pregnant?" I asked.

She nodded, "Don't know much; Skyla was able to get me in this Thursday to see Dr. Goodwin."

"You're pregnant," I whispered, still swimming in shock.

Maggie's face was painted with worry, "You're upset, aren't you?"

In her eyes, there was a shine, but they presented me with such a panicked look. I shook my head, stepped over to her, grabbed her face, and kissed her lips gently. She was pregnant with my kid. The pure happiness made me want to kiss every part of her. I was going to be a dad.

"Quite the opposite of upset," I kissed her forehead, "are you okay? I am sorry that I didn't ask."

Maggie gave a shy smile, "I am okay, no symptoms minus being late on my period."

"How are you feeling about this whole thing?"

It dawned on me that she might not be ready for this. It wasn't like we had been trying or fully had a conversation about this next step. Maggie had been through a lot, and I didn't want to make her go through with something that she wasn't ready for. As much as I was happy, if she wasn't, I was not going to make her go through this just for my sake. I loved her too much. If I made her, she would hate me, not to mention Skyla would probably kill me.

"Eh, it was very daunting at first, but then I realized this is something I want." I felt my body relaxed at those words. "I just was nervous to see how you were going to react."

I smiled and smoothed her hair down, "You know this is what I want. Is timing ideal? No, but we are having a baby."

Maggie smiled, "Sorry that you were the fourth person to find out."

"Huh?"

"Skyla and I went to get the tests, and she was the one who first read the sticks. So, technically, she was the first to know. Then, after sitting in the bathroom for ten minutes, Calvin wanted to know what was going on, so we told him." She gave me an apologetic look. "I am sorry."

Great, Calvin knew before me. I wasn't too surprised when she found out about Skyla. I would expect nothing less. Somehow, he was going to hold over my head that he knew before me, fucking Calvin.

"What time is your appointment on Thursday? I want to make sure I can come."

"Four thirty; Skyla is coming too."

I shook my head, "I figured."

"Are you sure you're happy about this, Jackson?" She asked with a serious face. "I can understand if you aren't; I am sure there are ways we can solve it."

"Maggie, I am beyond happy. I just care if you and the baby are healthy and safe." My lips pressed against hers lightly.

She giggled, "I love you."

I pressed my forehead to hers, "I love you, Maggie Kensinger."

Chapter Twenty

Reveals Aren't Always Happy

Maggie

I can remember the day my parents told Calvin and me that we were getting a younger sibling. We both were not happy at the thought, making Mom very upset, and Dad very pissed off. It wasn't a happy and joyous time.

There was this girl in our high school, a grade older than Skyla and me, and she got pregnant. Allison. She had been popular and loved by everyone, so she assumed everyone would be happy for her. Turns out, Allison's parents kicked her out, all her friends ditched her, and the baby daddy was some guy at Bemidji State who didn't even remember sleeping with her. Allison didn't get a joyous reveal. The last I heard of her, she was living somewhere in Iowa with the baby boy.

Reveals aren't always happy. They aren't what TV and books portray them to be. When I finally saw that the sticks were all pregnant-positive, it was silence in the bathroom. We both didn't know what to do and say, we just were thinking: oh shit. Our reactions weren't happy, they weren't pissed, they were surprised. Calvin acted the same way we did, left speechless because he didn't know what to feel or say. I was expecting Jackson to be the same way, but it wasn't.

I still hadn't figured out how I was going to tell my mom; something told me she wasn't going to be so happy. I remember her telling me the whole lecture that getting pregnant wasn't an accident. According to her, you knew what you were doing; you just must live with the consequences. I know for a fact she chewed Calvin's ass for months about getting Kara pregnant. I just knew telling her wasn't going to be a joyous one. I have no idea what my uncle would say, let alone Anika's thoughts or comments.

When I was walking through the front doors, the scent of that sharp cologne hit my nose. I turned around; there he was, walking behind me. How long had he been following me? My eyes scanned; too many people to see.

"Maggie," the way he said my name made my stomach do a flip. "You look beautiful," he walked up beside me; I was frozen, trying to decide what to do.

"Leave me alone," I said pathetically.

He walked in front of me, "You don't talk to me like that."

Finally, I was able to brush past him, prepared to feel the burning of his hand on me. To my surprise, he didn't reach for me, but I could feel his eyes on me as I kept walking toward the OB wing. Why hadn't he touched me? Why didn't he fight? My answer was in front of me; there she was, standing, arms crossed, with murder-driven eyes. Skyla.

As I walked up to her, she was still watching Daniel. I grabbed her upper arm and got her to look back at me. I gave her a nod, trying to indicate thank you, and it was fine. She shot one more look back at Daniel before following me.

There was still heat simmering from Skyla when we went back into the exam room. It felt oddly small and way too warm for my liking. I looked down to my stomach; over the last few days, I had begun wondering if the test had given me a false positive. What if I had gotten Jackson's hopes up? Or what if I was carrying a stillborn? I felt tears spring into my eyes; what if there was no life?

"Why are you crying?" Skyla asked, watching me with a straight face.

I looked between her and my stomach, "What if it's a stillborn? What if it's a false positive?"

There was sadness in those layers of all the different blues. "Maggie, you cannot start thinking like that. Wait for Dr. Goodwin to come in. They will probably draw your blood and then get that ultrasound. We can't start thinking negatively before anything has even started."

I took a deep breath, tears falling down my face. "I don't want to lose something I haven't even gotten yet."

Skyla smiled, grabbed my hands, and squeezed them tightly. "Dr. Goodwin is the best in the hospital, and you know that means something coming from me."

I gave her a wet smile, my makeup probably smeared. It was then the door opened, and a tall, African American woman entered. Her hair was in long braids, and her eyes had a golden hazel color; she wasn't much younger than my mother.

"Dr. Goodwin," I shook her hand, and then she leaned up against the counter. "So, sounds like we've got a little one on the way? Can you tell me what the date of your last menstrual cycle was, Maggie?"

I paused and thought about it, "The twenty-third of September."

It was then that Jackson finally came in; he was in his scrubs, sweating. Skyla was shooting him daggers as Jackson kissed me and stood on the opposite side of me.

"Dr. Calsen, I am going to assume you're the father." She said, with a warm smile. "Well, we are going to draw some blood to confirm, then we will do a pelvic exam, and lastly, an ultrasound. Nurse Cathy will be in to draw some blood, and I'll have you change into a gown. Sound like a plan?"

Nodding, Dr. Goodwin left us. My stomach finally squirmed at the idea of getting my blood drawn. That was the thing my family found funny: I could handle needles, shots, and blood, but getting my blood drawn was enough to get me to faint. I avoided it as much as I could, but there was no way for me to escape this one.

"Maggie?" Jackson wore a look of concern. "Are you okay?"

My eyes darted to Skyla, who knew exactly what was going through my head. "She can't stand blood draws."

Jackson laughed, "You're joking?"

I shook my head, slowly, "Don't judge me."

Sure enough, as if on cue, Nurse Cathy came in. Skyla squeezed my hand, nodding at me. Jackson awkwardly patted my shoulder as the process began. My eyes remained shut, and I counted to twenty; they couldn't be taking that much blood. Sure enough, they had to give me apple juice, as I was on the verge of passing out.

After giving me a minute to bring my blood sugar up and my color return, I slipped into my gown. Skyla forced Jackson to turn around, even though he protested that it was a moot point as to where we were at. However, when she finally gave him the death glare, he turned around, muttering something.

The pelvic exam is painless, easier than the blood draw. Jackson and Skyla remained up by my shoulders without even having to be asked. Once the exam was over, she stepped out to grab my lab results. I was able to change back into my clothes, and Jackson was forced to turn around again.

Dr. Goodwin returned a short time later, that warm smile on her face. "Blood tests confirm, you are pregnant, congratulations."

I felt my heart soar; it wasn't just in my head. I was pregnant, but then the daunting thought crept in: what if there wasn't a heartbeat? What if it was a stillborn? What if I miscarried? What if? I had to close my eyes and remind myself that I couldn't get lost in all those "what ifs."

"Now, I see that you are on fluoxetine; you will need to stop taking it." Fuck, that was something I hadn't even thought about. "I would recommend seeing your psychiatrist soon, and they can give more advice on how to move forward."

I nodded, making a mental note of setting up that appointment. Now, I am afraid because I had been taking my meds until today; what if that caused the baby harm? What if there was no heartbeat because of the medications?

"How far along is she?" Jackson asked, squeezing my shoulder. "Due date?"

Skyla rolled her eyes, "Relax, that is what the ultrasound is going to show and confirm what Dr. Goodwin already thinks."

Jackson gave her a smug look as I lifted my shirt, and the cold gel hit my skin. I felt goosebumps form on my skin as Dr. Goodwin smiled at me before placing the prob on my stomach. The room went silent as the sound of the machine filled it, all eyes on the screen.

I didn't see anything clearly, but Dr. Goodwin smiled and pointed. "There is the fetal pole and the gestational sac, so based on that, you are about seven weeks, which was my guess."

"What would be my due date?" I asked; it just looked like a blob with no defined shape.

"August twelfth would sound about right." She gave another smile to me. "We are now going to hear the heartbeat. Are you ready?"

I looked up at Jackson, who was just staring at the screen in awe. I then turned to Skyla, who was holding my hand and smiling down at me. Here was the moment of truth: no heartbeat equals no baby. I almost wanted to say no, don't check; I was too terrified about what the result was going to be.

Closing my eyes, I listened as the heartbeat filled the room, a strong and steady beat. I let out a gasp, and my eyes flashed open; there was a baby, a baby with a heartbeat. I felt my body shake as I sobbed into my hands, staring at my beautiful little blob. Tears poured down my cheeks and began to make everything slightly blurry.

Jackson came into my view and kissed my forehead. Skyla squeezed my hand and was grinning from ear to ear as she hugged me awkwardly because of the position I was in. I wanted to just close my eyes and soak in the feeling of relief and happiness. There was a heartbeat.

Over the next week, the motion sickness hit me like a truck. Every morning, right around four in the morning, I was over the toilet puking up everything in my system, it felt. I would spend the rest of the day drinking a lot of water and munching on carrots and salt crackers. I had not said anything to anyone at work; I wasn't really showing. However, I was already feeling my waistband on some of my clothes growing tighter.

Not taking my medication had been a strange adjustment. My psychiatrist suggested that I start seeing Kelly more frequently; twice a week would be ideal. Lucky for me, Kelly was more than happy to see me more and was just over the moon about me being pregnant. So that reveal was an easy and happy one, but I feared that it was going to be the only one like that.

Jackson had told his mother over FaceTime; she seemed to be just as happy as everyone else was. At the hospital, there was no word about my pregnancy, but I didn't know how long that would last. I also was concerned with how Daniel was going to take the news. Ever since I had told Jackson I was pregnant, Daniel seemed to be the last thing that was on his mind. For me, it was always on my mind.

He had made it clear what his intentions were when it came to me. I also knew, as he reminded me, he was capable of so much it was scary to think. I feel like just because I was pregnant did not mean I was safe; if anything, it made me more of a target, especially since Daniel was not the father. I feared he would stop at nothing to make sure that the baby was killed. The longer I could go without him knowing it was better, because it was no longer just me in danger.

The person I was dreading most to tell was my own mother. Her view was simple: there was no such thing as an accidental pregnancy. She also stated that kids were a direct consequence of having sex. My mom was a black-or-white thinker: you have unprotected sex, you pay the price, no ifs, ands, or buts.

Monday of Thanksgiving week is when I finally decided to tell my mom. Calvin kept saying that the longer I kept from her, the angrier and more upset she was going to be with me. Luckily for me, I had the week off, so I took this chance to see my mother.

As I did almost every time I pulled up to our house, I let out a gasp. The house was truly breathtaking; every detail had a purpose, a meaning. It was the dream home my mother wanted as she grew up without one. I would have to say my dad doing this for my mom was one of the most romantic things I have ever seen.

Growing up, my parents were not lovey, Dovey people. I think it had to do with how my mom's past; she was afraid to show love and care. My dad was any typical man; love and affection were a sign of weakness. Though, watching my parents, you knew they had a deep and respectful love for each other. They both were hard workers and, thankfully, had their separate fields in the medical world, so they weren't competing.

The thing I always laughed at was my father, according to my uncle, was not even a doctor. In the medical world, physical therapists were looked down upon, and not really considered hardcore doctors. My uncle had been a cardiothoracic surgeon before he stepped up to be chief when my grandfather died. Because my mom was a pediatric surgeon, both she and my uncle would give my dad endless shit about being a physical therapist.

When I was younger, I didn't know much about the difference, but when I got older, I saw that he was at the bottom of the medical food chain of doctors. Even if my mom gave him shit, she still would say he had Dr. in front of his name. My mom would have his back, even without him knowing, and my dad would do the same.

Since I haven't really been around for the last nine years, I don't know what their marriage was like. There was no doubt in my mind that they still loved each other, but I knew I was the tension and problem in the end. My mom may not be physically affectionate, but if she loved you, she would defend and stay loyal to you. If I had to guess, my parents probably fought a lot about me, which made me upset because those last years they could've spent living happily and the way they deserved. That was another fucked thing about life: time is against you.

When I got out of my car, there was a gust of bitterly cold wind. The temperatures had dropped significantly over the last week; we were barely getting to twenty degrees Fahrenheit on a good day. Being a native to this tundra, I was expecting nothing less. When the first snow falls, it will remain here until April. We only had four or five months of decent weather, well, hot weather to me. Skyla would moan and complain about the cold; she had never been a fan, and there was no way to convince her to like it.

My mom was expecting me; she was waiting by the front door as I slipped in. She, of course, looked perfect; her hair was curled, makeup was applied, and she wore jeans and a sweater. She did not look her age; her skin had very little to no wrinkles, and her hair still had natural golden tones. Her trick to it all: the bare minimum of products and light use of them and not wearing makeup most of the time helped.

"Do you want coffee?" She asked as I hung my coat up.

"I don't drink coffee, Mom."

She rolled her eyes, "What would you like to drink my child?"

"I am fine with water," I followed her into the kitchen, her favorite room in the entire house.

"So," she said as she handed me a glass of water, "I am assuming you have something important to tell me, otherwise you would not be here."

"You make it sound like I ignore you."

She gave a half-assed smile, "It feels that way at times, Maggie and you live in the same town. But I know I am your mom, and there are cooler people to be with."

"Well, I will do better to try and carve out time for you. Just because you're my mom doesn't mean you're cool." She grinned and took a sip of her coffee. "You are correct; there is something important I need to tell you."

Mom sat down at one of the barstools along the island with her coffee, "What is it?"

I started picking at my thumb, "I know what you're going to say, so please keep your comments to yourself until I am finished."

"Maggie Grace, what did you do?"

Ugh, I hated it when she would use my middle name; it usually meant trouble. "I am pregnant, and yes, it was an accident, but I am happy that Jackson and I are having a baby. So, you can be happy or pissed off, you can choose."

My mom sat there; her face was emotionless as she took in the information. I was waiting for her to stand up and start lecturing me about sex ed or how this is the consequences of my actions. I had braced myself for any possible outcome, but I did not prepare for this.

"Am I happy? No. Am I pissed? Yes. Am I hurt that you were nervous to tell me? Yes."

"I wasn't nervous!" I protested.

My mom sighed, "Honey, Jackson told me a few days ago. He wanted to take the initial anger from me."

My mouth dropped open, "What the hell?"

I was pissed. He told my mom. He told the one thing every daughter should tell their moms. Some girls dream of the different ways they would reveal their pregnancy to family, but that was never me. Still, what if I had something planned? He took that away from me, even if it was going to be anger and lectures.

"Romance isn't your thing, but I found it awfully sweet of him to do that. Especially since he had never faced the anger and wrath of me." Mom smiled at me, stood up, and walked over to where I was standing. "Maggie, you're a grown adult, and you have a steady job and relationship. If this is the next step for you, then it is."

As she stood next to me, I forgot how much taller she was than me. "So, you're not going to scream at me or call this baby a consequence?"

There was a sweet laugh, one that I hadn't heard from her in years. "No, it's my grandchild, so it is not a consequence, but I already let my anger go." She grabbed me by my shoulders gently. "So much has happened in this last year; we've lost more than I like to think in a lifetime. Instead of being upset, I am grateful."

"When you tried to kill yourself in college the first time, I didn't think you would be able to be in a relationship. I also believed that there was no chance of a normal life for you. I feared for how your life would turn out, afraid you would be left all alone. Then Jackson came into the picture, and I was finally hopeful, and then the shooting, your dad passing, it all went away.

"Then, Jackson shows up at the house with a sonogram of a healthy-looking baby, and instead of the brutal anger, I was graced with happiness. A rare feeling to have these days, so Maggie, I am excited for you."

I smiled at her, "Damn it, Mom." I leaned in and hugged her. "And I am happy too."

Maybe I was wrong: reveals can be happy.

Chapter Twenty-One

Risks Pay Off

Jackson

It was when Calvin and I were drinking at his place that he revealed why Maggie was avoiding talking to her mom. I was surprised that Julia Kensinger viewed babies as consequences of sex, which, in a way, she wasn't wrong. I thought maybe Julia said these things to scare her kids into not having sex, but Calvin said she still viewed it this way.

What I have come to learn about Maggie is that confrontation is something she will avoid at all costs. She was the opposite of Skyla, who craved it. That was just more proof they really were the ying and yang to each other.

I showed up at Julia's house early Thursday morning, and she was caught off guard. Her face was unreadable as I placed the sonogram on the table. I expected her to yell, but instead, she just stared at it. The silence was even harder to bear than the shouting I'd prepared for. When she finally met my eyes, I saw tears welling up, her lips trembling. Maggie looked just like her mom—so naturally beautiful.

Then Julia hugged me, crying into my shoulders. I held her close, feeling how thin she'd become since her husband passed. She'd lost so much weight, it was heartbreaking.

"Thank you," her voice was muffled, "for loving her for who she is."

After a few more minutes of me holding her, we shared a laugh, and she asked the basic questions about due dates and how I was feeling. I did explain to her why Maggie was afraid to talk to her, and there was no denying the hurt in her eyes, but Julia understood. I told her that Maggie had no idea I was there, so Julia needed to wait until she was ready.

Calvin paged me to meet him in the attending lounge on the third floor. I didn't have anything else better to do since I finished my rounds early. When I entered, I was met with a serious, pissed-off-looking, and pregnant Maggie Kensinger. My stomach lurched; she had talked to her mom.

"Aren't you happy to see me?" She said, a sourness in her voice.

"Depends. Have you eaten yet?" I teased, trying to lighten the mood.

Maggie remained pissed off looking, "Jackson," she sighed and crossed her arms. "Thank you." That was not what I was expecting. "I am glad you talked to Mom."

I smiled, "I figured I could take the brunt of her anger for you, since I haven't done anything to piss her off."

"Getting me pregnant doesn't make her happy."

"Oh, Kensinger," I embraced her into a hug, "don't lie, it turns you on to call me your baby daddy."

"Yuck," she pushed away, "you will NEVER be called that from me."

I kissed her forehead, "So this means I can't call you my beautiful baby mama." She made a face, and I grinned, damn the hold this woman had on me was insane.

Truthfully, since I had found out Maggie was pregnant, I had not thought of Daniel. Lucky for me, I really didn't see him or even have the chance to work with him. I know Skyla had to deal with him more than all of us, but she was the strongest one to do so.

As I was down in the pit, I offered to help Skyla as I had no surgeries, and that is when I saw him. It was always jarring to see Daniel, a reminder that he had violated her. It pissed me off to see him walk freely, but also knowing he was stalking Maggie. Fuck, I hadn't even thought about him finding out. What the hell was he going to do when he discovered she was pregnant? How was he going to hurt her? What would he do to the baby?

Shaking my head, I focused on the task in front of me. The longer Daniel remained in the dark, the better.

Chapter Twenty-Two

Thanksgiving Thrills

Maggie

Mom insisted that she make Thanksgiving dinner; she had conned my uncle into coming, along with Anika. Lucky for Jackson and Skyla, they both had to work, so they didn't have to deal with my sister. Unfortunately for Calvin and me, we were forced into going as neither of us worked.

I was up early in Skyla's room, as I had been puking my guys up. I was staring at my stomach in her mirror as she was yanking on her scrub bottoms, still half asleep. I knew she hadn't got much; in the twenty-nine years of living, I would be surprised if she's ever had a full night of sleep.

"Stop staring; it isn't going to help." She said as she pulled her long hair back. "You are going to gain weight; it is a natural part of being pregnant."

Narrowing my eyes at her through the mirror, I said, "I know that I am not dumb."

"I know you, Maggie Kensinger. Your brain is starting to worry about how different you will look. And somewhere deep down in you, you're afraid Jackson won't look at you the same."

God damn it, she really did know me. "It's just a lot of change," I mumbled.

Skyla rolled her eyes, "You've handled bigger changes before. Now, go eat your mom's food and bring me back some."

I spent the next few hours lying in her room, staring at the dark ceiling. I was not prepared for this dinner; who knew what Anika was going to have to say to me? Hopefully, she would still be too pissed to talk to me. My uncle, I was crossing my fingers, won't bring up anything about Daniel. I just wanted a smooth and easy-going dinner.

Knowing my mother, I would have to dress up. My mom had always been a big one about the presentation of self and making sure we looked at our best. I managed to find a baggy sweater dress that was loose-fitting; it was dark red, and I chose black knee-high boots to complement it. My hair remained down and wavy, and I wore a little more makeup than I was used to.

I met Calvin out in the living room; he was dressed in a nice brown button-up and black slacks. His hair was gelled and styled, and when he saw me, a smile spread across his face. It was crazy that his smile was identical to Mom's.

"Well, I do say you clean up nice." He joked as he slid on his dress shoes. "Are you ready for this nightmare?"

I rolled my eyes, "I want it to go fast and painless."

The drive was quiet, and neither of us was prepared to talk and converse with family. Oddly enough, Calvin had never been huge on these things. For family dinners, he would push his food around on a plate and not make conversation. I also remember at any major family functions; he remained hidden among the crowd. I found it strange as a kid. Why wouldn't you want to talk around family? Now, all these years later, I could understand.

When we got to Mom's, Calvin held the door open for me as we stepped in through the garage. There was a sprinkling of snow coming down, and it was in the teens, typical weather for Thanksgiving in Bemidji.

We both followed the sound of voices to the large dining room that had windows all around and a table that could fit fourteen or more. It was a breathtaking view as the snow fell; you could see it landing on all the pine trees that surrounded the house. Dad had really done a great job of finding and building the perfect home for Mom. There was no way she was going to leave this house; it was hers, and no one was going to take it from her.

My eyes finally scanned the room, and they froze on Daniel, who was sitting next to my uncle. My whole body tensed as his eyes met mine. What was he doing here? Why did he have to be here? He was family, my voice in my head said. I closed my eyes and took a quick breath before sitting across from Anika.

As usual, my sister looked pissed off that I was there. Her hair was down and perfectly straight, and she had an excessive amount of make-up on. She ignored me and smiled at Calvin, who was staring at my uncle; so much for a quick and painless dinner.

Mom came in. She, of course, was in a long sweater dress, and her hair was curled. "Oh good," she clapped her hands together when she saw her last two children had arrived. "I was just about to bring in the turkey."

Underneath the table, both of my hands were in fists. Even with my eyes down, I knew he was watching me. I could feel his stare on my skin. He still didn't know I was pregnant, and something told me that Daniel would be leaving here knowing I was.

Anika was watching me, "What the fuck is wrong with you?"

I narrowed my eyes, ready to snap back when Mom returned with the plate full of turkey. She beamed down at the table that had all her hard work and energy on it. For as long as I can remember, Thanksgiving was my mom's favorite meal to make. I know she didn't get to make it often, but when she did, she went all out.

"Well, before we begin dinner, Maggie, why don't you share with everyone your big news?" Mom said, smiling as she sat down at the head of the table.

I could feel all the eyes on me, fuck Mom, couldn't you have waited until we ate? My mouth went dry as the edges of my vision got fuzzy. Here were my final moments of being able to keep my child safe; after this, it was the both of us who were in danger.

"Maggie?" I heard my uncle ask. "Are you okay?"

Underneath the table, my hands were still in fists, and my knuckles were turned white. "I am, um," words were failing me as my eyes finally focused on him. "Um, Jackson and I are," my words faded again.

"Jesus, quit being a freak and spit it out," Anika said, annoyed.

Calvin stepped in, "Maggie and Jackson are expecting their first kid."

There it was: out in the open. My eyes remained on Daniel as I watched him process the information. I wanted to know what he was thinking or planning to do with me. His face gave no clue as I could hear my uncle saying something along the lines of congrats.

"Add to the list of things Maggie did to fuck up," Anika said as she rolled her eyes and took a sip of her wine.

"Do you always have to be a cunt?" Calvin fired back at her.

"Calvin," my mom warned as Anika stared at him in disbelief. "Let's try and have a good dinner."

Daniel finally spoke, "Well, I am glad that you are expecting, but don't you think it's inappropriate to be knocked up by someone you've known for a year?"

My mouth slightly dropped in disbelief. "You're joking, right?" I asked.

He shrugged, "I am just saying, I don't think your father would be pleased."

"What the hell?" Calvin said. "You're not our father, and quite frankly, your opinion doesn't matter."

Anika glared at me and then at Calvin. "Both of you knock it off. He is as close as a father to us at this time."

"He is as far away as a father to me or Maggie!" Calvin hissed.

"When did it become Maggie and me? You can't stand her, and you know everything she does is to seek attention. You were the one who said it." Anika snapped back. "She can't even stand up for herself! And to be honest, I agree with Daniel."

"Both, you need to stop." My uncle said, watching my mom, who was now upset. "Can we just enjoy dinner and debate about Maggie's pregnancy at another time?"

Daniel sighed, "I didn't mean to cause a fight; I was just stating an opinion."

"No one wanted your damn opinion," Calvin said. "I don't even know why you feel like you can state your opinion."

"Because," Daniel glared at Calvin, "your father was my best friend, and I care about you three like you're my own. I am concerned that maybe Maggie is making rash choices because of all the trauma that has happened."

Calvin stood up, "Some friend you are; after everything you've done, you have no right to evaluate Maggie."

"Knock it off," my uncle said, now glaring at him, "sit down and let it go."

I closed my eyes; my heart began to race. "I haven't done a damn thing but cared and looked out for all of you," Daniel said, standing up.

Calvin started to speak, but I clasped down on his wrist, making him stop.

"ENOUGH," I shouted, eyes scanning everyone in the room. "Thank you, Anika, for being so happy to have a niece or nephew. I'll remember to tell them what a bitch you are." I then looked to my uncle, "Thank you for the congratulations; I will pass it on to Jackson. And Daniel," even saying his name made my insides feel like ice. "I appreciate your concerns, but you have never been my father; I don't need one. And since you're not my psychiatrist, you have no idea if this was a rash decision."

Everyone was dead silent as they were all looking at me. My mom was crying; her perfect dinner was ruined. My uncle was frowning at me, Anika was shaking her head at me, and Daniel was staring at me emotionlessly.

"Now, I would like to eat the dinner my mother made. I don't care if it is silent. I am having a baby, whether you think it is right or not. The topic is done." I said coldly as I grabbed the ladle for the mashed potatoes.

The silence continued the whole dinner. My mom was sniffling every once in a while. Anika was glaring at me as if this whole thing was my fault, even though I wasn't the one who started the fighting. Calvin kept his head down and pushed around his food. My uncle kept giving Mom reassuring looks. As for Daniel, his eyes never left me. He was pissed and angry at me for many reasons: the pregnancy, the fact Calvin knew of what Daniel did, and then the way I spoke to him.

My stomach felt like shit, so I excused myself to go to the bathroom. I closed the door and locked it behind me. How was I supposed to stay safe? There was no way I could be protected the whole time; it wasn't plausible with everyone's schedules. There still wasn't enough evidence to indicate the need for a restraining order. Ignoring my reflection, I turned on the water and splashed some on my face. I was screwed.

After I managed to keep everything down, I opened the door only to be met by Daniel. He was leaning against the wall, waiting for me.

"So," he started as he took a few steps forward. "I think we are going to need to discuss some things." Daniel pushed some loose strands from my hair. "I don't ever want you to speak to me like that again." He growled into my ear. "And don't think you're safe because you are pregnant; you're still mine, and I will make sure it stays that way."

He pulled back, looking down at me. There was no hiding my fear, and Daniel loved every second of it. I could feel my hands shaking as I pressed myself against the bathroom door, hoping I could vanish through it. There was a sly smile on his lips, and I wasn't surprised to see him rock hard through his dress pants.

"Maggie?" My uncle came around the corner, his eyes dancing back and forth between the two of us. "Calvin wanted me to come check on you. Is everything alright?"

I glanced back at Daniel; that smile remained, but there was now a decent amount of space between us. Without answering, I put my head down and made my way back to the dining room. How was I going to protect the blob that was growing inside me if I couldn't protect myself?

Chapter Twenty-Three

Unsettled Changes

Jackson

Maggie had told me about what happened at Thanksgiving dinner. I was nervous about her being alone. I liked to think he was too busy at work to know her every move, but I would be a fucking fool if I thought that. He knew everything, he was watching her, and it made me sick.

Over the last weeks since Thanksgiving, Maggie finally was beginning to show, and I know it was bothering her. She had finally caved and told her principal that she was expecting, but she was waiting to tell her kids until it was more noticeable and when she would know the gender. There was a chance we might get to know the gender by New Year, and there had been debates on what we wanted.

"Personally, I want it to be a boy," Skyla said as she was sitting next to Maggie. "Girls are way too much work."

I frowned, "I want it to be a girl because boys are hell on wheels, especially if you two are raising him."

Calvin laughed, "He's got a point, but if you have a girl, she's going to have attitude on steroids with these two raising her."

"Hey, quit talking as if we can't hear you." Maggie snapped.

"Either way, the child will be screwed. Hell on wheels or attitude on steroids." Skyla said as she took a bite of Maggie's burger. "I vote boy."

Calvin took a swing of beer, "Can't disagree, boy."

I looked at Maggie, "What are you voting for?"

She shrugged and grabbed a fry, "I don't care, as long as it is healthy."

Christmas was a week away; it was crazy to me to think that this time next year, I would be a dad. My heart skipped a beat; Maggie was giving me a gift that I could not return. Everything I looked at online or in the store wouldn't be enough to show my gratitude.

There was a good inch of snow that was on the ground, and as I learned last year, it was going to be there until April. In the last weeks, I had the bathrooms finished and all the rooms upstairs painted. The next thing I was going to tackle was the kitchen; I was saving the basement for the end. I had told Maggie that the house would be ready before August, and we could move before she got too pregnant.

I know this was a lot of change for her. I caught her pinching her skin, where she gained weight. She had been monitoring everything she ate and had been going to therapy three times a week. Maggie was getting sick in the mornings only, but now she was experiencing vertigo in the evening. You could tell that she was getting frustrated as everyone was offering to help her.

The thing I had been noticing the most was her attachment to Skyla had grown. After she would throw up in the morning, Maggie would go and kick Calvin out and lie with Skyla. When I got home from work, both would be already eating and watching TV. They even went looking at baby shit and bought something to use for disposing of diapers. I couldn't help but be frustrated that all she wanted was to be with Skyla.

"You're overthinking it," Calvin said as I sat on the stiff couch at his place. "This is a lot of change, and the one thing that has been constant in her life is Skyla. Don't get upset about it."

I frowned, "She should be wanting to do stuff with me. I should be the one going shopping for baby shit."

Calvin shook his head, "Jackson, you realize that Maggie having a baby is changing everything, including her relationship with Skyla?"

"It isn't like they are going to never see each other again. We are having a baby; something tells me, at this rate, Skyla is going to be around the baby more than me."

"Do you realize that Skyla hates kids?"

That caught me off guard, "Huh?"

Calvin sighed, "Skyla can't have kids because of the abuse she had as a child. Lucky for her, she doesn't like kids and avoids being around them. She hates kids because she has no patience for them. There is nothing wrong with that, but if you think she wants to change diapers at three in the morning, you're wrong. She will love that child, but not like she loves Maggie."

"What does that mean for you?" I asked.

"I already had a kid; I can't stand the idea of losing another one. So, I am okay with not having any." Calvin said calmly. "It sucks not having the option, but I would still choose not to have any."

When I got home from Calvin's later that evening, I found Maggie curled up on the bed, clutching her green blanket, and fast asleep. I kissed the top of her head and climbed into bed. She instantly wrapped herself around my body and remained peacefully asleep. God, I hope our kid can sleep like her.

Chapter Twenty-Four

New Point of View

Skyla James

Was I mad at Maggie for getting pregnant? Fuck no. Was I irritated with Jackson being clingy? Hell yes. Was I upset because seeing Maggie pregnant made me think of Bentley? Yeah.

Growing up the way I did, you learned quickly that trusting others was not an option. You also learned that you are the only one who can take care of you. I firmly believe that I became a doctor to help people because I was never helped as a child. I also think my loyalty and love for someone must come from that as well. Bentley, well, he solidified why I couldn't trust anyone but Maggie.

To me, love was a fantasy; it was shit that I only read in books, saw on TV, or even heard in songs. My father, who I never knew, clearly wasn't in love with my mom, otherwise he would've been around. My grandma didn't love my mom or even me, or she would've been there for us. Even my mother didn't love me; she chose to put me in situations no child should ever be in.

Okay, maybe it was harsh to say she chose that, but it felt like it. The point is love doesn't exist. Then Maggie

Kensinger became my best friend and showed love. Sadly, with my fucked brain, I had a hard time believing at first she cared and loved me. But as the years went by, she was finally able to give me hope that maybe love wasn't a fantasy.

Bentley Ludwig came roaring into my life, and he got me to believe. He was the opposite of me in every way, and I think that is what drew me to him. And who the hell knows what made him come on to me? I was the school's biggest bitch. I had a hard exterior, and I parted the hallways like the Red Sea in that Jesus tale or whatever. The point was: that even though I was a freshman, everyone feared me.

I had been disliked since kindergarten, so I was used to it. What I wasn't used to was having someone approach me. The dumbass had a grin on his face when he walked over. I knew who he was; everyone did; another reason why he was the last person I wanted to come up to me. I still remember what I was wearing: an oversized hoodie and leggings with my hair in a braid that was half falling out. It was a Tuesday morning and sunny out, but bitter cold already.

The fucked thing was, even though I already hated him for coming up to me, there was this fire in my chest. There was no denying he was hot, with the prettiest eyes and hair that was in a perfect mess. Bentley had people always wanting to high-five and wave to him, but he was ignoring all those people, only looking at me. I was the only thing he cared about in that moment, and that is when I knew I was fucked.

It took a while, but he broke through my shell. And I was completely screwed. I was fully convinced love was real. I was living the dream, like a princess from a movie. I had broken the cycle of my family: I was getting married, going to have kids, and getting a college degree. Then, the news of not being able to give Bentley kids hit. He could say all he wanted about it not bothering him, but there was a disappointment; he didn't say it, but I could feel it.

Everything came crashing down when he killed himself. My life spiraled out of control; my emotions were not my own anymore, and I couldn't stop it. All that I had held in since I was a little girl came unloading out. I finally accepted it: love was a fantasy. And the only person I could rely on was myself. I didn't trust anything; if Maggie would hear it all, there's no way she would stay. It was me and me only.

Then, damn, Maggie Kensinger broke down my door and held me. We did end up paying a few hundred bucks because of that door, but I would've paid thousands for that door because it saved me. There was no letting Maggie go; she was someone I could rely on. I think I cried even harder at that moment because I finally was able to rely on someone but myself.

If people questioned why I was close to her, this was the reason why. The main one. So, everyone could fuck off, Maggie was my saving grace.

Chapter Twenty-Five

Run Like a Girl

Maggie

Graveyards are eerie no matter what time of the day or year. I hadn't been to one right before Christmas, but here I was, three inches of snow and twelve degrees. I was bundled up and had a picture of a sonogram in my pocket. Not that I had been close to my dad, but the hormones told me he needed to be informed. The damn baby was making me sentimental, the one thing I was hoping not to have in my pregnancy.

My dad's grave had a huge headstone, and beside his was a stone for my mom. I sat down in front of it; there were fresh flowers, and his stethoscope was hanging on the stone. I leaned forward and pressed my hand on it.

"Hey, Dad," I whispered, even though there was no one there. "I am sorry I haven't come to see you."

I was smart enough to know that all there was a body, no soul or conscience. I still wasn't sure if I believed in heaven or hell; how was one supposed to know? I have always been a logical thinker, so religion has always stumped me. I had grown up Catholic; my dad was raised this way. When he introduced it to Mom, she was all in. We went to mass almost every Sunday growing up, all of us dressed in the best clothes we had. Each one of us had been Baptized and Confirmed in the church as well.

For me, I did feel guilty that I didn't believe fully because I had convinced Mom I had. The whole concept of an afterlife didn't seem plausible, but it was a comfort for people. It stressed me more than anything.

"So, I know you would hate what I am about to say, but you're going to be a grandpa again." I laid out my most recent sonogram with the flowers. "I am sorry you'll never get to see your grandchildren, but they'll know you. Even though we had issues, you're still my dad, so my kids will know their grandpa." I smiled and wiped a tear from my eye. "I love you, Dad. Merry Christmas."

I leaned my head onto the headstone and felt more tears spill from my eyes. I know that we weren't close and what he did was unforgivable, but you only get one dad in life. Some people, like Jackson and Skyla, never got one. He was not the greatest person, but he was my dad.

As soon as I lifted my head, I heard the clapping from behind me. It was a matter of time before he would find me alone, but out of all the places, it had to be here. I turned around to see Daniel standing a few feet behind me. He was dressed in a long black coat and stocking hat.

"Beautiful," he said, smiling down at me. "Your father would be so disappointed in you."

I got up too fast, got lightheaded, and stumbled back. My eyes were scanning; there was no one. I was left alone in a fucking graveyard with the man who would rather have me dead than with someone else. How fitting. I wanted to know why he had a sudden interest in me. Why had he come back for me ten years later?

"You would know nothing about how my dad would feel," I said; I was about forty seconds run to my car, fast enough to get to.

Daniel laughed, "Your dad was my best friend, of course I know. I am disappointed in you."

My eyes darted to my car. Could I get to it? Should I run while pregnant? Would I be slower because I was? I was a fast runner, normally, but who knows in boots and a puffy coat?

"I am just confused while I am a sudden interest for you. You've been gone all these years, not giving a shit about me, and then suddenly, you're back for me. Why?" I needed to buy time while I figured out how to escape.

He stepped towards me, and my stomach flipped. "You think I didn't give a shit?"

"You went overseas, and I never heard from you; I would say that's a clear sign of not giving a shit." I stepped back, creating the distance again.

Daniel reached out and brushed his fingers on my cheek. "Seeing you stumble and lose it all, that was part of the plan. I remained updated on you through your mother, and she told me everything. I was thrilled to know you picked yourself up because then it would be my time to come and knock you down again. When your dad was sick, I knew the time was going to be perfect."

I let the words hit me, realizing it really was just a game all along. "So, I am just your plaything?"

He cocked his head to the side, "Plaything? No, you're my everything. When you were little, you were the prettiest thing, but I knew better than to move on with what I felt. I played along as someone you could trust; once you hit eighteen and got you alone, that was when I was able to make my move." I felt like I was going to be sick. "Once I got my taste of you, I couldn't stop, but what I enjoyed the most was seeing you fade away.

"I decided to up and leave after I left you destroyed. There was no chance someone could love you, not after what I did to you." He smiled and leaned into me, smelling me. "Mm, lavender and vanilla, like always."

Daniel brushed my hair. "Your life crumbled and spun out of control, all because I sparked the flame. When I learned you were getting back to your feet, it was time for me to return, especially when your dad was going to be out of the picture." He chuckled and brushed his thumb along my lip.

"That's why I came back, Maggie. It was the plan all along. You've been my everything since you were a toddler." His hands finally wrapped around my throat. "And then you think I will back down because some boy loves you? No," he squeezed my throat, "You… are… my… everything."

I couldn't breathe. "I will stop at nothing, to make sure you know that."

Before all my edges could go blurry, I kneed him in the stomach, making him stumble back, letting go of me. I seized the moment to run. I hated when men said women ran like a girl. We wouldn't have to if men weren't chasing us. I'd seen plenty of women outrun men. Heck, I'd outrun boys in school. But this run was different. This run meant the chance to save myself and my child. God be dammed if I wasn't going to give my all.

The snow was slowing me down, but I was able to reach the door and slam myself in. Daniel slammed against the driver's door, and my hands fumbled with my keys; they were shaking uncontrollably. I had focused too long on turning on my car, and I didn't even see him wind up to break my window. The glass showered down on me; I finally let out a scream as he reached for my throat.

There were glass shards all over my lap, and there were some stuck in between my fingers. I took my right hand, a sharp shard in my hand, and stabbed him in the arm. He stumbled backward, calling me a bitch. My foot slammed on the gas, and I sped out of the graveyard. I could feel my sticky blood, but there was no pain in my body. The cold air was blasting into my car from the window, blocking out my sobs.

I was afraid to look down on where I was injured. Was my baby hurt? I didn't know where to go or who to call. I braced myself as I looked in the rearview mirror; Daniel was clutching his arm on the ground. I didn't see a car anywhere near him, so I had a head start on him.

My hands looked bad, deep cut from the large shard I had stabbed Daniel with. There were tons of other small pieces, but the main source of blood was that cut. Once I was stopped at a red light, I was able to get a better look at the rest of my body. The puffy coat I had been wearing had stopped any shards from penetrating my torso. There was no surface damage to the baby.

Focusing on each turn, I was able to slow my heart rate down as I pulled into my driveway. I awkwardly got out and brushed any glass off me, the pieces nipping at my already bloody hands. My legs had a few surface scratches, but nothing deep. Immediately, I ran inside, locking the garage door and back door and deadbolted the front. I knew I was dripping blood on the floor, but I needed everything to be locked safely.

I rushed upstairs into the bathroom and delicately took off my coat, a sigh of relief seeing nothing on my torso. As I washed my hands, the searing pain raked through my body. Gasping, I forced myself to keep going. I needed to get the glass out and a bandage on the main cut. Tears were falling on my face as I wrapped my gaze (pros of having doctors that lived here) around the cut. The wound was radiating anger that I was stopping the bleeding. I wiped my face with my forearm, and my vision was getting hazy.

In the silence of my tears, Daniel's words echoed in my head. Since I was a toddler? Why me? How did no one suspect this? Why didn't I tell my parents? Since I was a toddler, I had been his target, his everything. I felt the vomit creep up and spewed out in the sink with warm water and fresh blood. I needed someone. There was no doubt in my mind who I was calling.

Chapter Twenty-Six

The Failure of a Brother

Calvin Kensinger

There is no such thing as luck; it either happens or it doesn't. Everything is already preset for you before you even open your eyes. You don't have choices; they have already been decided. By whom? No fucking clue, but fuck them. You don't have control of what happens; the world wants you to think so, but you don't. As I said, everything was preset for you.

Whoever made Maggie's choices, loved and hated her. They gave her hope and then took it away; I was all too familiar with that cycle myself. The moment I saw her name pop up on my phone, I knew it wasn't good.

The simple words she said: "I need you at home." I dropped the dumbbells in the gym and stormed out to my car, not even looking as I backed out.

In all the years I had been an older sibling, I don't think she had ever said those words. Anika most definitely had not, selfish bitch. It was insane how different my sisters were, but even how my love differed for each.

When our father disowned Maggie, I just followed suit. I had always felt there had been something more to the story, but for once, I got to be the golden child. I had fucked up so much in my youth that Maggie easily took the spot. Once I knew my place, I decided to embrace being the disgrace of the family.

It started as a weed, then cocaine, and then I met my downfall: meth. It felt good to be high; I didn't have to worry about being the only man in the family to inherit the hospital. I wasn't the oldest sibling with all eyes on me. I just got to be in my world, the one where nothing mattered. It was addicting to be in that world, hence why I was always in it. Then, when my baby girl died, I never wanted to leave that world. In that world, I hadn't lost the woman I loved and my beautiful daughter; it was just a nightmare.

That was the harsh reality I had to face in rehab. The withdrawals from meth were equally physically and mentally painful. I did my best to block out those days, but the pain was what I deserved; it was my punishment. I had to face the life I had been running away from, and that, in my opinion, was the worst pain I faced.

I let my pride get the better of me when Maggie's life went to utter hell. I assumed the worst of her because that is what selfish people like me do. Thinking she was weak made me feel powerful, like I had finally won the respect and love of my father. I finally wasn't the fuck up child, and it felt amazing, like I was back in that world.

Treating and talking about Maggie the way I did, made me more of an asshole than I already was. I had to live with all the words and actions I did to her. I failed once again in this life. I was ready to face the pain and punishment from this. Maggie surprised me by forgiving me instead of hating me. That was what made her different: she saw the good in others. That would be the main reason why I loved Maggie more than Anika; she forgave me when I didn't even forgive myself.

I had never felt connected to my youngest sister. She was always cold to Maggie and me, telling us several times we ruined her life because we had been born. Anika always got her way; she won every battle and fight with our parents. I was more embarrassed by her, even during my fuck Maggie phase. Anika was your typical, snotty, rich girl, and it disgusted me. She was selfish in the way that I am sorry was never in her vocabulary. Even I had said those words plenty of times. Anika believed it was her world, and we all lived in it, and she thrived on being a pure bitch, which is why she and I had never been connected other than by sharing the same last name.

I didn't expect Maggie or anyone else to forget what I had said and done. I was an utter ass, and there was no denying that, but I would be dammed if I were to fail again at being the big brother. What I didn't realize growing up was the oldest had to be the example and protector. Two things I failed to do.

Hearing Maggie reach out for help was my chance to show myself I wasn't a total failure, and that there was the hope of repairing the shit I had done.

A chance I knew I would never have again.

Chapter Twenty-Seven

Paralyzed Dreams Return

Maggie

Calvin got to my house, didn't ask any questions, and assessed the damage. Another bonus of living with doctors is they had suture kits on hand. I sat on the toilet as he worked delicately stitching the deep cut after he cleaned it. Then, he cleaned the smaller cuts and put small Band-Aids over them. Once he had cleaned up and disposed of all the mess, that is when I knew the questions were coming.

"The baby?" He was eyeing my stomach. "Did anything happen there?"

I shook my head, "My coat stopped any of the glass, and I was able to slow my heart rate. I am seeing Dr. Goodwin in a few days anyway."

Calvin wore a serious face. "What happened?"

"I went to see Dad's grave, alone. Then," I paused and took a deep breath. "Daniel showed up, and we got into an altercation."

I was expecting Calvin to blow up, kick something, and scream fuck. Instead, his face remained expressionless as he leaned up against the bathroom counter.

"He broke the window." Calvin's voice was flat as I nodded my head. "That is why your hand is cut." I closed my eyes and nodded once again. "How did you get away?"

As I spoke, the images flashed in my head. "I stabbed him in the arm with a shard and drove away."

"Mags, this is getting out of hand. He could've killed you, shit; he could've killed your baby."

I opened and narrowed my eyes, "You really think I don't know?" My harsh voice echoed in the bathroom. "His goal isn't to kill me; we know what the goal is."

Calvin crouched down in front of me. "Maggie, I don't know how to protect you and the baby."

I sighed, and my shoulders began to shake as I let myself crumble. The damn hormones were not helping in managing my emotions. Calvin wrapped his arms around me, and I sobbed into his shoulder. I was tired, so fucking tired of dealing with shit, after shit. No matter what I did, take my meds and go to therapy, I still was getting shit on. I don't know how much more I could take of this roller coaster of life I was on.

There had been plenty of times where I felt rock bottom; I thought losing my dad and being in a shooting within weeks of each other was the bottom. I knew that Daniel's return was going to be an issue, but I figured that I was protected. I wasn't alone in dealing with him. Somehow, this time was worse, because he not only hurt me, but many others I loved. I had never planned on getting pregnant at this age, but sometimes the best surprises were unexpected. The worst surprises were unexpected as well.

After spending fifteen minutes crying in my brother's arms, I ended up asleep on the couch. Calvin lay in the matching loveseat and watched some football. I was able to sleep knowing someone was near me; Daniel had officially scared me to the point where sleeping alone was not safe. I loved sleep; it was my way of coping, and now he had taken that away.

I was able to hear Skyla come in, but I kept my eyes closed. She and Calvin talked in hushed voices about what had happened. As I expected, she started to cry and sat at the end of the couch.

"God Damn it." She mumbled. "God Damn it, Maggie, I don't know what to do."

Being the coward I was, I kept my eyes closed. It was easier pretending to be asleep; people said truthful things when they didn't think you could hear.

"How do you think he's going to react when he finds out?" Calvin asked.

"Jackson is going to kill him. It isn't just Maggie anymore; it's their child too."

"There's no way she'd forgive him."

The silence settled around, and I finally let myself drift back into a deep sleep, knowing I was safe.

My dreams were back to being disturbing, but instead of waking up and screaming, I was paralyzed. I was unable to speak; all my mind was doing was reliving every moment with Daniel. I was brought back to the memories of when I was a child, and he lingered around. Daniel didn't move to the Denver area until I was nine. He was always around. My dad and him were inseparable; little did my dad know his friend was obsessed with his young daughter.

I don't know how long I was going in and out of these terrifying dreams, but it was a while. I was still on the couch, and the TV was on mute, some rerun of Sports Center. There was a candle burning on the coffee table. It was the Winter Candy Apple scent from the amazing *Bath and Body Works*. In the corner of the living room was a Christmas tree with just lights on it; it was not there when I fell asleep, along with Jackson, who was sleeping in the loveseat.

Even though I knew I was safe, my body was stiff, and my eyes were darting around, making sure Daniel wasn't there. I noticed the curtains were all drawn, wrapping me inside and away from him.

"Maggie?" Jackson said sheepishly. "Maggie, it's okay." He sat up, worried that I was still not responding.

"He isn't here," Jackson kneeled beside the couch and grabbed my hand. "Maggie, you're safe."

His touch sent flames through my body, defrosting the paralyzed feeling. I sat up and hugged him tightly, wanting to keep the burning warmth inside. At this moment in time, I was going to let myself feel safe, but deep down, I would never be safe with Daniel out there.

"I'm sorry," I whispered into his ear. "I'm sorry," I repeated.

Jackson's hand brushed down my hair. "I am not mad at you; I am relieved you're okay." He pulled away, grabbing my face. "And the baby is safe that we know of."

His thumb brushed away a tear that fell down my cheek. "I'm sorry."

"Stop saying that, you've done nothing wrong. This isn't your fault."

I nodded and closed my eyes. For now, I scraped away from Daniel's grasp. How long could it last? How long could I keep us safe?

Chapter Twenty-Eight

Different Connections

Skyla James

I remember when I came back from Thanksgiving break in college and saw Maggie for the first time after Daniel attacked her. I knew there was something wrong; her eyes were glossed over, and she was extremely pale. Any movement spooked her, like a deer out in the woods.

To this day, I regret not asking what happened, but it was alarming to see your best friend like this. Sure, I had seen Maggie upset, but this was different; she feared her own shadow. She had never been one that was overconfident, but never one to fear herself. Maggie, at one point, understood she was beautiful and had a kind personality. That set her apart from everyone in our school; it didn't matter who you were, she was always going to give you the benefit of the doubt. I had already seen the darkness of life, but it was refreshing to see someone like her.

After Daniel did a number on her, that is when Maggie changed. Sometimes, I wonder if she had never been abused, would she be the same? People change, but would her brain be broken? Would something else have happened to cause the Maggie we have now?

When she finally divulged what had been happening, I felt sick to my stomach. Memories of my abuse filled my head, fire filling me. She had to experience one of the worst things a human could do. My best friend, full of beauty, faith, and love for the world, had gone through what I had. It was when my fierce protectiveness was sent into overload then because that fucker had taken a piece of Maggie that I admired.

With that being said, I still loved my best friend for what she had become. I was still pissed that life dealt her this shit, but there were still parts of her that had faith. The way she was ALWAYS positive for me, made me still see the color and warmth the world had to offer. I had never admitted it out loud. Being a teacher made sense for her. It was her wanting to reassure the world wasn't at a total loss.

I don't know what I have done in my past life to deserve her. I felt guilty that I couldn't do more for her. I wish I could be as positive for her as she was for me. I wish I had a sliver of trust in the world so I could have faith, but I don't. That had all been taken from me as a child.

Daniel deserved to be six feet under, but I knew Maggie would never forgive me if I killed him. She said life would be shitty without me, that we had made a pact to do this life thing together. Me being in jail would destroy her, and she found such a peace with me; I didn't want to take that away from her.

So, as I sat there on the main counter in the pit, my eyes were focused on Daniel Dobson, who was doing a psych evaluation on a patient in trauma two; I had to remind myself Maggie needed me. And deep down, let's face it, I don't think I could do life without her.

Daniel had a bandage around his forearm, right where she had stabbed him. The story he told people is that he broke a mirror in his apartment. Such bullshit, but everyone bought that because there was no way Dr. Daniel Dobson could hurt another soul. Yeah right.

"Skyla," Calvin cut through my thoughts. "You ready to head home?" He was looking directly at me, ignoring all the nurses who were giggling like high school girls.

I tore my eyes from the saint Dr. Dobson to look at him. As usual, my heart raced just a little when Calvin looked at me with that cocky smile. Not too long ago, it used to piss me off; now, it was an intoxicating feeling.

It had been years since I had felt any sort of feeling towards a man. Bentley had been the only one who had broken through the mold. Now, Calvin has broken through more walls than I had up because of Bentley. Sometimes I wondered what made him put in all the effort to get me, especially since Calvin and I fought, and still fight, like cats and dogs. He never has been able to give me a clear answer, which was fine because I couldn't give him an answer to why I fell for him.

Without answering him, I hopped off the counter and grabbed my bag on the floor. My shift had been over for twenty minutes; I was just waiting for him since he insisted that carpooling was sexy. I hated having to rely on anyone for a ride, one of my biggest pet peeves. Once I had the freedom to drive my car, there was no way in hell I was going to rely on anyone to drive me. It took Maggie a while to understand she was never going to drive, but she eventually embraced being a passenger princess.

"What took you so long?" I grumbled as I walked next to him.

"My surgery ran late," he stated, "I am so happy to see you too, Calvin."

I rolled my eyes, "You're never going to hear that from me."

"No," Calvin wickedly grinned at me, "But I am going to hear you cry out my name later."

"You're fucking disgusting," I stated as we stepped out into the bitter cold.

Calvin put his arm around me, "Oh, you love it, don't deny it."

The crazy part was, he wasn't wrong. I had only consensually slept with two men: Bentley and Calvin. They both had their pros and cons, and I wouldn't say one was better than the other. It was just different. Bentley worshipped the ground I walked on and gave me everything. It was what everyone called puppy love. Then you had Calvin; he had respect for me but craved putting me in my place. As tough and bitchy as I was, it turned him on, knowing that I would let my guard down.

I loved them both, but they had come at different times in my life. My connection with each was drastically opposite; one I trusted and the other I didn't. Bentley had done the one thing he promised he'd never do to me: lie. He had lied about how bad his depression was and killed himself. All he left me with was a damn apology note instead of the life we had been working towards for seven years. He decided to lie, which meant he didn't trust me, and that is what hurt me the most.

The thing with Calvin was he understood that pain. He had gone through almost the same thing. He loved Kara, even if their relationship revolved around drugs. They had a daughter, a bond between them that never could be broken. I know they talked about having a clean future; he wanted to give her everything: a house, stability, and love. Both promised each other they would fight for that life; they were in it together.

Calvin told me the story about that night, a story he had never shared with anyone. Calvin trusted me, whereas Bentley didn't. To sum the story up, he had found drugs Kara had been using, and that was how the fight started. He felt betrayed, and all Kara would say was sorry. Instead of staying and listening to her plead about getting it together, he left and walked away. He had trusted her, getting clean and having that life for them, but for Heather as well. Calvin still trusted her when he left that night, only to learn Kara had betrayed him once again.

It was rare to find someone who could understand the grief I felt. I know Maggie tried, but Calvin had gone through the same thing: losing the one we loved most. We had both come to a point in our lives where there was no reason to find another. We believed that if we connected with someone else, it would be broken again, and the wound would be opened again.

My connection with Calvin was hard to understand, but the thing was, we understood the same pain. We both did not want to go through it again, which meant for the two of us we trusted each other because of that pain.

Chapter Twenty-Nine

One Hell of a Fighter

Maggie

Christmas had come and gone in the blink of an eye. It was an emotional holiday for my mom, so I did my best to cheer her up. I let her be the one to come with me for an appointment that would tell me if we had a boy or a girl. Skyla understood how much grief my mom was drowning in, so she had been the one who suggested it be my mom who went with me. Jackson was pissed, but I told him I would make it a special reveal just for him. He didn't seem convinced.

The whole drive over, Mom was chatting about how she had found out our genders. She wanted to be surprised about Calvin, so when he came out, she was floored that it was a boy. With me, she felt the need to know. As for Anika, my parents made a gender reveal cake, just the two of them. My dad had been disappointed in only getting one boy and even tried convincing my mom to have another baby, but she was adamant that Anika was the last one.

I was finally starting to show, making me feel self-conscious about anything I wore. My boss at work was over the moon about me having a baby, even though she had no idea about my personal life. At work, I tended to keep to myself; sharing information with strangers was like giving them a weapon to use against you. My students were happy and spent a lot of time coming up with baby names.

As joyous as everyone was, it was hard for me to feel the same way. It was coming up one year since Maxwell Fath had shot up the school. Internally, there was some fear that it would happen again, this time Daniel being the one. I had not been left alone since the graveyard incident. He had not been at Christmas at my mom's; he apparently worked the whole holiday.

It didn't matter where I went, but I was always searching for him. Now that he had confessed to wanting me since I was young, there was no way he wasn't stalking me. Knowing that he was watching my every move made my nightmares intensify.

As I was lying down, getting ready for the ultrasound, I heard someone knock on the door. Dr. Goodwin turned to the door, just as confused as my mom and me.

"Knock, knock," all the hair on my arms stood. "I was told Ms. Maggie would be in here."

Daniel cracked open the door; I jolted up as Mom went over to hug him. I pulled my shirt down and squeezed my hands into fists. This couldn't be happening, no. Not now, the one moment I am supposed to be excited about, and he has come to ruin it.

"Get out." I was frowning at him. "Get out, now."

My mom narrowed her eyes, "Maggie, he's just coming to say hi."

"I don't care. Get out of the room." My voice was shaky, and I could feel tears in my eyes. "LEAVE!"

This was the reaction he wanted. "All I wanted was to be here for this big moment, since your dad isn't here for this," Daniel said, walking towards me.

"GET AWAY FROM ME!" I screamed loud enough that everyone in the room flinched. "Leave," I whispered as tears were falling down my face.

My mom was frowning at me, Dr. Goodwin was wearing a concerned look, and Daniel was smiling with only his eyes. He fucking scared me.

"I am sorry, Dr. Dobson, but immediate family is only allowed." Dr. Goodwin said, eyes darting back to me. "You are upsetting my patient, so I must ask you to leave."

"He's family," Mom snapped. "Maggie's only upset because of the hormones."

I began picking at my thumb, "I don't want him in here."

My mom was giving me a disappointed look, but Dr. Goodwin held the door open for him to leave. There was a small grin on his face as he looked at me one more time. I let out a sigh of relief when the door closed.

"What the hell was that?" Mom looked pissed. "He was your dad's best friend; he loves you and is trying to be here for you."

In that moment, I wanted to tell her. He didn't love me like a niece; he was obsessed with me and always has been. Daniel destroyed me and triggered my downhill spiral of life. He had abused me, raped me, and stalked me. I wanted my mom to know the truth, but there was no way she would believe me.

"I don't want him anywhere near me," I said to her, picking harder at my thumb. "I don't give a damn who he is; I only wanted you here, Mom. If I had wanted an audience, then Jackson, Skyla, and Calvin would be here too. So, if you can't accept that, then leave."

Mom took a deep breath and sat back down in the chair with her arms folded. I looked back at Dr. Goodwin, who was staring at me, trying to understand my reaction. I laid back down and lifted my shirt, ready to get the hell out of here.

The whole drive home, I refused to talk to my mom. I didn't say anything; I just got out, slammed the door, and walked back into my house. Skyla was sitting on the kitchen counter eating a waffle, hair a mess, and still in scrubs. She was frowning at me.

"What happened?"

"Daniel," I said drily as I threw my bag onto the couch. "And, oh, by the way, it is a girl."

"He was there?"

I looked back at her, "Yep, and Mom got pissed because I screamed at him to leave."

"It's all a mind game."

"Yep, he got what he wanted out of me. Now, I cannot even enjoy that I am having a girl." I stomped up the stairs like a two-year-old.

"Maggie," I turned around to look at her; she was standing at the bottom of the stairs. "Your daughter is going to be one hell of a fighter."

I smiled and headed to my room and lay down on my bed. Daniel had gotten fear and fight out of me. I wonder if he banked on me being so upset. I know I couldn't be angry at my mom; she didn't know. Her reaction to him would be different if she knew, but I know it would kill her knowing the truth. My mom had been through enough; she didn't need this bombshell.

By the time Jackson got home, I had a cake baked and frosted. I was no professional baker; I used some box mix and food dye. Truthfully, the cake looked like shit. Hopefully, it didn't taste that way. Skyla was over at Calvin's, so we could have the house ourselves.

He smiled at me, "Look at you, baking me food."

"Oh yeah, I made everything from scratch." I rolled my eyes as he kissed me.

"Well, the good thing is you can't fuck up box mix cake." He took a lick of the frosting. "I am assuming my surprise in here?"

I grinned, "Yeah, I guess this is how my parents found out about Anika's gender. I thought it was pretty cute."

Jackson laughed, "That is what you think is cute? Out of all the romantic things, finding the gender of your baby through a cake is what gets to you?"

"Hey," I said frowning, "blame the hormones, damn it."

He shook his head and grabbed a plate from the cabinet above the sink. Jackson looked back at me, and I wore the biggest smile to reveal what our child was going to be.

Chapter Thirty

Happiness You Can't Take Away

Jackson

Lucky for me, Maggie was like me in wanting to keep a low profile. Most people these days want to do a major gender reveal party, not to mention a baby shower on top of that. I already knew this was overwhelming for her. However, when she told me her mom was going to the reveal appointment and not me, I was pissed. This was supposed to be something the mom and dad experienced, and it was another thing getting taken away from me.

When I got home from work, I was not expecting to see her in the kitchen with a fresh cake. She was wearing grey sweatpants, and an oversized t-shirt, and her hair was in two braids. There was little to no makeup on her face, and she was just as stunning as the day we met. I know Maggie was self-conscious about her body, but I found her sexier as her baby bump grew.

As I turned around from getting a plate, there was that smile. God, I hoped our child had her smile; it was so warm. I set the plate down and wrapped my arms around her. Maggie still smelled like lavender and vanilla.

"Why are you looking at me like that?" She asked, cheeks flushed.

"Just admiring," Maggie scrunched her face. "Alright, so do you want me to cut it or you?"

She grabbed the knife beside the cake. "I'll you do the honors, Dad."

I rolled my eyes and hesitated before cutting. Up to this point, I just assumed it was a girl, but what if it was a boy? I felt my heart race. Was I ready to be a dad? How was I supposed to raise a child, when I didn't know what I was even doing myself? I have barely made it this far in life; how was I ready to guide and support another life?

When I turned to look at Maggie, I was reminded that I wasn't alone. If she was terrified about this, she did not show it. She wore a smile and a gleam in her eyes; she was excited, making my heart slow down and relax. I cut through the cake and immediately saw the bright pink.

My jaw dropped, "You're joking!" I exclaimed.

Maggie took her finger and dipped it through the frosting. "I figured you'd be happy."

I leaned in and kissed her. We were having a girl. In that moment, looking down at her, I had never been happier in my goddamn life.

Chapter Thirty-One

1 out of 20

Maggie

When I think back to the morning of the shooting, I remember how normal everything was. I got ready the same way I always had. There was nothing that gave warning to what was going to happen. Bad things can happen whenever, and there is no way to predict them. I had no clue that morning that I was going to face a living hell. How was I supposed to know when I went to see my dad, that he was already going to be dead? I understood people with anxiety; the unknown is not comfortable. I know some people love the thrill; I would even say, at one point, I did it myself, but after all this shit, the unknown was scary as hell.

Everything was fine when I woke up. I took a shower and threw up as usual. I picked out a pair of light gray pants with an oversized black sweater. My choices of clothes were slowly winding down, which meant I was going to have to bite the bullet and buy maternity clothes.

I got to work, made the copies that needed to be made, and had my Google Slides up. All my Christmas décor had been taken down; just snowflakes remained hanging. Soon, I was going to have to put hearts up for Valentine's Day, a holiday that I could be fine without.

All my students were here today, and no one was late, which was rare for my kids this year. They all seemed to be in a decent mood, for it only being Tuesday. Everything was going okay; I was feeling okay. Nothing had indicated that I was going to be put through another hell.

It started when we were doing math, and I started to feel lightheaded. I decided to remain in my chair and play some counting songs from YouTube as I grabbed a juice box and some crackers. I figured I hadn't eaten enough and needed some fuel.

As my kids began working on their snowmen, adding worksheets at their seats, that is when the stabbing pain hit me. I grabbed my stomach; it was as if someone had taken a knife and cut through me. I closed my eyes, maybe this was that Braxton Hicks thing. Taking a deep breath, I returned to walking around, making sure none of the kids was just coloring their snowmen at will. A few minutes later, the pain hit again, but this time it wasn't as bad. As time went on, the pain eased.

After eating lunch and walking around outside for recess duty, that is when I felt the stickiness between my legs. My kids were hanging up their coats, all preoccupied, as I sat down in my chair and saw the blood. My heart stopped; I physically could feel everything stop. No.

"Ms. Kensinger?" Hailey, one of my students, said. "Are you okay?"

I blinked my eyes, and suddenly, the stabbing pain came back. Gripping my stomach, I doubled over and cried out. I wasn't in labor; I was having a miscarriage. This couldn't be happening. My body wouldn't betray me like this. I looked at the blood and then took in my surroundings. Oh no. The gunshots echoed in my head, and I could see blood running through the bottom of my door. I could hear the screams of my kids; I could feel the bat in my hands, and worst of all, I could see Maxwell's deformed body.

"Ms. Kensinger," Hailey said again. "You're bleeding." Her voice was muffled.

All that I was clearly hearing was the sound of the bat crushing bones. I needed to get out. What I was hearing wasn't real. The shooting wasn't happening again. The blood that I saw wasn't Maxwell's. It was mine. I needed to get to a hospital.

"Hailey," I said, trying to smile, "can you go down to the principal's office and say Ms. Kensinger isn't feeling well?"

"You're bleeding."

I nodded, "I know, honey, that is why Ms. Kensinger needs to leave."

"Are you okay?"

No, I wasn't. "Yes, I just need to go to the doctor. Can you go to the principals?"

Hailey took one more look at the blood staining my pants and headed out of the room. All my kids were watching me, eyes fixed on the blood.

"It's okay," I said, smiling. "Ms. Kensinger is going to go to the doctor; she's okay."

They were not convinced because they remained still. I luckily had my phone in my pocket; I grabbed it out and called Skyla, who answered on the first ring.

***

I had seen enough shows and movies that miscarriages were more common than others think. There are an estimated twenty-three million happening a year around the world. Out of that, about one million occur in the United States alone, representing about twenty percent of all pregnancies. You hear these numbers and think that it will never be me, but when you become one, your world shifts for the worse.

Skyla had picked me up from school, reassuring my boss that I wasn't in critical condition. Once, we were in the car alone, and that is when she frowned; we both knew what was happening. We didn't speak, instead we sat in silence as she drove. What were you supposed to say in a moment like that? I am sorry. What can I do? Silence was better.

We were able to walk in and get into an exam room on the OBGYN floor; they had already been alerted. I already knew what I was going to hear when Dr. Goodwin squirted the gel on my stomach. There was absolute silence in the room. Skyla covered her mouth, and I just stared at the monitor; the unthinkable happened.

"Maggie, I am sorry, there is no heartbeat." Dr. Goodwin said painfully.

"Check again," I whispered.

"Maggie, I have been checking for the last fifteen minutes." She said in a stern voice. "I am sorry, there is not a heartbeat."

I sat up and pressed my hands into my eyes; somehow, I had managed to kill my baby. What more damage could I do to myself?

"She was here not that long ago. What the hell happened?" Skyla demanded.

"From my best knowledge, the fetus might not have received enough or too many chromosomes." Dr. Goodwin said.

Once again, my fault. I had failed at keeping this baby alive. I could barely keep a damn plant alive, why did I think a baby live? I had done everything right; I drank enough fluids, I didn't take my medicine, I ate, I had regular appointments, and I even gave up Red Bull. Yet, somehow, I managed to kill my baby. My body betrays me once again.

It was then the scream and sob escaped me. I had lost my child, my baby girl. Why? What did I do wrong? What had I done to deserve this? Hadn't I been through enough? The abuse, the depression, the mood swings, the suicide attempts, the shooting, and losing my father hadn't been enough. Now, I am faced with the tragedy of losing my child. How was I supposed to move on? How was I supposed to have faith that I could get pregnant again and not miscarry? How was I supposed to believe good could happen to me?

The D&E, dilation, and evacuation, procedure was set to happen in an hour. I was moved to a different room, with a more comfortable bed. Skyla held me as I sobbed and let my pain be heard on the entire floor. She just smoothed my hair and squeezed me tightly. My baby was gone. I had been at eighteen weeks. I had kept her alive for eighteen whole weeks, not forty. I didn't even make it halfway.

I bit down hard on my lip; how was Jackson going to take this?

Chapter Thirty-Two

Hole In Your Heart

Jackson

Calvin was waiting for me when I got out of my last surgery of the day. He looked like he had just seen a ghost; that was how pale he was.

"Is this your last one?" Calvin asked, voice raspy.

"Yeah, what's up? You look like you're ready to shit yourself." I said, trying to lighten the mood.

"Get changed and meet me in the lobby." Before I could even ask him another question, he left.

What the hell? I scrubbed out and headed to the locker room to shower and change. Maybe he and Skyla got into an argument, and he needed to drown his sours. I also knew it was around time he had lost his daughter, so he could be upset about that.

I didn't think much of it; I took my time showering and throwing on fresh clothes from my bag. I headed down to the main lobby; Calvin was waiting with that grim look on his face.

"What's up?" I said as I approached him. "Who pissed in your Cheerios?"

Calvin frowned, "Jackson, I am sorry."

"Tell me what's going on," I demanded, now realizing this could be serious.

"Maggie's here, and it's not good," Calvin said, covering his mouth. "Jackson, she's lost the baby."

It was as if someone had pushed me off a cliff. My mind was processing as I fell, his words echoing in my head. The baby. Maggie had lost the baby. How? We had just been at our appointment not that long ago, and everything was fine. This had to be some sick, twisted joke.

I remember the night I found out we were having a girl; how happy we were. I remember kissing her and telling her how much I loved her. Maggie's laughs filled my head; we were finally happy, able to see a future that didn't involve complete darkness. Now, standing there, that happiness had blown away like a dandelion, into pieces.

"Is she hurt? What happened?" I asked, holding back the tears.

Calvin sighed, "Just follow me. Dr. Goodwin can explain better, and you can see Maggie."

His response did not answer my questions, but I followed him. My brain was trying to understand how my happiness had been taken away. I know I was no saint, and I had done my fair share of shit, but what had I done to deserve to lose my child? We didn't even get to meet her; we had been robbed of that chance.

Once we got onto the floor, I could hear Maggie's screams and sobs. I stopped walking and let her sounds penetrate my body. They didn't sound like the sobs and screams I had heard before; these were different. There was no life behind it, like everything had been taken for her. All hope and faith were gone, and you could hear it. If there was any chance for Maggie to believe in happiness, it was gone. She had gone through every nightmare a human could face.

Calvin was watching me with a painful look as Skyla stepped out of the room. Her eyes were bloodshot, and mascara was smeared. She ignored Calvin and walked straight to me, tears already painting her face. As soon as her arms were around me, I felt myself let out a sob.

"She's going to be okay," Skyla forced out and pulled away. "The D&E is going to happen here soon; you need to go in there. She needs you as much as you need her."

Skyla squeezed my shoulder, and Calvin patted me on the back. I opened the door, and Maggie lay curled up in an unnatural position. You could hear her heavy breathing, the sobs now quiet. She was facing away from me, afraid to turn around.

"Maggie," my voice cracked as tears were fighting their way out. "Maggie, please turn around and look at me."

I sucked in my breath when she finally was facing me. Those eyes were swollen and red as if they had been rubbed constantly. There was no life in them, nothing but the basic human eye, no Maggie in there. Both of her thumbs were bleeding from picking them, which she was still doing.

"I'm," her voice was hoarse, "am, so," she swallowed, "sorry, Jackson."

I grabbed her face with both of my hands, "Why are you sorry?"

She squeezed her eyes shut, as if looking at me was too painful. "She's gone."

"Maggie," tears were pouring down her face. "It is going to be okay," I whispered as I pressed my forehead to her. "We're going to be okay."

"No," she squeaked out. "Jackson, our baby is dead. I couldn't keep her alive. How am I supposed to be okay after this?"

I kissed her forehead, "You didn't kill our baby, Maggie." I said sternly. "Don't say that again. I don't know how to go on from here, but you DID NOT kill our baby."

Her lip was quivering, "Jackson," she whispered, "I am tired; I want to be done."

"You have every right to be tired," I pressed my face into her hair. "But you do not have the right to give up." She pulled away to argue, but I beat her to it. "No, you can feel that way, but you're not done. I can't lose you. I know that losing our girl is going to hurt like hell, but I will not lose you, and you will not lose me." I grabbed her hands as they were shaking uncontrollably.

I don't know how long we sat there, holding each other in silence. We both lost someone we never got to meet; that someone was half of her and half of me. How could you feel this heaping hole in your heart for someone who never took a breath on this earth? Why did it have to be us?

Maggie wanted to be alone when they performed the procedure, so I sat in the waiting room with Skyla. Calvin had gone to explain to his mom what was going on over the phone; she was visiting her sister. I knew this was causing all of us pain, but selfishly, no one would be in as much pain as Maggie and I were. I honestly think Maggie hurt the most, more than me.

When we got back to the townhouse, she went straight to her room. I closed the door behind me and turned on the lamp beside the bed. Maggie crawled into the bed, wrapping her green blanket tightly around her. I carefully laid down beside her; she was tracing the patterns in the blanket.

"Abbie June Calsen." She whispered.

I looked at her, confused, "What?"

Those lifeless eyes looked back up at me. "That is her name, Abbie June Calsen."

"What is the reason behind the name?" We hadn't even gotten to the point of talking about names.

Maggie shrugged, "June is Skyla's middle name. Don't tell her I told you that. Abbie is the girl who was killed in front of my room; the least I could do is name my kid after her because she's dead because of me."

"Maggie, you didn't kill her. Maxwell was the one who killed her." She turned her head back to her blanket. "I like the name, but Skyla June James?"

"She hates how it sounds, so she usually doesn't use it. I used to think mine was bad: Maggie Grace Kensinger."

I frowned at her, "That's not bad, but Skyla June? Why the alliteration?"

"Her original name was going to be Jacie June James." I made a face that could never be Skyla. "Thankful it was changed to Skyla."

I smiled and kissed the top of her head. "Abbie June Calsen, I like it."

Our little girl: Abbie June.

Chapter Thirty-Three

Good Vs. Bad

Maggie

Each day that passed, the hole in my heart grew bigger. You never realize how much you want something until it is taken away. When I found out I was pregnant, I had so many mixed emotions, but in the end, I was happy. Finding out it was a girl made it all feel more real but hearing her heartbeat brought out dormant happiness within. I had made that. Jackson and I made that. Then, my body destroyed her.

My work gave me two weeks of paid time off. In that time, I spent almost every day of the week in therapy. It took me a few sessions before I unloaded every bit of feeling I had.

I knew that life wasn't fair, fuck, I was aware of that. My question is, haven't I been through enough? For once in this cruel life, I was given a shimmer of hope, something that I could be proud of. I didn't hate my body; I had grown to appreciate the strength and beauty in it. A human was growing inside it, my little girl. Then, my body killed her, because why do I deserve something good?

Kelly sat through my unloading with her face blank. She didn't interrupt or ask questions; she just let me say it all. I hadn't felt like I could express everything to Jackson or even Skyla. Was it okay that I was so angry at myself that I wanted no one to talk to me? Was it selfish that I thought I was the one in the most pain? I felt that no one understood.

"You know that it is normal to feel this way?" Kelly finally said after I had let everything out.

I frowned, "I am a selfish person for feeling the way I do. How is Jackson going to forgive me? No matter what anyone says, it was ultimately my body that killed the baby."

"I am sure you've seen and read through every fact about miscarriages, but your body DID NOT kill your baby girl." Kelly leaned forward, looking me directly in the eyes. "I know that blaming yourself is easier than accepting that shit happens. It is hard to believe that if it is meant to be, it is meant to be."

I sat back and crossed my arms, "How can one believe in that? Am I just meant to be miserable? Because if that is the case, I am done. Who wants to be continually fucked at every corner?"

Kelly gave a heavy sigh, "You are not meant to be miserable. You are a person who has had shitty things happen to them. But you are also a person who has had good things happen, too."

"Please," I scoffed, "I have had more shitty things happen than good."

"So, you are telling me that getting Skyla as your best friend is a shit thing?"

"No."

"What about Jackson?"

"Of course not."

Kelly smiled, "Your mind fixates on the bad and decides that is all that has happened to you. It is not your fault your brain does that."

"My brain wasn't always like this," I said, anger filling my chest.

She nodded, "You're correct; trauma has that effect."

"How the hell do I fix this?" I asked.

Kelly smiled warmly, "Therapy, medication, patience, and hard work. Will it ever be fully cured? No. Mental illness is about learning to survive."

"What if I am done surviving?" I asked.

"Then you know exactly what I would have to do." She said sternly. "Maggie, you are surrounded in darkness, and no one blames you for feeling the way you do. You would lose too much if you gave up. Live. It sucks, but there are moments in this life worth experiencing, all the shit ones."

"To sum up everything: I am fucked in the brain because of trauma, and there is no cure. So, I must learn how to survive all the shit to experience for the few moments of so-called happiness." I said bitterly.

She was frowning, "Favorite memory with Skyla, describe it."

I opened my mouth but stopped. What was my favorite memory? In the fifteen-some years we had been best friends, is there just one moment that was my favorite? There were so many, I could spend days talking about all my best times with Skyla.

"See, there's too many, aren't there?" I narrowed my eyes at her. "Tell me about your favorite memory with Jackson." Once again, I opened my mouth to answer but was stumped by many good ones. "Tell me your favorite one with your mom."

"Okay, okay, okay," I said, putting my hands up. "I see what you are getting at."

Kelly smiled, "I am not saying you don't deserve to hate life, but you need to be reminded of the good."

There was good, just so much worse. How is one supposed to ignore the bad when it gets thrown in your face? I spent the rest of the day sitting at the kitchen table, writing out my best memories with Skyla. It was sunny out, but cold as usual. It was close to Valentine's Day, and that's when I started writing out my favorite memories.

When Skyla and I were nineteen, she and Bentley were fighting, and so she was locked up in her room blaring Evanescence for the whole afternoon. She ditched her classes the whole day, whereas I went to mine. When I came home in the evening from my last class, *Call Me When Your Sober* could be heard through the apartment walls. She was going on nine hours of this, so I knew shit was bad. I was able to score a beautiful bouquet at the grocery store. I snagged a few bottles of her favorite

Starbucks Frappuccino drink and got her a gaggy Valentine's card.

There was nothing special about it; I didn't put it in a basket or anything. I just pounded on Skyla's door until the music stopped, signaling me to come in. She was lying in the middle of the room on the floor. Her clothes were all over the floor, her bed unmade, her curtains drawn shut, no lights on, and just one candle lit on her bedside table. Skyla's music speaker was on her desk, which had a mess of textbooks and notebooks. She was in plaid sleep shorts and Bentley's *Bush Light* shirt. Her hair was splashed out around her, framing her on the floor.

"What do you want?" She groaned.

I switched on the lights, "I got you something." She was squinting her eyes when she turned to look at me.

"You got me flowers?" She sat up slowly, eyes locked on them. "Why?"

I sighed and walked over, and plopped myself on her bed. "Yes, I got you flowers, coffee, and a card. I know Bentley fucked up, so it's the least I can do for you on this God-awful holiday." I threw the flowers on her lap. "Happy Valentine's Day, bitch."

Skyla smiled at me and laughed. "Happy Valentine's Day, to bitch. Sorry to disappoint, but I got you nothing."

It was such a random memory, but it was a memory that made the hole in my heart shrink a bit.

Skyla was healing a heart she didn't break once again.

Chapter Thirty-Four

Vanishing Like Smoke

Jackson

I didn't take time off work. I didn't want to be stuck at home, reminded of the tragedy. It was better to be busy, but for Maggie, being alone was better for her. I know she had been going to therapy every day of the week, which seemed to be helping. For me, pushing down the memories and emotions worked better. I had never been to therapy outside of rehab; I felt like it did nothing for me.

Was my heart broken that my baby girl was dead? Yes. I was also gutted to see the effect it had on Maggie. Not for one moment did I blame her. She didn't do anything; at the point of conception, it was already determined our girl wasn't going to make it. The likelihood of this happening again was incredibly low, and Dr. Goodwin reassured us of this. Maggie had gone through a lot of testing and examinations. She was determined to find out what was wrong with her. As I guessed, there was nothing wrong on the surface; everything looked healthy.

Even with all the science, I knew Maggie was fully convinced she was the reason we lost the baby. She hated her body before, but now she despised it. Everything she wore was baggy, hiding the monster she believed in.

Maggie refused to let me touch her and avoided any talk with me. At least she was doing this to everyone, including Skyla.

She had been back at work for a few days now. She was gradually building her routine, and I was hoping letting me touch her was part of it. I missed her warmth and the comfort I got from her touch. I just wanted my Maggie back; something told me, this time, she was not coming back.

Chapter Thirty-Five

Hiding In the Tundra

Maggie

Having a stalker means they don't take time off. I had been drowning in grief, but I was still aware of my surroundings. The few times I had been leaving my therapy session, he was watching me from his black Mercedes with the window down. When I met his eye, he would give me a grin and drive off.

There had been times when I was in the middle of teaching a lesson at school, and there he would be up against my car. I had even seen him lingering outside the house, causing me to close all the curtains in the house. It seemed as if he wasn't at the hospital; he was watching me. The scary thing wasn't him following me; it was the fact he did not approach me, even when I was alone.

In the few weeks I had been back at work, I was able to find myself slowly getting into life again. It had been hard the first few days at work, having to explain to my kids what happened to my baby. Therapy helped every day; I noticed that I was talking and interacting more with the people around me. The loss of my child would weigh heavily on me, an added demon to the list. It wasn't something that could be washed away by alcohol or work; no, you had to face it and learn to live with it. I was afraid that Jackson was trying to do just that, but alone. Hence, why was I waiting in the hospital cafeteria for him?

There was a shocked look on his face, followed by a half-assed smile. He was in nice navy scrubs; they molded his body beautifully, and his hair was messed up from wearing a scrub hat. Jackson made his way to where I was sitting, and I stood up and kissed him lightly on the lips.

"What do I owe the pleasure, Kensinger?" He asked as he sat down next to me.

"Am I not allowed to come visit you?"

He shook his head, "You are; it is just not what I was expecting, given how everything has been."

"I am worried about you," I said slowly, nervous to upset him. "I am nervous we are growing apart."

Jackson's face was blank, making my stomach sink. "You are worried about me?"

"Jackson, I know what happened is causing a lot of pain for the both of us. I am sorry that I have been selfish in keeping to myself. I am sorry that my body failed you. I suck at communicating, so this is the best you're getting, but I am worried this will be the nail in the coffin." I said these words super-fast as heat rose to my cheeks.

He was silent, watching me as my breathing increased. I was hoping for an immediate response if nothing is going to happen to us. His not saying anything was one of my fears about his responses. In my brain, sirens were going off, alerting me that something bad was about to occur.

"Maggie," he sighed, and that is when I took off.

It had been a while since I had run, and my legs ached as I did so. I managed to easily slip by people and not look back to see if he was following me. My fight-or-flight instinct had kicked in. The sirens in my head were growing quieter the farther I ran. I didn't even bother going to my car; instead, I headed towards the main sidewalk and headed down it.

The weather was still cold; maybe it hit about twenty degrees today, but it was sunny. There was a sharp wind that I was running into, making it more challenging. It also didn't help that I was in boots, jeans, and a long coat.

Did I have a clue as to where I was running? Hell no. I just knew it was better to take flight than sit there and hear what he had to say. I didn't want to face the fact that this would be the end of our relationship, and the reason for it was because of me. I was used to being the problem in every situation, but this time, I was far more ashamed than ever to be the reason something ended.

Since Jackson had come into my life, I hadn't imagined life without him. I assumed there would be no after us. We had such a connection that I knew I was never going to find another guy, not to mention I would even allow myself to let a guy in. I didn't want to face an after-Jackson life, hence why I ran for my life.

My breathing remained steady as I found myself on the outskirts of town, headed towards Lake Marquette, south of Bemidji, right along Jefferson Avenue. There were at least a few inches of snow on the ground, and my boots were starting to get soaked as they were not intended to stand in the snow.

Once I hit Lake Marquette, I turned around to see if anyone was following me. No one. A part of me was pissed Jackson didn't follow me, telling me that we weren't worth fighting for. Then, there was a part of me that was happy he didn't because I didn't know what to say. I was going to be mad if he did or didn't follow me because my mind couldn't decide what to think.

Lake Marquette was one of the ten thousand lakes in the state of Minnesota. There was a reason the state was called "The Land of Ten Thousand Lakes." Lake Marquette was a lot smaller than Lake Bemidji, but bigger than Lake Irving, which was connected to Lake Bemidji. The point was that there were plenty of lakes in the area I lived in, and I had no connection with Lake Marquette.

I sat down at the end of the lake, closest to the road. As expected, it was frozen, so there were no peaceful sounds of the water, but also no fishy smell. The road around was not popular travel, so leaving me with just utter silence out in the middle of nowhere. I laid myself down, feet hitting the ice, head surrounded by snow.

There were so many places in this world I had seen and so many I hadn't seen. Either way, there was something special about northern Minnesota. I know many people had never been here, but in my humble opinion, they were missing out. It didn't matter what time of year, around here, it would always leave you speechless. What I have learned from all the traveling I've done is that every place has something. My home here held the beauty of silence. An escape from the fucked world.

I didn't expect anyone to find me. Like I had said, I had no connection to this lake. I had maybe been here once or twice as a kid; otherwise, I had nothing that would indicate this being my haven. Another bonus is that in the great northern woods of Minnesota, there were plenty of places to hide if you did not want to be found. Hence, deep down, that is what I wanted: not to be found.

Maybe, after all, I had been through abuse, suicide attempts, a shooting, losing my dad, and having a miscarriage were just reminders that I was better off alone. Maybe it was my karma from all the bad shit I had done in my life, finally catching up to me. Maybe being alone was the key to my survival. Jackson disappearing from my life was just another reminder that I, Maggie Kensinger, deserved to be alone for the rest of my life.

The key here was I didn't want to be alone. I had come to peace with the idea of dying alone, but that was all before Jackson came in. He was able to show me that broken people can love, but now, I was left questioning if two broken people can survive each other.

I had no idea how long I lay there; my body had become numb. But when I heard footsteps behind me, it was already starting to get dark out.

"You know, you're too predictable," Skyla said as she plopped down beside me.

I frowned up at the sky, "There was no way in hell you knew I was here."

She laughed, "No, it took me a few tries, but I knew you didn't want to be found, so go somewhere no one would think."

"And out of all places, you thought of Lake Marquette?"

"Like I said, it wasn't my first choice, but your footprints gave away on the side of the road."

I turned to look at her, "You should've been a detective."

Skyla smiled, "It's fucking cold, let's go."

"No."

"Excuse me?"

"I said no, I am not moving."

Skyla grabbed my arm and yanked it. "Out of all the ways to die, I am not letting you freeze to death. Get your ass up now."

"Skyla," I shook her arm off me. "I'm done. I am so over this shit of life."

"So, you're telling me I am not worth you living for?" Her words cut so deep that my body shuddered. "I mean nothing to you." There were tears in her eyes. "Maggie, you giving up this time means everything we've been through meant nothing. You and I have experienced hell in different ways, but we were able to smile and laugh together. Am I not worth living for?

Because you are my reason for pushing forward each day."

At that moment, I crumpled as I launched into her arms. We were not huggers in our friendship, but this moment was a time we needed to.

"Of course you are, you dumbass," I whispered.

She squeezed me tightly. "Now is not the time to be selfish; it is my turn for that."

Even if Jackson were to vanish from my life, I still would have the best thing that has ever happened to me: my best friend.

Chapter Thirty-Six

Trauma Changes You

Jackson

I had frozen and fucked up. How could she possibly think we could grow apart? If anything, it just made us connect on a deeper level. I know that I had been distant from her, but I didn't know what to say to convince her I didn't blame her. It wasn't about blaming; science wasn't on our side this time. I should've said something instead of being silent, but my brain was trying to protect itself from thinking about life without her. I didn't want there to be an after Maggie.

In all the time I had known her, I don't think I had ever seen the flight mode kick in with me. It was not a great feeling to know that I jump-started that trauma response; it was like you had just been punched in the ball sack. Maggie fled faster than the stupid Road Runner from *Looney Tunes*. I didn't know if I should follow her; what if she wanted to be alone? I didn't want to piss her off. Something deep down told me, yeah, she wanted me to follow her.

By the time I got to the front of the hospital and located her car, panic set in. Maggie's phone, keys, and purse were in the front seat. I looked around the car to see any signs of a struggle, but there was none. Plus, I knew Daniel was working; I had seen him doing a psych exam on the third floor. So, if Daniel didn't have her, where the hell would she have gone?

I ran back inside and checked my schedule. I had no surgeries for the rest of the day, plus I was off in an hour anyway. I grabbed my coat and headed to my car; where would she have gone?

I dialed Skyla's number, knowing she was off. "What do you want bitch boy?"

"I thought we were past the name-calling?" I responded, annoyed. "Is Maggie home?"

"We will never be done with name-calling. And no, she was going to see you at the hospital."

Not good. "I know; I am just asking if she had made it back."

"What did you do?" Her whole tone changed. "Calsen, I am dead serious; what the hell did you do?"

"She tried talking to me, and I froze, and she ran off." I gritted through my teeth as I unlocked my car. "Her car and phone are still here."

"You fucking dick." She hissed onto the phone. "Is Daniel working?"

I nodded as I turned on my car, "Yes, he's here; she is on her own. What do I do?"

"You've done plenty. You stay at work, and I'll clean up your damn mess." I could hear shit being thrown around.

"Too late, I am in the car."

Skyla hung up without another word. She didn't sound too alarmed, so maybe I was overreacting, but it didn't feel like it. My mind was trying to think where she could have gotten on foot. Where would she go?

I drove by the townhouse; Skyla's car was gone. I went downtown; there wasn't anyone by the lake. I checked all the bars and restaurants. Fuck, I even went into Walmart and walked around the whole store, she wasn't in there. I finally went to my house; there were no footprints in the snow. I quickly went into double check, empty. Now I was in full panic mode; where had I scared her off too?

Right about the time I was about to scream, a text from Skyla popped up on my phone, declaring she was at home. I felt all my tension released from my body at that moment; there was no need to scream; she was safe. The realization set in that now I had to face her. How was I supposed to explain my reaction to her words? Let alone have her believe it.

When I walked into the house, Skyla was glaring at me from the couch. Calvin avoided my eyes as he sipped on his beer in the kitchen. Maggie was nowhere in sight.

"Lake Marquette. You sent her running over six miles because you froze." Skyla hissed at me.

"It's not like I wanted to freeze." I fired back at her. "I know I screwed up; I didn't expect her to go running!"

She stood up, "Communicating period makes any of us vulnerable. Your response of silence confirmed a deep fear and reminder that everyone leaves."

"Maggie didn't give me a chance." I stepped towards her, pissed. "She just took off, and I assumed like I was everyone else."

Skyla got close to my face, "Maybe she ran off because you haven't given her a reason to believe you would stay." Her voice was low and furious. "You've been avoiding her like the damn plague; no wonder her mind goes to thinking you'll leave."

"She's been avoiding all of us." I spat at her. "Don't act like she hasn't treated you differently."

Skyla laughed, "You don't get it; she trusts me. I have seen her at the lowest of the lows, and never once did I hesitant or freeze."

"You think you are better than everyone just because you've been around longer?" I yelled.

Calvin stepped forward, "Calsen, walk away."

"No, she doesn't get to stand here and claim Maggie is hers only. Believe it or not, she can have more than one person in her life."

Skyla stood toe to toe with me. "Let's face the fact, Jackson, in the end, she will always choose me. A burning house and she had to pick between the two of us; it'd be me. Being each other's person will do that. It doesn't mean she can't love you; what it means is her love is different from you and me. I am so tired of telling you: I am not the threat; I am the damn ally."

I looked down at her, fire in my chest. "You've been nothing but a thorn in our relationship."

"Calsen, back away, now." Calvin grabbed my arm. "I know you don't mean that."

I shook my head, "It is true; can't you see how toxic she is?"

"KNOCK IT OFF." Maggie's voice was loud and turned all our heads; she was standing at the bottom of the stairs. "Calvin, let go of him, and Skyla, step away."

Even though Skyla was trying to wear an exterior of steel, you could see the wounds in her eyes. I had finally crossed the line. Calvin was looking at me with such disappointment, but nothing beat the way Maggie was looking at me.

"I am only going to say this once, Jackson; she will always be my first choice. She had multiple chances to walk away from me, but instead of stepping over me, she helped me out. You're a guy and don't understand how two-faced women are, so when you find one that truly is defending the knives from going into the back, you do your damndest to keep them around.

"I know it is hard to understand and swallow; Bentley struggled with it, too. To me, it isn't toxic; it is loyalty and love. So, if you want the chance to still be around, face the fact that she isn't the threat." Maggie's words were like icicles penetrating my skin. "Apologize, now. If I ever hear or must explain this again, you will never see me again."

If my face could speak, shame is what it would say. I don't think I have ever seen Maggie furious with me. What the fuck was I thinking? That was the thing, I wasn't. I was so angry at myself that I took it out on anyone around me. It was no excuse for saying what I said. As much as it bothered me that Maggie would pick Skyla any day of the week, I admired it more than anything.

In this world, it was hard to find genuine people. It felt like everyone was looking out for only themselves. To get what they wanted, they would stab their blood and friends in the back. I saw this firsthand, experienced it firsthand. I felt guilty about what I had said, but I couldn't take it back.

I looked at Skyla, begging that my face looked as sincere as I felt. "I fucked up, I am sorry."

Skyla nodded, "I'm sorry for picking a fight.'"

Maggie looked between us, "Are we good?"

Skyla and I turned to each other and said, "Yes."

Maggie turned and went back up the stairs, leaving us all ashamed as to what had just happened. Calvin clapped me on the back and gestured for Skyla to follow him up the stairs and to her room. They both left, Calvin turning to give me a sad look.

I closed my eyes and slammed my fist into the counter. The only person that I could be pissed at was myself. I had been the one to start this whole thing. Just another reminder of what a shit person I was.

"Jackson," her voice was soft as I turned around to see Maggie back at the bottom of the stairs.

I turned around, embarrassed again that she had seen my frustration. She walked over to me, not breaking eye contact. Her hair was wet, like she had just gotten out of the shower, and she wore baggy sweats and a hoodie.

"Maggie, I am sorry."

She stopped right in front of me. "I am sorry, too. I shouldn't have run off like that."

"I shouldn't have frozen."

"Jackson, are we growing apart?"

My mouth dropped open, but determined not to make the same mistake, I said: "I don't understand how you can think that is possible. Maggie, we were going to have a baby, a connection that will never go away. I am sorry if I have given you the impression that I didn't want you; that is the farthest thing from the truth."

"I am sorry that I assumed." She whispered, afraid to meet my eyes.

I reached out and tilted her chin up at me. "You know how I feel about you. I know you second-guess it because it is hard for you to believe. I meant what I said that night: I want you. Even if you're not okay, I am not running. I made a promise that night, a promise that I intend on keeping."

She gave a small smile, "Look at you being romantic."

I laughed, "Look at you ruining the moment."

Maggie leaned in and hugged me. "Your romantic shit is starting to charm me."

"Marry me." The words came out of my mouth before I had a chance to think.

She didn't move; she remained hugging me. "Ask me with a ring and being down on one knee, and it will be a maybe."

I laughed and kissed the top of her head. Yeah, there was no fucking way I wanted a life without Maggie Kensinger.

Chapter Thirty-Seven

Once Upon A Time

Maggie

People in books and movies always say they know when life-changing moments happen; I call bullshit on that. For me, they always come out of the left field. I didn't expect to meet Jackson on that plane. I had no clue Skyla, and I would be best friends after all these years. There was no way for me to know that my father was going to die when he did. The point being, you never know when shit is going to happen.

When I got home from work one Friday night, Jackson was the only one home, but the house was dark. When I got upstairs, my door was shut, and locked. I frowned; what the hell?

I pounded on the door, "Calsen, open the damn door."

I heard him chuckling from the other side, "What word are you missing?"

"Please open the damn door," I said, annoyed.

When Jackson opened the door, I was hit by the smell of fresh mint. He wore a goofy grin on his face as I took him in. His body was perfect, muscular, and toned, but his skin still had a hint of tan. He towered over me, making me feel protected when he wrapped me in his arms. Jackson also had perfect white teeth that complimented his smile, which would make any heart melt.

"Kensinger, liking what you see?" He said with a cocky tone.

I rolled my eyes and walked by him and into the room that was lit by a few candles. I stopped and turned around; he was leaning against the door frame.

"Hoping to get laid?" I asked as I sat down on my bed. "I must say the candles are a nice touch."

Jackson laughed and stood in front of me. "I am glad to know candles are a way to turn you on."

I frowned, "Okay, why the candles?"

He smiled down at me, "Well," he pulled something out of his pocket, "I believe your exact words were: if you have a ring and get down on one knee, you might get a maybe." Jackson lowered himself to one knee. "So, a ring as requested."

He opened the box, and I felt my heart beat so loudly. I think every girl dreams of getting married at one point. I know I always imagined getting engaged in the mountains or some shit like that. As I got older, the idea of marriage made me scrunch my nose. Now, here I was, a man on one knee with a ring that he seemed to have plucked out of my dreams.

"How," I whispered, eyes locked on the ring. "How did you know?"

It was a pear-cut ring, but instead of a white diamond, it was a pastel blue diamond. The band was white gold with small diamonds around the main diamond, a halo. It literally was what I wanted, exactly what I dreamed. I didn't want it to look like every ring you saw; I wanted it to be different. It was strange to see the thing you had only dreamed about in front of you.

Jackson was smiling, "Who do you think told me?" I smiled and laughed as tears fell down my face. "So, you've got the ring and me down on one knee. Now I can ask, Maggie Grace Kensinger, will you marry me?"

There was no point in stopping the tears. "Yes," I breathed. "Yes, I will marry you, Jackson Calsen."

My hand was shaking as he slid it on. I wrapped my arms around his neck as he lifted me. He spun me around like a princess from one of those movies. When he sat me down, I looked down at the ring, still speechless. I had never seen anything like it, just the way I wanted it.

"I must say, it was complicated getting it right." He said as I looked up at him. "But it was worth every second to see your reaction."

In one motion, he grabbed my neck and kissed my lips, moving down to my neck. Goosebumps immediately formed on my skin as his fingers tugged to pull off my long sweater. I pulled away and let him take it off. His mouth traced my collarbone before unclasping my bra, exposing my breasts, which his mouth went to right away.

Laying me down on the bed, he tugged off my leggings as I eyed him hungrily. He kissed the insides of my thighs sweetly and gently. When he finally met my clit, I let out a sigh of relief as he sucked on it. My hands dug through his hair as I slowly slid two of his fingers into me. It had been way too long, and there was no way my body could handle the amount of pleasure it was going to face.

Jackson pumped his fingers in and out of me while still moving his tongue in perfect sequence. I could already feel the tension building and my legs shaking. God damn it. Sensing I was close, he slowed his pace, making me whimper and rake my nails through his harder. When my eyes met his, he picked up his pace again.

"Fuck." I whimpered as my eyes rolled to the back of my head, and my body took the full blast of my organism.

When I opened my eyes, there he was, sucking on his fingers, tasting me, watching me. In a swift motion, I sit up and crawl to him, pulling down his jeans. His dick was rock hard as I aggressively pulled his boxers down. Before he had a second to think, my tongue went from his base to the tip, causing Jackson to suck in a breath.

Once I had him all the way in my mouth, he groaned, and his fingers went to my hair. I glided my tongue along the sides, and I fluttered my eyes up his as he began to move himself inside my mouth, hitting the back of my throat. Tears sparked in my eyes from it.

He took this moment to guide my mouth off his dick by using my hair as reins. Jackson kissed me, as I lay back down. He had no issue sliding inside me, but it did cause my back to arch.

"God damn it," Jackson mumbled into my ear. "You're so fucking tight."

I felt myself squeezing as he kicked into gear, thrusting in and out of me. I don't even want to think of when he was inside me last; it had been too long. Jackson's lips traced the side of my neck. I could already feel the tension forming between my legs. Sensing this, he began to move faster and hit my G-spot perfectly. I let myself ride the wave of pleasure as he continued moving in and out of me.

When he finally finished, we both lay on the bed, tangled together. Jackson traced the curves of my body as I closed my eyes, his touch still as electrifying as the day we met. Assuring me that this feeling would never go away.

Chapter Thirty-Eight

Palm of Her Hand

Jackson

When I think back to the day that I first saw her on the plane, I couldn't have even imagined this was where we would be. At that point in my life, I was content to be alone, but then there she was. Maggie shook up my world and for the better. I had known, after hugging her and blurting out the one question you should think before saying, there was no way I could function in a life without her.

Maggie didn't strike me as the traditional type, and she didn't seem like the girl who would want a basic ring you could find at any store. I honestly didn't know if she would want a wedding where she walked down the aisle; for all I could know, she would want a courthouse wedding. Even worse, she might want to get married in Vegas. I was too afraid to ask her these things because I had already fucked up twice asking Maggie to marry me without thought. This final time was going to be planned.

I didn't tell anyone my plans; I had started browsing online for rings and in the shitty mall. The ring for Maggie was not going to be found in Bemidji, let alone online. I knew that, eventually, I was going to have to talk to Skyla, but I didn't know how she would feel about me asking Maggie to marry me. Both of us had done a great job over the last month, avoiding having any kind of conversation. Skyla was spending more and more time at Calvin's, which made it easier. Luckily, at work, we really didn't see each other either.

The weather was slowly warming up; February had come and gone, and March was upon us. The temperatures were now in the twenties and thirties, with an occasional forty-degree day. The sun seemed to be out more, which helped the lake slowly melt. All the ice fishing huts had been removed, and the college students were no longer parking on the lake.

After weeks of being stubborn and searching for rings, I knew it was time to approach Skyla. I figured talking to her in a public setting was going to be safer for me, just in case I needed witnesses to my death. So, I found myself at the hospital cafeteria, where, as usual, Skyla sat alone, picking a plate of fries and reading something on her phone, alone. The crazy red hair was piled into a bun, and she wore minimum makeup.

Before I had even reached the table, she said: "What do you want, Calsen?"

I paused; her tone wasn't cold but wasn't welcoming. "I need to ask you something."

She looked up at me, debating, and then shook her head. "Go ask Calvin."

"It pertains to Maggie, and I am pretty sure Calvin has no idea what his sister wants for a ring." I snapped at her.

Skyla stared at me, blinking her eyes. "Why do you think I would help you?"

I groaned and sat down across from her. "I get what I said and did was uncalled for, and I am an asshole. So, I am sorry; please help me in finding a wedding ring for your best friend."

"I'll think about it." She said and went back to whatever was on her phone.

"Skyla, I've been searching for the last few weeks. Please, I am begging you, help me." God, I was pathetic.

She looked at me, grinning. "You're begging me?"

"Yes, I am."

She sat back, crossing her arms. "Why are you wanting my help? What do I get out of it?"

"I'll give you full credit."

"Deal," she said and clapped her hands together. "What do you want to know?"

I sighed, "Everything. Does she even want a wedding? I don't even know what kind of ring she'd want. I know you know her best."

"Glad you came to that realization." Skyla snickered. "Even if she tries to deny it, Maggie wants a wedding. As for the ring, well, be prepared to spend a shit load on it."

The shit load was right, but worth it. Skyla described the ring and was able to show me some images of the shapes and what the hell a halo was. It had to be custom-made, and it took some time; I had to go and pick it up from the jewelry store in Minneapolis. It was exactly what Skyla said, and even she was stunned by the beauty of it.

Next, I had to learn from Skyla, that Maggie was not going to be one who wanted a big and flashy wedding. Small with some traditional touches. I breathed a sigh of relief, learning that she did not want to get married in Vegas. In fact, Skyla said Maggie found those weddings to be trashy as they were usually a drunk fest.

Skyla was the one who was able to tell me Maggie would want it private. After everything that had happened to her, she wanted to keep the happy moments away from everyone so they wouldn't get tarnished.

"A long time ago, she talked about getting proposed to at like a national park like Rocky Mountain or Glacier," Skyla said while she was admiring the ring. "I think now, the more intimate it is, the more she will appreciate it."

I had been nervous; any guy who says they weren't is a liar. The whole day, I was preparing for Maggie to say no, make a face, or, worst of all, laugh. I picked a Friday night to do it so she wouldn't have to get up early in the morning; I wanted to savor every moment of our engagement night. Not to mention that Skyla and Calvin were going to be at one of the bars downtown waiting for us.

Traditionally, I did ask Calvin for permission to marry his sister. He was not fazed by my question, which told me Skyla had already kept him in the loop. I had coffee with Julia Kensinger and asked for permission, and she started to cry. I had even gone to Mitch Kensinger's grave and told his gravestone what I was planning to do. I never formally met him, but I knew that deep down, if he had known the truth behind Maggie's choices, he would've never wasted those years of not talking to her.

When Maggie saw the ring, her reaction was priceless, and I will forever hold that image in my head. It was a mix of shock, happiness, sadness, and excitement in one. But what did me in was when she looked at me and said yes. All the worry and panicking had been for nothing. Maggie Kensinger had agreed to be my wife; she was officially mine.

After we lay together, holding each other for a while, I told her we had to meet Calvin and Skyla. She groaned as she started digging through her closet, her bare ass for my sight. I knew she could feel me watching because Maggie flipped me off before stepping into a skintight, long-sleeved, purple dress. It cut deeply into her back, along with the front. The dress barely fell below her ass cheeks.

Without looking at me, she went into the bathroom, muttering about how she was going to take too long. I smiled. Maggie was my fiancée, and she still had all the spunk and feistiness. It took me all of two minutes to get back into my jeans and black shirt. It was about another ten minutes, and she came back with curled hair, freshly applied makeup, and red lips. God damn. Not to mention, her ring perfectly complemented her eyes, making it stand out.

"I want you again," I came up behind her, kissing the top of her head. "We can keep them waiting."

Maggie shook her head as she slid on black heels. "I think we've kept them waiting long enough."

When she finally straightened up, my hands gripped her ass. "I want you again."

"You get to have me for the rest of your life," she rolled her eyes and brushed past me. "If you get enough alcohol in me, maybe you'll score."

We ended up downtown within the next twenty minutes by Uber. Calvin and Skyla were sitting in a booth near the pool tables and darts. She was dressed in a mini skirt and a strapless top with her hair perfectly straight and down. I watched as she ran up to Maggie and embraced her in a huge hug. I slid next to Calvin, who was just shaking his head and sipping his beer.

There was a decent amount of people here. It was mostly college kids, some who didn't even look old enough to drink. Most people were out on the dance floor, a bunch of guys were playing pool, and very few people were throwing darts. Dim lighting made everything seem mysterious and hidden. The music was playing some kind of rap song that was loud enough to feel the vibrations in my chest.

"You know," Calvin leaned and yelled, "I'll kill you if you hurt her."

I laughed as he handed me a beer; we were both watching Maggie and Skyla. They were huddled close to each other, looking at Maggie's ring. They both were lost in their worlds, completely forgetting everyone in the room.

When Maggie glanced at me and smiled, my heart skipped a few beats, and a fire burned inside my chest. She had me in the fucking palm of her hand, always. I was screwed.

Chapter Thirty-Nine

Choose The Right Answer

Maggie

Growing up, my favorite fairytale was *Beauty and the Beast*. Though the story was dark, it still had a happy ending. After getting engaged to Jackson, I just assumed that I would get the happily ever after shit. As I said, there was a lot of dark crap in my favorite fairytale, and look how it all turned out: happy ending and marriage. That was just another damn lie your childhood tells you.

Truthfully, in the weeks that followed my engagement, there were plenty of smiles and happy shit. My students were all over the moon over my ring, along with every person who saw it. It was absolutely breathtaking to look at every morning; I would find myself just staring at it. Every detail that I had imagined was right there on my finger; Jackson had captured the dream that Skyla had described. Just proving how much both loved me.

There were the same questions: of when's the date? Big or small wedding? Destination wedding? When is your bridal shower? All that I said, no idea. I hadn't really given much thought to the wedding itself other than the dread of planning it. I knew it was going to be small and private, but after that, I had no clue. Jackson and I hadn't discussed details as we were either working opposite shifts or having sex.

When I had found out I was pregnant, the idea of having sex repulsed me. Then, I miscarried, and we were floating apart. The night he proposed to me was the first time we had sex in months. It was a connection I had missed, and I could tell Jackson felt the same. He made me feel safe, seen, and loved. He knew my body better than me, and he sure as hell knew how to please it. We were in the honeymoon phase of our engagement, which is why I didn't expect what happened next.

In April, the weather in Bemidji is very bipolar. One day, it will be sunny and sixty degrees, and the next, it could be snowing. So far, most of the snow has melted, and things have started to get green. However, there were still plenty of chances for a random snowfall. It was Saturday, sunny but in the low fifties, and I took this opportunity to go on a run.

Everyone was working, so I was left to myself. I pulled my hair into a high ponytail and threw on leggings and a long-sleeved shirt. Despite everything that had happened, there was not one thing I can say positively about my body. There were still stretch marks, and I could easily pitch fat all around. Jackson could say how beautiful my body was all he wanted, but there were flaws, not to mention it was the very thing that destroyed my baby.

Shaking my head, I pulled my headphones in and walked out on the back patio as I slung my backpack that was filled with water, my phone, first aid kit, and pepper spray clasped to the outside. I stretched my arms and legs quickly and jogged down the path toward the trail that was wrapped around the lake. I headed north, towards the more woodsy and hidden parts of Bemidji, away from the town.

My headphones were blasting some song by *Twenty-One Pilots* as I slowly picked my pace up. In school, I had been on the track team for three years. I hated track season; it came after basketball, and I usually was pretty fed up with sports as I played volleyball in the fall. The track was just purely running, which made it my least favorite. Skyla only played basketball; she despised running for fun, so there was no convincing there. Volleyball was too girly of a sport with bows and shit; not her thing, either.

I could've gone to Bemidji State for basketball, but there was no way in hell I was staying here. Skyla was given a full ride to Bemidji State as she scored a thirty-five on her ACT, which she will brag about. Like me, staying here was hell, and we thought Colorado was the coolest place to go. In our time living there, it was nice as you got all four seasons and plenty of outdoor activities to keep you busy.

About three minutes in, I had yet to meet another person, which wasn't unusual. The more north you went, the fewer people and more nature. I should've known he had been following me, but like I said, I was in this happily ever after mindset. Such a foolish girl I was.

Before I heard or saw anything, I could smell the sharp cologne. I could feel my feet slowing as my heart began to beat loudly. Too scared to turn around, I squeezed my eyes shut, came to a stop, and felt the burn on his hand on my shoulder.

Afraid to turn around, Daniel came into view, smiling like a predator about to dig into his prey. I remember the first night he raped me, the way I was caught off guard, not to mention all the fights I put up. There was no sleep as I lay on his bed, shoulders shaking as tears fell. Daniel's arm was wrapped around my waist, unable to escape. Little did I know that was only the beginning of a lifelong nightmare.

"Maggie," he pulled my headphones off, "princess, why are you scared?"

I hated that he called me that; it was a nickname that my dad had called me as a young girl. I knew Daniel only used the name because of that.

"Get away," I said pathetically, not being able to meet his eye. "Please."

His fingers brushed my cheek, and he leaned in close, "Oh, that is the last fucking thing I am going to do."

Growing up, Daniel wasn't around all the time, but for every holiday or major family event, he was there. Calvin kissed the ground he walked on, and Anika had the biggest crush on him. As for me, I respected him at the time and found his work interesting. That was the reason I was so keen on studying under him. Now I knew why he was eager to have me start right away.

I tried stepping back, but he wrapped his fingers around my throat. "Please," I begged. "Let me go."

Daniel laughed and tightened his grasp. "Look at you, begging like the pathetic bitch you are." He crashed his lips to mine, and my body got ridged.

Throbbing images came into view. My skin burned, and I tried to move, but everything was still in me. White noise filled my head as images of all the times he forced himself upon me. The pain of the bites between my legs and the rough feeling of him inside me produced screaming and trashing internally, but externally, I remained like a statue as he kissed me.

As he lowered me to the ground, my body became numb; it already knew what was going to happen. I said before the body has its way of protecting you from trauma; mine was shutting down completely. The fight-or-give-up sense in me had chosen the latter; it always did when it came to Daniel. It was sickening knowing that I had given up, but wouldn't you after everything? Rape. Attempting suicide. Having a miscarriage. School shooting. Your father deteriorates in front of you, and then you are the one to find him dead. I had more than enough reason to give up.

"I find it funny that you truly thought you could escape me," Daniel said as he tugged down my leggings. "I will be the one who has you forever, Maggie."

He thrust inside of me, and that is when something sparked. I could finally feel everything that was going on, my body influencing me to fight. My mind was set on giving up as it had always been, but my body had a different idea, a new response I had never felt before.

Avoiding the sight in front of me, my hands were searching the ground around me, trying to find a weapon to save me. Keeping my eyes squeezed shut; my fingers found gravel from the path. I just needed to find a bigger chunk or a rock I could hit him with. All that I could find were crumbs, and panic rising in my chest; I was going to have to figure out a different plan. In the last seconds, before giving up, I finally found a stone that was big enough to fit in the palm of my hand. Without giving much thought, I wound up, opened my eyes, and used my strength to hit Daniel in the face.

As he stumbled back, I took my chance to escape as I got my feet, pulling my leggings up and beginning to run. I knew I wouldn't have much time, but when Daniel reached for my ankles, I was caught off guard. My face met the ground hard, pain stinging. I tried to crawl forward as he pounced on top of me.

"You little bitch." He mumbled as he turned me to face him. "You really think you can outrun me?"

Daniel was laughing as my body was squirming. My brain was trying to come up with a new plan before he would get back inside me. My backpack was still on me, and then the idea came; my arm awkwardly reached for my pepper spray that was hooked on one of the zippers. Without thinking, I sprayed it in the direction of Daniel. He stumbled back, screaming in pain as I kept spraying as I stood up. This was my chance as I took off sprinting.

There was no looking back as I kept my head down and ran as fast as I could. My legs were sore, but that was only going to fuel me to get back to the house. I wanted protection, and nothing made more sense than Skyla's gun, which she kept locked up in her room. If Daniel was to try anything, the gun gave me the ultimate protection.

Sweat was dripping down my back, and the sun was burning my skin. My head was spinning in a thousand-plus directions; there were muted sirens going off in my head, and I could barely process what was in front of me. Thankfully, my feet knew where we were going, and I eventually found myself fumbling with the back door. This is when I realized I had been crying this entire time. The tears were stinging as they fell onto my shaking hands.

Once I had got into the house, I locked the back door, drew the curtain over the window, and raced up the stairs and into Skyla's dark bedroom. I slid under her bed and got the lockbox. I typed in her combination, which was the last four of her mom's social security number. The safe popped, and I grabbed the handgun, kicked the box under the bed, and barricaded myself in the closet.

Pitch black surrounded me as the throbbing in my head eased up. I leaned my head back and slowed my breathing. I was locked in a closet, holding a gun, prepared to kill. Kill. It then dawned on me that I held a weapon that killed kids and teachers I worked with. A weapon that had nearly taken me out and my students. The sounds of the gunshots rang out, and the images of

Maxwell's deformed body appeared. I let out a scream and dropped the gun.

I pulled my knees to my chest and started to count up to ten and back down to zero. It had been something I had done for comfort, but now I was doing it to control the urge to take the gun and end my life. Death would be easier than constantly running from something. I squeezed my eyes tightly, knowing that it was selfish of me to think that suicide was the answer to my problems.

It was an answer, but the wrong one. My answer was something called help, an answer I hesitated to use but ended up being the sole reason I lived.

Chapter Forty

Courage and Bavery Are Parallels

Calvin Kensinger

Almost every neurology surgeon I had met had some sort of God complex. I think that is what drew me to this field; I held the mobility and thoughts of a person in my hands. I was the only one who could work on the brain or spinal cord; you can't replace those. Hearts you can, brains no. So, having that power made me feel like I was God.

Growing up, I used to think I was going to end up like my dad, but as I got older, I realized that physical therapy was the laughingstock of medicine. At least my mom's field of pediatrics had more respect. Neurology was a field my dad despised because of the attitude they had. And I knew he was furious when I told him, but I had spent my whole life pissing him off; why stop now?

I had always figured Maggie would follow in Mom's footsteps. Paediatrics had its challenges; you were operating on kids, with parents making the decisions. You had to have more patience, composure, and a personality to work with kids. I had never been a kid person; when Kara told me she was pregnant, I was nervous because what if I disliked my child? Of course, Heather was perfect, and I loved her, but the idea of working on and with kids all day long sounded like absolute hell to me.

Maggie shocked me when she wanted to go into the psychology field. In my field, we fixed the problem in the brain; we didn't try to understand why behind everything it did. Of course, both of my parents were proud, even if my dad talked mad shit about psych being a joke. He had no room to talk, and he was a fucking physical therapist, a joke to the medical field.

It made sense why Maggie ended up being a teacher; she had the same composure and patience our mom did. Her smile was so welcoming; it was the same one as our mom's. I didn't need to be told by anyone that my sister was a well-liked teacher. Maggie was smart, but she was creative. I always envied how interested she was in books, drawing, and writing. I didn't see things the way she did; I was practical and closed-minded. No matter what she had decided to do, Maggie was going to be successful.

I happened to be getting coffee from the attending lounge on the third floor when my phone buzzed. I had ignored it the first two times it rang, convinced whoever it was would just leave a message. I groaned as I dug into my pocket to reveal Maggie's name on the screen.

"Hello?" There was heavy breathing, but no words. "Mags?"

I heard her take a shaky breath, "He raped me."

My blood went cold. The coffee cup in my hand spilled all over the floor. My jaw was locked, and there was heat rising in my chest. I had to have heard her wrong. How did he get to her? How was she able to get from his grasp?

"Where are you?" You could hear the anger in my voice. "Where is he?"

Maggie was clearly holding back tears, "I am at home locked in Skyla's closet."

"Is he there?"

"I…" she let out a small sob. "I don't know."

"I'm on my way; stay there. Do you have anything to protect yourself?" She was silent for a second. "Maggie?"

"I have Skyla's gun."

The fuck? "What do you mean?" I shook my head; this was a conversation for a different time. "Doesn't matter, I will be there in ten."

I hung up before she could speak. I didn't bother cleaning the mess; I knew it would get cleaned up. There was no time to grab Skyla or Jackson; for all I knew, Daniel was in the house. I didn't care if she pleaded or screamed for me to stop; I was going to kill him. He had painted himself all these years as a mentor and family to us. Little did the rest of us know what he was truly after: Maggie.

Sliding my way past people, ignoring nurses calling my name, and bypassing my uncle, who was in the front lobby, I was able to sprint to my car. When I worked, I left my key fob and wallet in my car; I was too lazy to bring them with me. My luck of not getting robbed had been going on for all these years, so it was no surprise when I got into my car; my stuff was where I left it.

Not even bothering to look both ways, I backed out of the spot and switched to drive aggressively. My tires squeaked as I made my way out of the parking ramp. I didn't know if time was a factor, but I was sure as hell, I wasn't going to risk it. I blew through stop signs and red lights, not giving a fuck if the cops pulled me over. I was getting to Maggie, and there was no way even they were going to stop me.

When I pulled into the driveway, I had surveyed and noticed nothing out of place. I slammed the door shut and opened the garage with the code, bracing for the possibility of him being right there; it was empty, along with the entire house. I had looked everywhere, and there was no sign of struggle anywhere, which meant this rape didn't happen here. Not to mention, there were no broken windows or bust doors, so clearly, he wasn't in there.

Walking back into Skyla's room, I surveyed the floor to see a safe open and half kicked under the bed. I walked over to the closet and kicked it open, not even bothering to warn her. She let out a scream, and the gun was shaking in her hands. Maggie was pressed up against the wall; her eyes were wild as they looked at me. She was sweating, and her eyes were red, but there was swelling and cuts on her arms and cheeks.

Maggie dropped the gun and let out a cry as I lunged forward to her. I wrapped my arms around her and felt her body ease up. Her cheeks were puffy with small scraps of gravel. Along her forearms were the same scraps, but a little more pronounced.

"What happened?" I whispered as I pulled away to take a better look at her cuts.

"I went for a run," she managed out as tears poured from her eyes. "He was there, and it happened." Her voice cracked, when saying the last word.

As far as the cuts, none looked to be deep, but the swelling on her cheeks was clear from a fall. "How did you get back here?"

Maggie pointed to her backpack next to her, and that is where I saw the pepper spray. "I just ran and locked myself in here."

"What do you want to do?" I asked.

"What?"

I sighed, "There is still evidence of sexual assault on you, which means we could do a rape kit." Maggie bit down hard on her lip. "Or I can let you shower and change, and we can pretend it didn't happen."

She was quiet as her eyes looked down at her hands. I knew what she was going to say. I would never understand why she just didn't turn him in and fight, but I had learned to respect people's choices. I wanted her to get the rape kit done; this was her chance to stop him before he killed her.

As per usual, my sister had a way of still surprising everyone. "Take me to Sandford to get it done."

I frowned, "What?"

"Take me to Sanford to get it done." She repeated.

At that moment, I was washed over with relief, anger, and sadness. The anger that I had for what Daniel has done will never go away. I was sad that it took her getting raped again to finally stand up. I was relieved she was taking the first step.

Holding out my hand, she took it and stood up. It was then you could see the rips in her leggings for them being yanked down with force. You could also still see the gravel dust and pebbles as well. Maggie truly came straight to the closet. I helped her down the stairs, and I checked outside to see if there was a sign of Daniel before I led her out.

The whole drive, Maggie was focused on her hands, staring at her engagement ring. With some luck, it seemed like it hadn't been scratched at all. I kept stealing glances, trying to gauge what was going on in her mind. I knew better than being able to read minds, but I wanted to know everything that happened and what she was thinking. I wanted to know what I was going to kill Daniel Dobson for.

When I parked, I walked over and opened the passenger door for her. Instead of getting out, she remained sitting with her leg bouncing up and down. Her eyes were full of tears and fixed on the ring. I felt my heart sink to see her in this pain. I felt guilty that I wasn't there for all the times before and even felt shittier for the way I talked about Maggie. There isn't a whole lot that I remember from early on in my childhood, but I can still see and feel the day my parents brought her home. Like all babies, she looked like an alien, but when she opened her eyes and attempted to smile at me while I held her, that is when the protective instinct came over me. Well, she didn't need protection, as she could hold her own, but I had been ready until I failed.

"Mags?" She looked over at me. "Do you want me to call him or Skyla?"

She shook her head, "I don't think I can do this."

I stepped over to her and gently took her hands in mine. "You can do this; I will be here the whole time. I know this is hard, but I am proud of you for getting this far." I gave her a small smile. "I believe in you."

Avoiding my eyes, she stepped out of the car. We walked side by side into the emergency room. It wasn't like Bemidji was a big town, so everyone knew who the Kensinger descendants were. It was almost as if we all had a label that said KENSINGER. So, as soon as one nurse caught sight of us, it was like the game telephone, and soon they were all looking at us.

"Can I help you?" An older nurse asked, eyes flickering to Maggie.

"We need a rape kit done." Maggie beat me to it.

When we were secured into a closed-off room, I told Maggie I was going to call Skyla. She nodded and pulled her knees to her chest as she waited for a nurse to come. I stepped out and dialed Skyla's number.

On the third ring, she picked up. "Where the hell are you? I thought you had surgeries this afternoon."

"You need to come to Sandford." I started, and Skyla was silent; I could hear people talking. "Maggie and I are at Sandford; you need to be here for this."

"What happened?" She whispered.

I closed my eyes and swallowed, "Daniel raped her, and she has agreed to have a rape kit done."

Skyla was silent for a few minutes; I knew her mind was running a mile a minute. "I'll be there soon. Do I need to get Jackson?"

"No, I think it should be just you."

"I'll see you soon." She hung up, and I walked back into the room where Maggie was still sitting.

"What's going to happen?" She asked as I stood next to her.

I wrapped my arm around her. "Let's just get through this, and then we can figure everything else out."

Maggie looked up at me. "Thank you, and I love you."

I curled my lip into a smile so she couldn't tell how sad I was. "I love you, Mags."

Maggie leaned her head against my arm, and then the nurse came in with all the shit needed. I squeezed her shoulder and turned around as this four-plus hour-long procedure began.

Chapter Forty-One

Reminder of Mine Own

Skyla James

I still can remember clearly the first time I was sexually assaulted as a kid. Those kinds of memories you shove into something called a Pandora's Box. You do your best not to open the box because it is easier to pretend it didn't happen instead of dealing with it. But sometimes, feeling the pain from those memories outweighs the pain you feel in this shitty life.

If you look back at the few pictures that were taken in my childhood, you can see when my innocence was stolen from me. There is a look you get in your eyes that screams for help. No one helped me. I was the girl whose mom was a drug addict, so there was no point in helping someone like that. After years of realizing no one is going to help, you lose that look in your eyes, and something changes. For me, that is when my anger surfaced. It was easier to be a bitch, and this is why I was one.

I should've known when coming back from Thanksgiving break my freshman year that Maggie had that look in her eyes. A part of me believed I was too afraid to believe what I was seeing. There was also another part that was denying that anything like that could happen, not with how protective I was of her. I don't know what I would've done if she had told me that Sunday. At the time, I had nothing holding me back from setting the world on fire, so I guess that I would've cut Daniel's dick off or some shit like that.

When she told me, I knew I had fucked up, that her eyes were calling for help like I had all those years. It still eats me alive that I ignored the cry for help. It was just another thing I shoved in my Pandora's Box. A psychiatrist would have a field day going through everything in that damn box, but now that I was twenty-nine, I felt no need to drag it out and fix what was inside.

I hated Sandford. They were like chain hospitals all over Minnesota. I felt like everything was cookie-cutter there and that they would hire anyone. In reality, Sandford reminded me of the hospital where I was treated for attempted suicide, so that is where most of my hate stems from. I knew why Maggie had chosen here, though. Just because she had taken the first steps in standing up to Daniel didn't mean she was prepared to face the truth with her family.

By the time I got there, Calvin was waiting for me outside the room. I ran into his arms and felt tears forming in my eyes. Calvin smoothed my hair down and, kissed the top of my head, and let me into the room, where he remained outside.

Maggie was lying there in a hospital gown; the nurse turned around, grabbing something. I walked over and stood next to Maggie as she looked up at me, the help screaming in her eyes. I gave her a pathetic smile as I grabbed her hand and squeezed it. I was not leaving her side; she was taking a big step.

A step I never took for myself.

Chapter Forty-Two

Anger Is an Unpredictable Emotion

Jackson

I had concluded that when Skyla and Calvin were both up waiting for me at home, something had happened to Maggie. My heart rate rose as they both looked somber while I took my shoes off. What the fuck could've happened? Calvin and Skyla exchanged a look before she disappeared upstairs, leaving us alone.

"What the hell is going on?"

"Jackson," he sighed, fighting back what looked like tears. "He got to her."

Everything froze, as if you had hit the paused button on the remote. There was silence as you could no longer hear. It could mean many things when Calvin said: 'He got to her.' I knew my mind went for the worst; Daniel had killed her. But if that were the case, we would not be standing in the kitchen; we'd be in the hospital. My mind then went to the next worst thing: he raped her.

I squeezed my eyes shut and opened them up slowly, hitting play on the remote. "He raped her, didn't he?"

Calvin leaned forward onto the counter. "Yes, he raped her. We had a rape kit done at Sandford."

There was too much to feel, so I went with the most swallow feeling. "Why the hell wasn't I called?"

"She hasn't decided what she wants to do," Calvin said, frowning. "But she at least had the kit done."

I ran my hand through my hair. "She's got to go through with it. Next thing we know, he's going to kill her."

"You can't force her into that, you know that. Jackson, we just need to be patient with her."

"HOW ARE WE SUPPOSED TO WORK WITH HIM?" I exploded.

Calvin shook his head, "I don't know, but can we just be grateful Maggie is in one piece."

I leaned back on the fridge and let out a shaky breath. I should be grateful my fiancé was safe, but there was such an anger that I couldn't contain. In my mind, Daniel deserved the rage that was in me. I wanted to do such violent things to him that even made my stomach churn thinking about it. Skyla and Calvin had to feel the same way, but now, how are we supposed to sit back? If I saw him, no one, not even Maggie, was going to stop me.

Skyla came back down the stairs. She was freshly showered and dressed in Calvin's shirt, which went past her mid-thigh, and no pants underneath. She nodded her head in the direction of the stairs, silently dismissing me.

With my head swimming, I climbed the stairs and slipped into her bedroom. There were a few candles lit, the room smelling like vanilla, but no lavender. Maggie was curled up in the middle of the bed with her green blanket wrapped around her. I carefully sat down on the edge of the bed, not wanting to wake her up. She looked so peaceful, breathing softly. My eyes were drawn to her engagement ring, still there, perfect.

Right as I was about to lean in and kiss her, those eyes snapped open. They still took my breath away, even though you could see the mix of pain and cry for help. I immediately spotted where the damage was on the outside. My stomach did a flip, and the fire exploded in my chest.

Maggie sat up, a worried look on her face. I took in that she was wearing a Bemidji State crewneck and grey sweatpants. Her perfect body was shielded by these baggy clothes.

"Jackson?" She whispered as her hand brushed the side of my face.

I leaned my head into her hand, "Maggie, I can't," I started, afraid of what to say.

"Day by day." She whispered and gave a weak smile that still warmed me. "Today is over."

Maggie laid back down, and I followed suit, letting her curl up against me. I brushed my fingers through the golden hair and watched those eyes flutter back to sleep. I felt her body relaxed, a sign that her body knew it was safe. With me, that is all I ever wanted was for Maggie to feel safe, not just mentally but physically. Right here, her body finally told me that was the case. I smiled and kissed the top of her head; I had her safe and sound...for now.

***

It was not a shocker that Skyla was the only one who knew the full details. I think it was better that way because if I had to hear it all, I would be in jail. Same with Calvin. All that had been shared was that Maggie was on a run when he cornered her. The way she escaped was with a stone and her pepper spray. Maggie had barricaded herself in Skyla's closet with the gun none of us knew existed.

"Since when do you own a gun?" Calvin asked her as we were walking to work that Monday.

Skyla shrugged, "Since you started fucking me. Got it in case I needed to shoot your dick off."

I smiled while Calvin rolled his eyes. "You think he's going to be here?"

That was the dreaded question all of us were facing. I knew Maggie would never forgive us if we confronted him, but there was only so much resistance one can have. She had not decided what she was going to do. I was pissed because the obvious answer was to go through with the police report, but Maggie was still hesitant. Skyla had to remind me that it was still her choice and not ours.

I fucking hated it when she was right.

Strangely enough, Maggie opted to go to work, saying it was going to get her mind off everything. She had to beg me not to confront Daniel, and she even doubted that he would even show his face now. I was just hoping she was right, and I wouldn't have to break my promise to her. The anger that was boiling inside me, I didn't think I was going to be able to stop myself.

I wasn't even fully dressed and ready for rounds when my pager went off. My stomach sank when I realized it was Chief Kensinger wanting to see me. What could he possibly want from me? Once I finished getting dressed, I headed up the stairs and to his office. To my surprise, we were not alone, Julia and Calvin Kensinger were there. Calvin looked pissed off, while Julia wore a look of concern. The chief was just glaring at me as he gestured for me to come in.

"So," his eyes darted between Calvin and me, "would either of you like to explain why my head of psychiatry is on medical leave for the week?"

Jesus, a week? "No." We both said.

"What happened?" He growled.

I looked at Calvin, who kept his eyes glued to the floor. Did the chief really think we had something to do with it? Is this my chance to expose the bastard to what he was doing? I knew better than to, but the opportunity was right here.

"Daniel told me, if I wanted an explanation, I should speak to my son and his best friend." Julia fired out, looking right at Calvin. "So, someone better start talking."

He was baiting us. "I don't know anything," I said as, in reality, I had nothing to do with the injuries he suffered. "I have rounds and surgery this morning, so can I be excused from this conversation?"

The chief stood up and narrowed his eyes. "If I find out that you had anything to do with this Calsen, I will fire your ass."

"He had nothing to do with it." Calvin finally said. "I don't know what psycho lies that piece of shit is telling you, but neither of us had anything to do with his injuries." He stood up and shook his head. "Honestly, whatever happened, he deserves it."

Without another word, Calvin grabbed my shoulder and ushered me out with him. I followed him without another word until we got to the nearest lounge, and he slammed the door and ran his fingers through his hair, clearly stressed out from that conversation.

I crossed my arms, trying to be calm. "He is baiting us."

"You don't think I know that? Of course, he is. It is all part of his game. He wants you out of the picture so he can take Maggie all for himself." Calvin kicked the side of the couch. "For all we know, he might as well kidnap her."

The hairs on my neck stood; I had never even thought of that possibility. "I don't understand, why her? He never seemed to be a problem when you guys were younger."

Calvin squeezed his eyes shut and took a deep breath. "Jackson, he's been obsessed with her since he first met her."

I couldn't even describe the feeling I felt. It was beyond disgust, with a mix of anger behind it. Maggie had been a fucking child when Daniel met her. This whole time, it was her. Daniel's end goal was Maggie. It had been for years.

"How do we know that for a fact?" I asked, hoping it was some bullshit he made up. "It isn't like he showed these signs all those years ago."

Calvin sighed, "Jackson, he told Maggie. He told her from the moment he laid eyes on her, he wanted her to be his and his only. It explains why he was so eager to have her study under him; it was finally his chance."

"What do we do?"

"We have to give her time."

I shook my head, "She's had time; at this point, she is making the decision he can have her."

"You honestly believe that?" Calvin snapped at me, fury on his face. "You think that is what your fiancé and MY sister want?"

There was too much anger inside me. "By her not doing anything, that is what it feels like."

"You're a fucking prick; you really don't know her at all." Calvin stepped towards me.

"You have no room to talk; you tossed your sister to the side the moment she wasn't perfect." I hissed as I made a step to him. "You don't get to paint me as the villain here because you fucked up at being a brother."

It happened fast, Calvin punched me hard in the jaw, knocking me off balance. As I said, there was too much anger for me to just let it go. I lunged at him, tackling him to the ground. My fist met his face at the same time Calvin kneed me right in the balls, sending shooting pain through my body.

"You're not the knight in fucking shiny armor." Calvin punched me in the gut. "Who did she call when Daniel got to her?" He laughed drily. "Me, not you!"

I got back up on my feet and, rammed him into the wall, and uppercut him hard so that I could feel his blood on my skin. It was also that moment I could feel the swelling on the side of my face and my own blood seeping inside my cheek. He had got me good. I then was yanked back and pushed to the corner. Skyla stood looking between us in absolute disgust.

"WHAT THE FUCK IS WRONG WITH BOTH OF YOU?" She yelled so loud it felt like the room was shaking. "THIS ISN'T A PISSING CONTEST."

I narrowed my eyes at Calvin, who had blood on his face. "He started it."

"I don't give a fuck who started what." She seethed, looking back at me. "This is exactly what Daniel is hoping for, so quit playing the game."

Calvin rolled his eyes, "Skyla, I highly doubt this has anything to do with that bastard."

"You guys don't get it. He wants everyone to start fighting and turning on each other. Everyone knows that Maggie gets overwhelmed, and her response is to take flight and not fight. So, he's hoping that everyone around her gets mad and causes her to flee and get her alone." Skyla shook her head and sighed. "Maggie, at the end of the day, must make this choice, and we must respect it. If either of you love her, you know everything I have said is right."

I looked over at Calvin, who was watching me. Anger does strange things to people. It was an emotion I tried to avoid because you never know what can happen if someone is angry. Clearly, I had no issue fighting with my best friend; as much as Calvin pisses me off, I would have never laid a hand on him. The look he was giving me now told me he felt the same. We both knew we fucked up.

But anger is a dangerous emotion. An unpredictable one at that.

Chapter Forty-Three

Surprised Reaction

Maggie

There are pros and cons to everything in life, including having the last name of Kensinger. Growing up, there were a few events I remember having to be at; they were awful. Mom dressed us up in nice clothes, and we had to be on our best behavior. My shoes were always too tight, and my dress would be ugly pink and yellow colors. I hadn't had to be at any gala or event since I was in high school, and I figured since Dad passed, I would never have to again. As life has it, Mom was hell-bent on having a gala to raise money for mental health awareness.

It had been about a week since my interaction with Daniel. Tensions were high this whole week, especially between Calvin and Jackson. I was still pissed at them both for fighting, but I also knew they were only fighting because I hadn't made a choice yet.

Many people don't understand how complex the choice is when it comes to abuse. Most of the time, you don't want to remember it, so it is better to brush it under the rug. Another thing is that the attacker scares the absolute shit out of you. As a woman, you also must be prepared to be accused of lying or making it up. There are so many parts to making this choice, but eventually, you'll come to one. Most of the time, people disagree with the one you make.

The entire time we were in the party room of the nicest hotel on the water, all I could think about was how my choice would affect everyone. Mom was talking about how she wanted shit set up and the why behind it all while Calvin and I sat in the corner, not listening to her. My eyes were focused on the water as Calvin was scrolling through his phone.

The first thing was that Mom would not believe Daniel was capable, or it would be her last straw before a complete mental breakdown. She had been through so much that causing her more pain would spin me into a lifelong guilt. I also knew that all these years, Daniel was prepared for me to speak out, so what did he have up his sleeve? The last thing was I didn't want to relive it.

"So glad my children are listening," Mom stated sarcastically as she crossed her arms. "This is a big deal; we could raise thousands for research."

Calvin sighed and pushed his phone into his pocket. "You say this every time, Mom. We both have been through this process way too many times."

I glanced at Mom, who was narrowing her eyes at us, and went back to looking at the lake. "I just want to be able to help those who are at war with themselves, like Maggie."

"Excuse me?" I turned and frowned at her. "People like me? You want to help people like me?"

Mom frowned, "Of course, Maggie, I want to help anyone I can. I just happen to experience this on a more personal level."

I scoffed, "You can't say you've experienced a damn thing at being at war with themselves."

I knew, as soon as the words left my mouth, they were going to be bullets to my mom. Of course, she understood what being at war with yourself felt like. Between the abuse she endured as a child, losing a sister, nearly losing a daughter, and, to top it off, the man who saved her from drowning in complete sorrow died. Mom knew depression better than anyone; she had to overcome all of that, not to mention her job itself had been mostly depressing.

Mom sighed, "You are not the only one suffering."

What a shitty daughter I was. I turned and looked back out to the lake, trying to focus on the different hues of blue. I was too cowardly to look at my mom.

"It starts at seven o'clock tomorrow night?" Calvin asked, trying to break the tension.

"I expect you both, plus Skyla, here by six thirty." Mom said, and the sounds of her heels clicking away filled the room.

Shaking my head, I turned and looked over at my brother. "There's no way I can unload another traumatic thing to her."

"I think you forget how strong Mom is."

"There is only so much one person can take before breaking." I closed my eyes. "I can't hurt her anymore."

Calvin gripped both of my shoulders as I looked up at him. "It will hurt her more that you keep this from her."

"Pain is still pain."

He rolled his eyes, "Mags, no one said you had to deliver the news right away. If you want to go forward with pressing charges, you don't have to tell Mom right away."

"I don't think I want to," I whispered, avoiding his eyes. "Who knows what he has up his sleeve? You and I both know he's prepared for me to make this move, but I am as far away from being prepared. Those who are prepared are the ones who come out on top."

Calvin's face remained stoic, "Whatever you decide, I support it. But for what it is worth, I know you will come out on top."

If only it were that easy to believe. I was filled with too much fear of the unknown, not to mention how scared I was of Daniel himself.

***

Jackson was pissed that he couldn't come to this gala, even though we all kept telling him it wasn't as glamorous as he thinks. Sure, the food and drinks would be good; otherwise, we would have to spend our time talking to people who were only there to make an appearance. Calvin had stated to him multiple times that he would rather be working like him than going to this stupid thing. Skyla was only going because Mom made sure she wasn't scheduled, which pissed Skyla off because it meant she was going to have to get dressed up. It wasn't like a nice dress for an everyday thing; nope, it was like prom attire.

Lucky for me, I had a few of these outfits in my closet in case Skyla and I ended up at one of the fancy nightclubs in Denver in college. Otherwise, all my clothes were either teacher-appropriate or casual. Skyla had one dress that fit the category; it was the dress Bently chose when he took her to an expensive place in Denver for their last anniversary.

I was standing looking at myself in the mirror when Jackson came into the room. It was a black dress that clung to my body and fell to the floor. My whole back was exposed, and it loosely hung at my neck, showing quite a bit of my chest and all my shoulders. He stared at me with his mouth open as if he had never seen a woman before.

"Quit looking at me like that," I mumbled as I sat down on the bed.

He came and stood in front of me, still gawking at me. "Holy fuck," he whispered as his fingers brushed my cheek. "Now I am really pissed I'm not going."

I shook my head, "Oh, you'll be fine; you'll get me naked whenever you want."

Jackson went and closed the door and took off his shirt, sending heat to my cheeks. I don't think I'll ever get over seeing him shirtless. His body was effortlessly sculpted; you could trace his muscles. Jackson still had tan skin, so drastically different from me, white as hell.

I stood up as he walked back towards me, eyeing me hungrily. He slid off his shorts and gripped both sides of my face. I could already feel myself melting into him. Jackson kissed me softly, carefully unclasping my dress at the neck and letting it drop, exposing my breasts.

"Correction," he whispered in my ear, "I get you when I want."

He pinched my nipple, seeing the goosebumps form on my skin. I ran my hands along his torso, skin perfectly smooth and soft.

"You can't ruin my makeup," I whispered as his lips nicked my ear. "Skyla will kill you."

Jackson chuckled, "She won't be able to tell."

That is when he tugged down my dress until it spilled around me. All that I had on was my heels as he took every inch of my body. It was then my eyes met where his cock was bulging, my lips curled into a smirk. The moment my hands yanked at his boxers was when Jackson laid me back down on the bed. Before anything else could happen, his tongue met my clit, and my back arched. Fuck, my hands raked through his hair as he pumped two fingers into me. I had to bite down on my lip to stop my screaming out his name. I looked down between my legs, and there were those perfect dark brown eyes looking directly at me.

My back arched, and my legs were shaking as the orgasm hit me. My eyes rolled to the back of my head, and a wave of pleasure and satisfaction rippled through my body. Before I could ride out the warm feeling, Jackson thrust inside me, and that is when everything changed.

I was no longer in my bedroom lying on my plushy comforter. The sun was hitting my face, and the feeling of rock and gravel was beneath me. There, in between my legs, was Daniel, his hands gripping my throat.

"STOP!" I screamed.

Snapping my eyes shut, I could feel the burn from where his hands had been. I felt the stinging in my hand when he punched my car window. My scars were throbbing on the insides of my thigh. His words cut through my brain: princess, mine, pathetic. My body curled into a ball as tears were trying to surface, and my heartbeat was the only thing I could hear.

Slowly, my senses came back to reality; I could feel the plushiness of my comforter. I could smell Skyla's Rue 21 perfume, which she had worn for as long as I could remember. I could hear a book page being turned. Carefully, I let my eyes open, meeting Skyla, who sat on my bed with my book in hand.

"You know, I am not really into hockey smut, but damn, this shit has got my clit throbbing." A laugh escaped me as I sat up; my dress was still on the floor, so there I lay nude. "I wouldn't bother covering; I've seen this view plenty of times."

Gently, I pulled my dress back over my body, feeling safe with being covered. I let my eyes lock themselves in the mirror; my make-up remained intact, and my hair had been brushed through and adjusted. There was a wild look on my face, one that reminded me of a girl running for her life in a scary movie.

"Where did he go?" I asked.

"Work, he was scared shitless, so he went running," Skyla said, standing up. "Maggie?"

I glanced back at her, "He didn't deserve that."

"Maggie, you were raped not long ago; your body had a natural response to trauma."

"I don't remember having these problems, so why now?"

Skyla sighed and rested her head on my shoulder. "You have someone who you are engaged to; that's the difference. You had got yourself out and opened to let him in, but Daniel came back and brought you back into the dark. Your body doesn't know the difference; it assumes you're in danger all over again."

"We are going to be late, aren't we?" I mumbled.

Skyla chuckled, "Yeah, but better late than never."

Clinging onto her hand, we made our way out the door and to where Calvin was waiting in his car. His eyes lit up when he saw Skyla. She was dressed in a cream-colored dress that was strapless and clung to her body. The long red hair was curled and bright against the dress and her tan skin. For whatever reason, minus having Sicilian ancestors, she was able to have a deep tan during the summer months.

We both climbed into the back seat, and I saw Calvin looking at me through the rearview mirror. I gave him a subtle nod, assuring him I was alright. We drove to the hotel in silence, all of us dreading this party.

Little did I know there was more to dread than just the party.

Chapter Forty-Four

Swallow Me Whole

Maggie

I will give my mom this: she knew how to throw a party. If she had not become a doctor, she could've made a living off being a party planner. My mom was concerned about every detail there was, which set her apart from most people who hosted parties. Every little thing was a big deal, and she stressed each, but in the end, it was always worth it. This party was no exception.

There was valet parking, which was unnecessary; it wasn't like it was that big of a walk. Inside, there were signs with flowers leading us into the big banquet room. Calvin walked in front of us, adjusting his tie. It was a decent crowd; music was playing, and the lights were dimmed. You could see the buffet lines and the bar with a few bartenders. I scanned the room and found my mom surrounded by people; as always, she looked calm and beautiful. She was in a long-sleeved green dress, and her hair was pulled into a neat bun, and she wore dangling earrings.

The lake looked breathtaking, as usual. The wall was lined with windows, exposing the view. The sun was slowly making its way down, changing the colors in the sky to various oranges and purples. There were a few boats out and people fishing off the sandy beach on the far right. The doors to the outside were wide open, letting a soft breeze in and also helping with the heat from all the people.

The colors were green and gold, reminding me more of a forest. There were tables set up with big centerpieces of greenery and candles. The buffet ran along in front of the view of the lake. There was a variety of food, from cocktail wieners to sandwiches to steak kabobs. Not to mention, on the far back wall was a line of different pastries and cakes.

"I am going to get drinks; what are you two wanting?" Calvin said loudly.

"Water." Skyla and I said in unison.

"Boring." He rolled his eyes and slid past people to get to the bar.

It was like three seconds before Skyla, and my mother bombarded me. She gave us big hugs and introduced us to several people, whose names I didn't give a shit knowing. Skyla wore a painful smile; she hated people, not to mention strangers. I did my best to give a convincing smile.

Calvin came back and was sucked into talking with total strangers. The conversations varied from talking about my dad to what the hospital needed. I had no clue what the damn hospital needed, so I gave some bullshit about funding for a lab. Most of the people I talked to assumed I was a doctor and seemed to be disappointed to find out I was just a Kindergarten teacher, Typical.

Skyla kept giving me death looks to come and save her, but any time I got a chance to head over to her, another person would introduce themselves. My attention would be drawn back to having a conversation with a stranger. Calvin had always been good at talking to strangers; he definitely got that from Mom. My dad was more like me, reserved and not comfortable in public settings. Mom brought out a more social part of him, but even then, it still was clear the discomfort my dad felt.

My feet were beginning to throb as time did not exist when constant strangers were jockeying in line to talk to me. I knew some time had passed because the sunlight was slowly fading away, revealing more purple to the sky. I had no idea where Skyla or Calvin was; we seemed to have floated apart from each other. There were too many people for me to budge my way through, so I decided to excuse myself from a conversation with a man who knew my dad, and I was able to get outside.

The air felt good in my lungs as I walked towards the water and up on the dock. Everyone was busy inside the party, which left me alone with peace. I awkwardly got off my heels, and I plopped my ass down on the edge of the dock. I leaned my head back and watched the stars slowly make their appearance. You could hear the yells of children from the other beaches on either side of the hotel. There were hums of boats that were still out on the water. It was a typical spring night in Bemidji.

"You know, you craving your alone time makes you such an easy target."

My stomach sank, and the smell finally hit my nose. I was able to get myself on both feet to stare at Daniel. The blood stopped rushing in my veins; my heartbeat paused. My mind was frozen, unable to think.

I had assumed that Daniel would still be out on medical leave. I assumed wrong, as usual. Here he stood, dressed in a tux and hair gelled back. The cologne smell was stronger, indicating he had put more on. He blocked the entrance to the dock, leaving my only escape to jumping into the lake. The water had to still be cold; it had not gotten any warmer than sixty today. Goosebumps formed along my skin, thinking of the cold water.

Once, when I was eight, we went tubing on the lake, and I fell off. My dumbass didn't secure my life jacket, so the force of hitting the water made it slip off. I plunged under the water, surrounded by the ice-cold lake. I had got my way to the top, but the waves from the boat smacked me in the face, causing me to struggle for air. I was convinced I was going to drown, but my dad had come in and saved me. It took a while before I even dared to go near the water.

"I see you're engaged," Daniel said, nodding his head and shaking hands. "Funny that you think you can escape so easily."

"What do you want from me?" I asked, trying to keep my mind on my near-traumatic drowning.

Daniel laughed, "Are we really going to do this song and dance all over again?"

"I am getting married."

"That's cute, but not going to happen." He stepped forward and gripped my hips, the burning pain shooting from his touch. "You think that is what is going to save you?"

I tried to move; he moved one of his hands to grip the back of my neck. "Let me go," I whispered.

He shook his head as his other hand met my breast, and Daniel sighed. "Maggie, you were always going to be mine. I knew from the moment I held you as a child." My stomach formed a tight knot. "My love and attraction only grew as I watched you age into this woman."

His lips were by my ear; my body was officially frozen with the disturbing images forming in my head. I think of the memories of Daniel growing up; he always had been kind but avoided most physical contact with me. It would've never crossed my mind that he had been sickly attracted to me. All those years when he would smile at me, it wasn't because he was an uncle; it was because he had been in love with me.

"Daniel, let go of me, please," I said, swallowing back down the vomit that was trying to escape me. "Let me go." As I shook him from me, he stumbled back and laughed at me.

In one smooth motion, he grabbed my waist and slammed my body into the dock. I let out a scream as everything was dizzy. I snapped my head back, and it hit the metal part of the dock. I began to stumble backward; my world was spinning, and three Daniels were standing over me, smiling.

"You really think you can escape?" He said, crouching down in front of me. "Oh, princess, so young and naïve. See, you never stood a chance, and it excites me to think you could."

The dock itself felt like it was rocking back and forth as if we were on a boat. I leaned to the side and threw up, not having the strength to hold it back. Between the motion sickness and my head pounding, I didn't stand a chance of fighting off the vomit. Wiping my mouth, I looked back up at Daniel. I had to find a way out. I wasn't going to give up, not after everything I had been through.

"Let me go, Daniel," I said as I stood up, stumbling as balance was no longer a thing for me. "It's over, you don't have me. I am marrying Jackson, and I am going to have a FUCKING life without you in it."

I began to move forward, but now both of his hands clutched around my throat. "You're not going anywhere. You're mine, Maggie, always had been. No one is going to take you away from me. I'd rather kill you before that happens."

Tears were forming as his grasp tightened around my windpipe. There was that fire in Daniel's eyes from the first night he assaulted me. The look that had haunted my dreams all these years was now in front of me. I gasped for air as I began to feel lightheaded.

"You don't get to have a life without me." He whispered in my ear.

This was not how I wanted to die, not by his hands, but I could feel everything getting heavy. This was how it ended: Daniel winning by making sure only he could have me. I heard my name being shouted in the distance. I felt my eyes rolling back into my head as

Daniel shoved me off the dock; I took what would be my last breath.

Instead of seeing all the memories, I was hit with every emotion there was. And then it was nothing but darkness.

Chapter Forty-Five

You Can't Save Her

There was some kind of sense that Skyla felt that made her look out to the dock. A gut-wrenching scream escaped her that made everyone stop and look in the direction she was. Everyone gasped as Skyla kicked off her heels and went running towards the dock, Calvin not far behind.

"MAGGIE!" She screamed, running with everything she had in her. "MAGGIE!"

When Daniel turned around, gripping Maggie's throat still, Skyla came to a halt. There was a wicked grin on his face, which reminded her of Bill in all the years he abused her. Her body went cold as the memories she had pushed deep down were surfacing. Daniel looked like Bill, and that made everything freeze.

Daniel pushed Maggie off the dock; her body was already limp before hitting the water. The sound of Maggie meeting the water shocked Skyla back to life. Calvin ran past her and collided with Daniel, who was laughing like a lunatic from one of those murder shows. A fire burned within Skyla; she should've killed Daniel when she had the chance. She narrowed her eyes on him and launched herself onto him, pinning his neck to the dock.

When turning to look at Calvin, he dived into the lake, leaving it to Skyla to handle the bastard. She looked down at the man who had destroyed her best friend, the man who reminded her of her worst nightmare.

"You think you can save her?" He croaked out, still wearing that vicious smile. "She was already out before hitting the water."

Skyla shook her head and turned to see the crowd that had formed on the beach. "SOMEONE CALL 911."

She looked back down and punched him hard so that she could hear his nose breaking. That had gotten him to shut up and the urge to fight back. Daniel lunged towards her throat, but she rolled off him fast and kicked him hard in the ribs, letting out a cry as two people came past her to hold down Daniel. Skyla then looked to see Calvin surfaced from the water, holding Maggie.

Calvin knew the lake was still shallow enough that Maggie hadn't fallen too far. He didn't even hesitate to jump in; he couldn't lose Maggie, not this way. He remembered when Maggie almost drowned when they went tubing; he was scared shitless, just as he was now.

Opening his eyes underwater stung, but he was easily able to spot Maggie floating. When he reached her, you could already feel how cold and stiff she was; it reminded him of when he came home to find Kara and Heather dead. He was not going to lose Maggie. Swimming with the resistance to the water and the extra weight of another body, it took him longer than he liked to get to shore.

Flinging Maggie's body down on the sand, he immediately began to check for signs of breathing, which was a waste of time, because she wasn't. Without hesitation, Calvin began to perform CPR. This is when Skyla crumpled to her knees, eyes drowning in tears as she gripped Maggie's lifeless hand.

The next moments were such a blur for everyone. The two men who had grabbed Daniel were security for the hotel, and they restrained him. Julia Kensinger was sobbing on her knees, watching her daughter being resuscitated. When the EMTs arrived, Maggie had to spit up some water but remained still. Calvin snapped at the poor EMTs as he continued CPR as they got in the ambulance. Skyla remained clinging to Maggie as they got her hooked up.

"No, no, no," she kept mumbling. "This isn't how it goes; you don't get to die on me, Maggie Kensinger."

Calvin called clearly and shocked Maggie, and they all looked at the heart monitor. It was a very slow beat, but there was a heartbeat. Skyla let out a cry and laugh of relief as the male EMT got some more warming blankets on her. Calvin was watching the slow beats his sister's heart was making; he knew she wasn't out of the woods.

Once they got to the hospital, they were going to have better answers as to the chances Maggie could regain consciousness. It also dawned on them that they were going to have to tell Jackson. Skyla and Calvin settled on paging him to the pit as neither of them wanted to leave Maggie, whose heartbeat was now up to twenty-six beats a minute.

The ambulance doors swung open, "Twenty-nine-year-old Jane Doe,"

"It's fucking Maggie Kensinger." Calvin snapped as he got out, followed by Skyla.

"What the hell happened?" Chief Kensinger asked as they quickly wheeled Maggie to trauma bay 2.

There was no secret to keep, so there was no need to hide. "She was choked to death by Daniel and thrown into the lake."

Chief Kensinger's stomach sank, realizing how everything fit together. He looked back down at his niece; she was pale, with her lips still blue. Daniel did this.

"Someone," Jackson Calsen stopped speaking as he entered the room.

His face fell as he came up to Maggie's head, tears pouring down his face as he gripped her face. She was so cold, she felt like ice. He kept his hands on her face, hoping they would bring her warmth. Skyla was clinging onto Maggie's hand, and Calvin stood over her, barking orders at the nurse and his uncle.

"We can't perform anything on her," Chief Kensinger said as he watched Julia Kensinger come into the room. "We are family, Calvin; step away and let Dr. Gilis do his thing."

"No," Calvin snarled, "I am not letting anyone fuck up my sister."

Chief Kensinger shook his head, "Exact reason why we don't perform on loved ones."

Calvin was about to snap back when Maggie's heartbeat shot up. Everyone turned to look down at her as she flashed her eyes open. No one could speak as her eyes darted all around her, trying to settle on someone or something.

There were too many people to focus on, so Maggie settled on Skyla, who was finally starting to say something to her. Calvin began saying something, but Maggie didn't move or speak. And Jackson felt his stomach sinking; what if she was paralyzed? Calvin was thinking the same thing and went to tap her feet; everyone held their breath as Maggie reacted. As soon as he told her to press down, she did nothing. The only thing she seemed to do was have reactions and not follow commands.

"Oh my god," Skyla said as Maggie finally lifted her shaking hand to point to her ear. "She can't hear."

Chapter Forty-Six

No Heaven or Hell

Maggie

Death was strange. Growing up, I just assumed when you died, everything went dark, and there was nothing. That is when your thoughts and who you were as a person vanished. I fully prepared myself to be at peace, but that was not the case. In truth, I was engulfed in endless darkness but was left with all my thoughts. All I could think about was not dying and about how much I wanted to get back. I had wanted to die most of my life, but right now, all I wanted was the chance to live. My mind was fighting my body to stay alive for once.

Searching through the darkness, trying to find light, reminded me of walking around with a tight blindfold. It dawned on me that there would never be light again, and all that I would be left with was my fucked-up thoughts in the dark. A punishment that will live on for eternity for all the sins I had done. No God to save me. No hell to welcome me, too. Just darkness and my thoughts.

It was quite a shock when my eyes flung open to meet an intense bright light. Not to mention, when all the faces appeared in front of me, none of them were clear. Everything in my body hurt, especially my heart, not to mention how cold I was. It was Skyla's face that came into focus first. Red surrounded her eyes as she was looking at me with those unique blue eyes. When her mouth moved, I heard nothing; in fact, I didn't even hear buzzing. That is when I snapped my eyes to look at Jackson, who looked like he had lost everything. I wanted to smile or tell him that I was awake and it was going to be okay, even if I wasn't convinced myself that was the case.

I could feel people touching my feet, and Calvin came into view. He was soaking wet and looked frazzled. Did he jump into the water for me? Why wasn't he covered with a blanket or something? Did anyone see what happened? How long was I out? Too many questions that hurt my brain.

Skyla was trying to say something to me, but I heard nothing. Had I lost my hearing? With pain, I lifted my hand, shaking violently, and pointed at my ear. Her face turned to horror as she looked at Calvin and said something. That is when he investigated my ears and then motioned for my uncle to come into view.

There was a worried look on Jackson's face. I opened my mouth to speak, but nothing came out; it burned. He shook his head, trying to tell me not to talk. I couldn't speak. Why did my throat hurt? Why was my head throbbing like someone was hitting me with a hammer? It was then the image of Daniel in front of me that jolted my body. I tried to scream, but nothing could come out.

That is when my heart took its last break.

Jackson

Maggie was looking at me, trying to speak, but I shook my head. Her windpipe was crushed, and it would cause her more pain and recovery if she tried to speak. Her eyes were searching mine as if they were trying to tell me something. I brushed her hair away from her eyes, trying to soothe both of us.

When Calvin had investigated her ears, he could see there was spinal fluid that was leaking from her ears. That exact moment was when Maggie tried to scream, and she flatlined right there. Skyla screamed as Calvin pushed her back from Maggie. I had already begun chest compressions without hesitation; there was no fucking way I was losing the only thing that was keeping me alive.

As the chief called for us to clear, I almost didn't. I wanted to feel her jolt back to life. I wanted to be the first thing she felt, but I cleared and let him shock her heart. There was nothing; I resumed chest compressions as the chief charged again and called clear.

Please, Maggie, don't die. Not this way. I am right here; don't give up now. Maggie, the most selfish thing I will ask is to live for me. Live for the chance of us.

The shock hit her body, and there was silence. Please, please, please. Skyla covered her mouth and sank to the floor, crying out in agony. Just as I was about to start compressions again, there was a beep, then another, and another. Julia Kensinger cried out, and I felt myself let out a deep breath I hadn't realized I was holding.

Chapter Forty-Seven

Defy the Odds

Maggie

Time didn't exist. It started with just hearing people talk, and then it became blinking my eyes before going back to sleep. Whenever I opened my eyes, the room was dark. The machines were beeping. Skyla would always be sleeping with her head resting on my legs. It hurt to take in anything more, and then I would fade back into a sleep. Every time I opened my eyes, I immediately felt like I needed to close them again. At first, it was because it ached everywhere, and now it was more because I was afraid of what would come next.

I had suffered some kind of brain injury, and what caused my hearing loss was the spinal fluid that had been leaking. My heart flatlined twice. I had not breathed when coming out of the water but was able to in the ambulance. I vaguely remember the bright light and the faces; I just remember the feeling of my heart breaking and then that endless fall in the dark.

From what I gathered was that Daniel was sitting in jail on attempted murder charges. My mom had been angry with Jackson, Skyla, and Calvin for keeping this from her. I think the anger was better than dealing with the guilt she had to be drowning in.

It had been easier to sleep and pretend that everything was just a dream, but I knew facing reality was going to have to come. So, when I opened my eyes, I was surprised to find that I was alone. I blinked a few more times before my sight confirmed I was the only one. I carefully looked up to see the TV was playing hockey; it said it was the finals, which meant a decent amount of time had passed.

Looking down at my hands, I noticed that my wedding ring was on with no damage. It still looked as perfect as the day Jackson got down on his knee and asked me to marry him. I let myself soak in the feelings from that day, one of the happiest days of my life. The happiest days of my life: getting engaged, graduating college, the day Skyla and I spent all day snowboarding in Winter Park, senior prom night, the day I met Skyla, when my dad helped me practice to beat Jimmy Keller in basketball, and the day mom danced and sang with me all day when I was feeling down at six years old.

Happiness is such a rare thing. Even though I could name so many happy memories, there were like a thousand more that were sad. You just will your mind to look at the happy ones, which is no easy task.

"Hey, sleepy head," Skyla walked in with a slice of cheesecake from the cafeteria. "Nice to see you awake."

I smiled at her; it hurts to use these muscles. "I am happy to be awake." My voice was still hoarse, but at least I was able to talk. "Daniel?"

Skyla plopped herself down in the chair next to my bed and grabbed my hand. "He's still in jail, can't make bail. You are going to press charges?"

"It's going to have to be done, but I am not worried about it right now," I said softly; my throat began to hurt.

She smiled, "I have something to tell you." I frowned, and a laugh escaped her. "It's good, promise."

Releasing my hand, I felt something in my hand. I unclasped my hand, and there it lay. My mouth fell open in shock as I looked back at her. Tears were forming in her eyes, and her cheeks were flushed.

"You're joking?" I whispered.

"No. Confirmed and everything." Smiling at her as, tears fell from her eyes.

In my hand lay a pregnancy stick that read positive. "I am going to assume Calvin is happy?"

Skyla shook her head, "I wanted you to be the first one to know, so I don't know."

I smiled, "You really are my best friend."

She wiped the tears from her face as she laughed. "I am glad you're alive because I have no clue how I could do this life without you."

I don't know if I would've made it this far without her. I know for a fact that if I never scored Skyla as my best friend, life would have been shitty. I would have never known what love was or what it meant to have a soul sister. It is something special to have. I am glad I am alive to see my best friend get the life she deserves.

More than anything, I am happy to see what was next for us in this fucked life.

Chapter Forty-Eight

The End?

Calvin Kensinger could spot an addict from a mile away. It was a talent that he wished he didn't have because he only acquired it from being one himself. It made him wonder how many people had looked at him during those years with disgust or pity, because that is how he looked at addicts now, which was hypocritical. No one ever said Calvin was a great person; this was just another flaw for him. And lord knows people have a shit load of flaws, some on the surface and some below.

The pit was calm for a Tuesday night as Calvin was covering for Skyla. It had been a few weeks since Maggie was released from the hospital, and when he discovered that being a dad was back on his job description. In the years since he lost Heather and Kara, he had come to peace with not ever having another child. Skyla had moved on from the news of not being able to have children. Yet, here they were, sixteen weeks along with a child.

As for Maggie and Jackson, they had officially finished the house, and she was moving in. They had picked a wedding date, making sure it was after the baby was here, so Skyla was not going to be bloated and fat in the pictures. Calvin had sold his apartment and was living in the townhouse with his pregnant girlfriend.

Things were falling into place; at least, that is what everyone was assuming.

The TV above the nurse's station flashed with breaking news. This caught my attention as it was local and not national. The news lady, who Calvin had fucked once upon a time, appeared with a somber look on her face.

"Pardon our interruption, but we have some local breaking news." Everyone was now looking at the TV, "I am here to report there has been a breach at Beltrami Jail; it is reported that five inmates have escaped and one security guard killed. One of the inmates who escaped was Daniel Dobson, who is facing charges of attempted murder of a local woman, and police caution that he is a threat and anyone that has…"

Calvin had already stopped listening, and his stomach dropped. Meanwhile, Skyla and Jackson were watching a UFC fight when the news cut in. Skyla made a rush to find Maggie in the bedroom as Jackson remained stunned.

Oddly enough, when Maggie got out of the shower, she had this urge to peak out the window. When she did, she wished she hadn't. There in the light of dusk, in her backyard, Daniel Dobson stood, smiling up at her.

At the same time, Maggie's phone chimed with a text:

You've been a naughty princess, and those who are naughty deserve to be punished. This is far from over.

Indeed, it was far from over.

www.ingramcontent.com/pod-product-compliance
Lightning Source LLC
Chambersburg PA
CBHW011148310726
48973CB00010B/2824